广东商学院学术文库

大 众 诗 学

——卡尔·桑伯格诗歌及诗学研究

张广奎 著

中国社会科学出版社

图书在版编目（CIP）数据

大众诗学：卡尔·桑伯格诗歌及诗学研究/张广奎著.—北京：中国社会科学出版社，2008.6

ISBN 978 - 7 - 5004 - 6964 - 3

Ⅰ.大… Ⅱ.张… Ⅲ.桑伯格，K.（1878～1967）—诗歌—文学研究 Ⅳ.I712.072

中国版本图书馆 CIP 数据核字（2008）第 120218 号

策划编辑 卢小生（E - mail：georgelu@ vip. sina. com）
责任编辑 卢小生
责任校对 韩天炜
封面设计 高丽琴
技术编辑 李 建

出版发行 中国社会科学出版社
社　　址 北京鼓楼西大街甲 158 号　　　邮 编 100720
电　　话 010 - 84029450（邮购）
网　　址 http：//www. csspw. cn
经　　销 新华书店
印　　刷 北京新魏印刷厂　　　装 订 丰华装订厂
版　　次 2008 年 6 月第 1 版　　　印 次 2008 年 6 月第 1 次印刷
开　　本 710×980 1/16　　　插 页 2
印　　张 16　　　印 数 1 - 6000 册
字　　数 258 千字
定　　价 30.00 元

Contents

Acknowledgements

This book is a revised edition of my doctoral dissertation. At its publication, I first feel grateful to my supervisor Professor Ou Hong, and some other scholars and friends.

When I was matriculated as a doctoral student by Sun Yat-sen University in 2002, I was immediately attacked by a kind of ignorant fear, because, at that time, frankly and honestly speaking, I hadn't done much in learning and lacked systematic knowledge about literature. In the three years (2002–2005), I had been haunted by the fear that became an impetus driving me forward step by step and little by little. Unfortunately and regretfully I could not have erased it completely from my mind, but it has turned much weaker (and weaker) than before. I know the lingering ignorant fear still exists and will be forever a drive for me.

Who on earth directed me to have cut down the ignorant fear to a less degree? Who enlightened me academically? Who gave me more space to develop? And who bestowed me more chances to reflect on my missteps and deficiency in learning and personal behavior, to meditate and reexamine myself from time to time? He was and is Professor Ou Hong. He influenced me in many aspects. But, here with thanks, I also apologize to Professor Ou for my imperfections of the three years' study. According to him, academic research is a piece of long-term and persistent work and needs much perseverance. So I take, and I have to take, my doctoral dissertation as the first step to learn to walk in academia.

Before more thanksgiving to some others, I am indebted to Professor Zhang Ziqing from Nanjing University, who read through the whole book and put forward some constructive opinions for this revised edition just before the publication, which avoided some deficiencies in the book.

And my thanks are given to my family. During the years, my family suppor-ted me both materially and spiritually, which I will feel conscience-stricken if I do not mention them. I feel proud for having such a loving big family including my father Zhang Guilin, my mother Tang Jifei, and my dear wife Wang Guangy-ing who had been supporting our nuclear family with her own salary but without any help from me for three years, while she sacrificed opportunities for further study to develop herself.

Then, my special thanks go to the following friends and classmates: Long Jingyao who gave me a special help; Pu Durong who generously bought many valuable books for me from Ireland when he was there as a visiting scholar in Trinity College, Dublin; Li Chengjian and Lei Yanni who also got some precious books for me when they were in England; Sun Jicheng who is one of my best friends studying in Peking University and got me the first essential materials a-bout Carl Sandburg when he was in Stockholm, Sweden; Chen Xiaohong and Chen Shangzhen who read through my first rough draft and put forward some use-ful suggestions; and lastly, Zhang Xueying and Shen Jie who did much sundry work for me and us all.

Last, but not least. I dedicate this doctoral dissertation to my maternal grandmother who nursed me for a long period during and after the Chinese Cul-tural Revolution when my parents were busy teachers. And though in coma in her last days, she had murmured my infant name at times and could still recog-nize me just on the last second day before she died on Tuesday, January 25, 2005, and it was the third day morning after I got home in Xuzhou when I fin-ished the first draft of my dissertation in Guangzhou. I wish she rest in peace in heaven.

Chronology

1878   Born January 6, Galesburg, Illinois, first son of August and Clara Sandburg, Swedish immigrants. Baptized Carl August.

1891   Leaves school after eighth grade. Works at various jobs, including newsboy and milk–delivery boy.

1892   Works as shoeshine boy in barbershop.

1894   Takes second milk–wagon job.

1896   Visits Chicago for the first time.

1896   Sees Robert Todd Lincoln (the eldest son of President Lincoln) at fortieth anniversary of Lincoln–Douglas debate, Knox College, Galesburg.

1897   Rides boxcar to Iowa, Kansas, Nebraska, Colorado. Works on railroad section gang, as farm hand, dishwasher, and at odd jobs.

1898   Serves as apprentice to house painter, Galesburg. On April 26, enlists in Company C, sixth Infantry Regiment, Illinois Volunteers. Serves as private in Puerto Rico during Spanish–American War. Returns to Galesburg. Enrolls as special student in Lombard College, Galesburg.

1899   Appointed to West Point in May. Fails written examination in grammar and arithmetic. Enters Lombard College in September. To support himself, serves in town fire department. Becomes business manager of the *Lombard Review*.

1900   Works in summer selling Underwood & Underwood stereoscopic photographs, with Frederick Dickinson.

1901   Editor–in–chief of the *Lombard Review*. With Frederick Dickinson, edits *The Cannibal, the Jubilee Year Book*.

1902   Leaves college before graduating to wander over country, selling Underwood & Underwood stereoscopic photographs. Attested for riding rails without ticket, serves ten days in Allegheny County jail, Pittsburgh.

1903   Returns to Galesburg. Writes articles for column called "Inklings & Idling" in the Galesburg *Evening Mail*. Writes editorials for the *Galesburg Labor News*. In December has first poetry and a few prose pieces published in a booklet by Asgard Press, *In Reckless Ecstasy*.

1905   Becomes assistant editor of *Tomorrow Magazine*, in Chicago, which also publishes his poems and sketches.

1906   Becomes lyceum lecturer on Walt Whitman.

1907   Publishes "A Dream Girl" in The Lyceumite. As associate editor of The Lyceumite, in Chicago, writes the series "Unimportant Portraits of Important People. " Asgard Press publishes *Incidentals* in November. Delivers lectures on Whitman and Bernard Shaw at Elbert Hubbard's Roycroft Chapel. In December becomes organizer for Social Democratic Party

1908   Goes to Wisconsin as district organizer in the Lake Shore and Fox River Valley district. Asgard Press publishes *The Plaint of a Rose in January*. On June 15 marries Lilian Steichen, schoolteacher, also a Socialist. Speaks for the Socialists at a large Chautauqua at Marinette, Wisconsin. Campaigns through Wisconsin aboard "Red Special" with Socialist candidate Eugene V. Debs during Presidential campaign. Writes pamphlet *You and Your Job*, published by Social Democratic Publishing Company, Milwaukee.

1909   Lives in Appleton, Wisconsin, from January to April. Moves to Beaver Dam, then to Milwaukee, where he becomes advertising copy writer for Kroeger's Department Store. Later in the year becomes a reporter for the Milwaukee *Sentinel*, the Milwaukee *Journal*, and the Milwaukee Daily News. Writes "Letters to Bill" and tuberculosis article for *La Follette's Weekly Magazine*. Tours Wisconsin (forty-five cities) with "flying squadron" of Anti-Tuberculosis League.

1910   Father dies March 10. Emil Seidel, Socialist mayor of Milwaukee, appoints him to post of private secretary. In August resigns to become city editor of the Milwaukee *Social-Democratic Herald*. Works for Victor Berger's Political Action. Asgard Press publishes *Josefly: An Appreciation*. Socialist party reprints

You and Your Job.

1911   First child, Margaret, is born June 3. Three articles, "The Man and the Job," "Making the City Efficient," and "My Baby Girl," are published in *La Follette's Weekly Magazine.*

1912   Writers articles for Victor Berger's Milwaukee *Leader.* His article "Where Is My Girl To–Night" appears in *Woman's New Idea Magazine.* Contributes two articles to *The Coming Nation.* Moves to Chicago in September. Joins *Chicago Evening World* staff briefly.

1913   Goes to *The Day Book, Chicago,* then *System,* a management magazine, for which he sometimes writes under the pseudonym R. E. Coulson. In December goes to the *American Artisan & Hardware Record,* writing under the pseudonym Sidney Arnold.

1914   Returns to *The Day Book.* Has some poems published in the March issue of *Poetry: A Magazine of Verse.* Wins Helen Haire Levinson Prize for best poems of the year. Moves to Maywood, a suburb of Chicago, in the fall.

1915   Writes two articles on "That Walsh Report" and three on "Fixing the Pay of Railroad Men" for *The International Socialist Review. Reedy's Mirror* publishes article on Margaret Haley.

1916   Has four poems printed in *The Little Review in April. Chicago Poems* is published by Henry Holt. Daughter Janet is born June 27.

1917   Covers labor conference for the American Federation of Labor at Omaha, in July, and Minneapolis Labor Convention. Joins Chicago Daily News in August. "The Four Brothers," first published in *Poetry,* appears in *Chicago Daily News* in October. Publishes article, "The 8–Hour Rail Drive," under pseudonym Jack Phillips in *The International Socialist Review.*

1918   Quits Chicago *Daily News.* Goes to the Chicago *Evening American* for three weeks, then joins Newspaper Enterprise Association. Does series of ten articles on "Books the Newspaperman Ought to Read" for Pep, an NEA magazine. Goes to Stockholm in October. Daughter Helga is born November 24. *Cornhuskers* is published by Henry Holt. Returns to New York before Christmas.

1919   Assigned to NEA offices in Chicago. *Reedy's Mirror* publishes " Baltic Fogs" in April. Rejoins *Chicago Daily News* as labor reporter; is later appointed motion–picture editor. Shares Poetry Society of America prize with Margaret Widdemer. Harcourt, Brace and Howe publishes *The Chicago Race Riots*. Covers American Federation of Labor Convention in Atlantic City in June, and the Gary, Indiana, steel strike, where he goes with William Allen White. Writes series on shop–steward system in the garment industry. Moves to Elmhurst, a suburb of Chicago.

1920   Gives lecture–recital at Cornell College, Mount Vernon, Iowa. *Smoke and Steel* is published by Harcourt, Brace and Howe.

1921   Share Poetry Society of America Annual Book Award with Stephen Vincent Benet.

1922   Publishes first book for children, *Rootabaga Stories*, and a new volume of poetry, *Slabs of the Sunburnt West*, both brought out by Harcourt, Brace and Company (later Harcourt, Brace & World), the publisher of the rest of his major work.

1923   *Rootabaga Pigeons*, his second book of stories for children, is published.

1926   *Rootabaga Stories* is published in France by F. Rieder & Company, Editeurs, as *Au Pays de Rootabaga*, translated by Leon Bazalgette. Magazine serial rights to *Abraham Lincoln: The Prairie Years*, called "The Unfathomed Lincoln," are bought by *Pictorial Review*.

1926   Two–volume *Abraham Lincoln: The Prairie Years* is published on Lincoln's birthday. Buys summer cottage at Tower Hill, Michigan. *Selected Poems*, edited by Rebecca West, is published by Jonathan Cape, London. Mother dies in December.

1927   Publishes a collection of folk songs, *The American Songbag*. Buys five–acre lot in Harbert, Michigan, on which to build large year–round home.

1928   Is invited to read as Phi Beta Kappa poet at Harvard. Receives Litt. D. from Lombard College. In spring, moves into new house at Harbert. Publishes volume of poetry, *Good Morning, America*. *Abe Lincoln Grows Up* (the first twenty–six chapters of *Abraham Lincoln: The Prairie Years*) published.

1929   Receives Litt. D. from Knox College. Publishes biography, *Steichen the Photographer*, and book for children, *Rootabaga Country*.

1930   *Potato Face* and poems for children, *Early Moon*, are published.

1931   Receives Litt. D. from Northwestern University. Sister Martha Goldstone dies.

1932   Leaves Chicago *Daily News* in May. Publishes biography, *Mary Lincoln: Wife and Widow* (with an Appendix by Paul M. Angle) .

1934   Lectures at University of Hawaii.

1936   *The People, Yes* is published in August.

1938   *Lincoln and Whitman Miscellany*, an essay, is published by Holiday Press, Chicago. Sandburg is awarded the Order of the North Star by the King of Sweden.

1939   Four–volume *Abraham Lincoln: The War Years* is published.

1940   Wins Pulitzer Prize for history. Is elected to American Academy of Arts and Letters. Delivers six Walgreen Fund lectures at University of Chicago. Receives Litt. D. degrees from Harvard, Yale, New York University, Wesleyan University, and Lafayette College.

1941   Essay *Bronze Wood* is published by Grabhorn Press, San Francisco. Receives Litt. d. from Syracuse University and from Dartmouth College; LL. D. from Rollins College. Grandson John Carl is born December 3.

1942   Writes weekly column for Chicago Times Syndicate, commentary for U. S. government film "Bomber," foreign broadcasts for office of War Information, captions for *Road to Victory* (Museum of Modern Art, New York) . *Storm Over the Land* (excerpted from *The War Years*) is published.

1943   *Home Front Memo* is published. Granddaughter Karlen Paula is born June 28.

1944   Publishes *The Photographs of Abraham Lincoln* (with Frederick Hill Meserve). Brother, Martin Sandburg, dies April 7.

1945   Moves to Connemara Farm, Flat Rock, North Carolina, in late fall.

1946   Birthplace at Galesburg, Illinois, is dedicated. *Poems of the Midwest* (*Chicago Poems* and *Cornhuskers* together in one volume) is published by World

Publishing Company, Cleveland.

1948　Publishes novel, Remembrance Rock. Goes to Hollywood to help in planning it as film. Receives LL. D form Augustana College.

1949　*Lincoln Collector*: *The Story of Oliver R. Barrett's Great Private Collection* is published.

1950　Receives Ph. D. from Uppsala University, Sweden. Publishes *Complete Poems*, which wins Pulitzer Prize for poetry. The *New American Songbag* is published.

1952　Receives American Academy of Arts and Letters gold medal for history and biography.

1953　First volume of autobiography, *Always the Young Strangers*, is published. Attends Carl Sandburg Day banquet in Chicago, January 6, on seventy-fifty birthday. Receives Poetry Society of America gold medal. Publishes *A Lincoln Preface*, which was intended for, but not published as, a preface to *The Prairie Years*. Receives Tamiment Institute Award for *Always the Young Strangers*.

1954　*Abraham Lincoln*: *The Prairie Years and The War Years*, a condensation of the six volumes in one, is published. Receives scroll from Civil War Round Table in New York.

1955　*Prairie-Town Boy* (a version for children of *Always the Young Strangers*) is published. Writes prologue to *Family of Man*, a volume of photographs selected by Edward Steichen, published by the Museum of Modern Art, New York.

1956　Is paid $ 30,000 by the University of Illinois for his manuscripts, library, and papers. Receives Humanities award from Albert Einstein College of Medicine, New York. November 18 is proclaimed Carl Sandburg Day in Chicago. The first of sixteen schools named after him opens in Harvey, Illinois.

1957　*The Sandburg Range*, an anthology of his work, is published. Carl Sandburg elementary School opens in Wheeling, Illinois.

1958　Is made "Honorary Ambassador" of North Carolina on March 27, Sandburg Day, at a luncheon in Raleigh, North Carolina. Sister Mary Johnson dies July 29.

1959   Delivers Lincoln Day address, February 12, in Washington, D. C. , before a joint session of congress attended by members of the Supreme Court, the Cabinet, and the diplomatic corps. Goes to Moscow with Edward Steichen under State Department auspices for "Family of Man" exhibit. Meets Ivan Kashkeen, Russian translator of his work. Travel to Stockholm for Swedish–American Day and award of Litteris et Artibus medal from King Gustav. Carl Sandburg High School opens in Mundelein, Illinois, and Levittown, Pennsylvania: Carl Sandburg Elementary School opens in San Burno, California.

1960   Goes to Hollywood as consultant for film "The Greatest Story Ever Told. " Publishes two paper–bound volumes of poetry, *Harvest Poems* 1910 – 1960 and *Wind Song*, poems for children. Carl Sandburg Elementary School is dedicated in Minneapolis. Carl Sandburg Junior High School opens in Elmhurst, Illinois. Receives citation from U. S. Chamber of Commerce as a Great Living American "for lasting contribution to American literature. "

1961   *Six New Poems and a Parable* is published by the University of Kentucky Press. Carl Sandburg elementary schools open in Rockville, Maryland; Pontiac, Michigan; Rolling Meadows, Illinois; Springfield, Illinois.

1962   Designated "Poet Laureate of Illinois. " Writes Foreword for *To Turn the Tide*, a book of John F. Kennedy's speeches. Carl Sandburg Elementary School opens in Joliet, Illinois.

1963   *Honey and Salt* is published on January 6, his eighty–fifth birthday. Receives International United Poets Award as "Hon. Poet Laureate of the U. S. A. "

1964   Receives Presidential Medal of Freedom from President Lyndon B. Johnson.

1966   Carl Sandburg Junior High School opens in Glendora, California.

1967   Dies July 22 at his home in Flat Rock, North Carolina (and the author hereof was born on July 30, 1967, which might be the lot of this study) . Carl Sandburg Elementary School opens in Littleton, Colorado. Carl Sandburg Junior College opens in Galesburg, Illinois.

Abbreviations

AS: *The American Songbag* (New York: Harcourt, Brace & Company, 1927)

AYS: *Always the Young Strangers* (New York: Harcourt, Brace and Company, 1953)

C: *Cornhuskers* (Mineola, New York: Dover Publications, Inc. , 2000)

CP: *Chicago Poems* (New York: Dover Publications, Inc. , 1994)

CPCS: *The Complete Poems of Carl Sandburg* (San Diego, New York and London: Harcourt Brace Jovanocich, Publishers, 1970)

CS: *Carl Sandburg* (Cleveland and New York: The World Publishing Company, 1961)

CSB: *Carl Sandburg: A Biography* (New York: Charles Scribner's Sons, 1991)

CSLW: *Carl Sandburg: His Life and Works* (University Park and London: The Pennsylvania State University Press, 1987)

EWC: *Ever the Winds of Chance* (Urbana and Chicago: University of Illinois Press, 1983)

GMA: *Good Morning, America* (New York: Harcourt, Brace and Company, 1928)

HP: *Harvest Poems* 1910–1960 (San Diego, New York and London: Harcourt Brace & Company, 1988)

LCS: *The Letters of Carl Sandburg* (New York: Harcourt, Brace & World, Inc. , 1968)

PDG: *The Poet and the Dream Girl* (Urbana and Chicago: University of Illinois Press, 1999)

PY: *The People, Yes* (San Diego, New York and London: Harcourt Brace

& Company, 1964)

SR: *The Sandburg Range* (New York: Harcourt, Brace and Company, 1957)

SS: *Smoke and Steel* (New York: Harcourt, Brace and Company, 1920)

SSW: *Slabs of the Sunburnt West* (New York: Harcourt, Brace and Company, 1922)

WS: *Wind Song* (New York: Harcourt, Brace & World, Inc. , 1960)

Introduction

In recent years, pop culture study is one of the academic hot spots. When we think of American culture, what first comes to our mind is often the pop culture: McDonald's, Coca Cola, Levi's, Disneyland, Michael Jordan, Julia Roberts, and so on. Why do we think of these? It is only because of their popularity—their being widely accepted. What is pop culture? Pop is short for popular. The origins of pop culture can often be traced to popular movies, television shows, and music stars or sports figures. They are accepted by a large group of people. Pop culture is usually promoted by business and advertisement. And it is in close connection with the acceptance of the broad masses of the people.

Since popular poetics belongs to culture, it must bear the features of wide acceptance by the masses, too. For deep investigation, let's investigate what role literature plays in society. It has been all the time a discussion and a debate. But most people tend to agree that literature should functionally play an active role for the instruction of the people in society. And due to this, if we take now a point of view from pop culture, firstly, Carl Sandburg's popular poetics could be attributed to his common origin, his role as a minstrel, his frequent appearance on TV screen reading aloud his poems, and his frequent participation in socialist activities benefiting the common people; secondly, it is because of his colloquial and musical language, common theme and popular poetic style, which could be and actually were accepted widely by the people in many aspects.

For deep and profound investigation in Sandburg's popular poetics, history must be traced to the period from 1878 to 1967, the life span of American poet Sandburg, when America experienced many great events, chronologically including Spanish American War (1898), World War I (1914-1918), the Great

Depression (1929-1941), World War II (1939-1945), Korean War (1950-1953), and finally, Vietnam War (1965-1975) . The first four are found to influence Sandburg and his poetry deeply: Spanish American War in which he was involved as a private, WWI, the Great Depression and WWII, which are all reflected in different places of his poetry and dominate his philosophy in life, social activities and literary creation. And it was just under this turbulent age and serious American situation that Sandburg came to grow into the people's poet and a great writer.

Sandburg's literary creation, generally speaking, can be traced back to 1904 when he had his first poems and some prose pieces published by Asgard Press in the form of a book under the title of *In Reckless Ecstasy*. In 1905, he decided to work in Chicago as an editor-journalist for *Tomorrow Magazine* and *The Lyceumite*. But the year of 1908 saw him leave Chicago for Wisconsin. He worked there as a political writer, a lecturer and an organizer for the Social Democratic Party. And it was there that he met his dream girl Lilian Steichen and married her. As a socialist, he worked hard for his belief. Then, four years later in 1912 he moved to Chicago a second time, but this time Sandburg worked and lived there till 1945 when he and his family fulfilled a long-dreamed move to Connemara Farm near Flat Rock, North Carolina.

During the Chicago years Sandburg got in much in literary creation. He published widely as a poet, biographer, journalist, children's writer, novelist, musician, folk singer and collector of folksongs. In 1914, *Poetry: A Magazine of Verse* published some of his poems, containing his landmark poem— "Chicago" winning much fame for him. Then, *Chicago Poems*, his first and best-known major book of poetry, was published in 1916. And then were published *Cornhuskers* (1918), *Smoke and Steel* (1920), *Slabs of the Sunburnt West* (1922), *Good Morning, America* (1928), and *The People, Yes* (1936), with the last one being his most popular single book in which his solicitude for the people, his interest in folk speech and expression became a clear feature of his poetry. And it was just *The People*, Yes, the most representative and powerful work, that hammered him finally and mostly into a poet of the people.

As a poet, especially in the collections of his poems mentioned above, Sandburg speaks directly and compellingly of the commons, a vigorous and enduring group of composite characters embodying Sandburg's free-verse portraits who he thinks "will live on" and "move eternally". Throughout his life, he kept thinking about the people. In practice, he went into the people; and in poetry, he described the people. The ordinary persons are a central topic among his poetic lines and held a special and prominent place in his mind. So the distinguished American poet Lee Bennett Hopkins[1] profiles Sandburg as "Sandburg wrote poetry about people—men, women, children people like you and me."[2] And he thinks of Sandburg as "Americas 'poet of the people'"[3], while an author of a newspaper says Sandburg is "often acclaimed as 'the poet of the people' for a body of work that spoke to all reaches of humanity" in an article with the title of "A letter-perfect plethora for our young abecedarians."[4] And American scholar and writer Joseph Epstein[5] even dissertates Sandburg as a poet of the people with a direct title "The People's Poet"[6] in the world-widely renowned academic journal Commentary in New York, in which he explains why the author thinks that Sandburg is truly the people's poet. The article covers 6 pages of the issue of the journal. On the basis of the materials at hand, it is likely the longest thesis discussing Sandburg as the people's poet. In spite of this, there is no one who studied and studies Sandburg as the people's poet in a comprehensive way. So, in this dissertation, the theme of Sandburg's being a poet of the peo-

---

① Lee Bennett Hopkins, born in Scranton, Pennsylvania, on April 13, 1938. His famous collections include *Days to Celebrate* (Greenwillow, 2005) and *Oh No! Where Are My Pants? and Other Disasters* (Harper Collins, 2005).

② Lee, Hopkins. *A Poetry of Workshop: In Print of Teaching Pre K-8.* Norwalk: Jan. 2005. Vol. 35, Iss. 4; p. 74.

③ Ibid..

④ Basbanes, Nicholas. A letter-perfect plethora for our young abecedarians. Worcester, Mass. : Aug 10, 2003. p. 5.

⑤ Joseph Epstein, 1937 – , a famous scholar and an emeritus lecturer in English and writing at Northwestern University, born and educated in Chicago, and also a writer of some books such a books of essays and short fiction including *Envy, Snobbery: The American Version, Narcissus Leaves the Pool, Life Sentences, and so on.*

⑥ Epstein, Joseph. The People's Poet. *Commentary*: May 1992, Vol. 93 Issue 5, p. 47.

ple and his popular poetics will be demonstrated in details in relatively full–scale aspects.

Sandburg's fame as a historian began when he wrote his great six–volume biography on Abraham Lincoln. He believed that previous biographies had idealized Lincoln too much. Two–volume *Abraham Lincoln: The Prairie Years* was published in 1926 on Lincoln's Birthday; and the four–volume *Abraham Lincoln: The War Years* was published in 1939. This is the most important one of his prose pieces; for these he received the Pulitzer Prize. And by many historians, scholars, and critics the books are considered to be not only the most literary but also the most authentic Lincoln biography written to that time.

Some of his other main works during his prime years include his autobiography: *Always the Young Strangers* (1953); poetry: *Complete Poems* (1950), *Harvest Poems: 1910–1960* (1960), *Honey and Salt* (1963); novel: *Remembrance Rock* (1948); books for young folks: *Rootabaga Stories* (1922), *Rootabaga Pigeons* (1923), *Abe Lincoln Grows Up* (1928), *Early Moon* (1930), *Prairie–Town Boy* (1955), *The Wedding Procession of the Rag Doll and the Broom Handle and Who Was In It* (1967).

In order to explain his achievements, the following prizes he gained can be of some help. In 1914 he won Helen Haire Levinson Prize for best poems of the year; in 1919 he shared Poetry Society of America prize with Margaret Widdemer; in 1940 he won Pulitzer Prize for history and was elected to AAAL (American Academy of Arts and Letters); and in 1950 he won Pulitzer Prize for his *Complete Poems*. Then he received AAAL's gold medal for history in 1952 and later got the same medal for poetry in 1953. Sandburg was also awarded the Presidential Medal of Freedom in 1964. Being a poet, Sandburg was also popular as a historian biographer. He has been recognized as the people's poet only second to Walt Whitman[1].

---

　① Walt Whitman, 1819–1892, American poet whose great work *Leaves of Grass* (first published 1855), written in unconventional meter and rhyme (free verse), and in common people's language, celebrates the self, the common subjects of common people, universal brotherhood, and the greatness of democracy and the United States. And this influenced Sandburg much in his poetry.

Although Sandburg was and is widely accepted as both his status of being a poet and the identity of being a biographer, to specialize in his poetry is the main discussion to support his place of the people's poet herein. Then, what about the study of Sandburg? As we know, though he was very popular and once a focus when he was alive, after a rough literary review by searching (in December 2004) two authoritative academic journal databases as illustrations (one is American, the other is Chinese), the study of Sandburg and his poetry is found to be limited, let alone the topic chosen here (Though there are some related commentaries in other academic journals). In American database–Gale: Literature Resource Center, the topic or related ones found are mostly book reviews, or on some specific poems; and no articles of overall critique about Sandburg as a poet are given, except, to instance, the thesis "A Poet of Common–Place", which numbers only 1759 words in the text by computer statistics and was published (as the footnote here annotates) in 1920, the year of his *Smoke and Steel* being published in New York.

Another example is in China. By searching CAJ Full – text Database with keywords and titles from the year 1994 to 2004, in total there are 12 articles within 10 years, ten of which are written by Professor Meng Xianzhong from Weifang College, Shangdong Province; among the ten only one paper in theme involves Sandburg's poetry. Professor Meng translates Sandburg's ten poems without commentary, while others treat Sandburg's general life, literary creation, and other aspects. One of the other two, analyzing the poem "Fog" only, discusses Sandburg as a poet with the title of "Carl Sandburg and Imagism", and another one labels Sandburg as an American industrial poet.

As to the expression of "popular poetics", some scholars mentioned the concept before. Andrew J. E. Bell from University of Nevada, Las Vegas once put forward the term in "The Popular Poetics and Politics of the Aeneid". He says: "Modern analysts have not always been ready to ponder whether in fact Vergil's artistry succeeded not only in pleasing the community at large but thereby also in communicating aesthetically a regime's legitimacy." (*Transactions of the American Philological Association*, Vol. 129. 1999, pp. 263–279.), from which we see artistry (popular poetics included) should please the community. In China, Mr. Wang Xuehai also referred to it in 2002 in the article "Roses Far Away from Society and the Masses: Interrogating Belles Letters", saying that the growing and developing of belles letters involve an open process of popular poetics. (*Exploring and Contending.* 2002, No. 1.)

Generally, the study of popular poetics and of Sandburg's poetry and poetics are very limited. Therefore, there is still more space for further study about Sandburg the poet, esp. in China. The author hereof wishes if the study could be an addition to Sandburg study in China's academia, and if his poetry and his popular poetics could be a reference for Chinese contemporary poets' creation to bring the importance of the common people into prominence in their poetry and draw more attention to dumb millions, that would be pleasing and of a little significance; and if it could be somewhat fresh and creative in international academia, that would be the author's wild wish.

For this purpose, the dissertation attempts to demonstrate that Sandburg's origin, socialistic tendency, common poetic subjects, language drawn from his fraternal people, and his own and unique style contribute to his affinity with the people and popularity as a people's poet. However it is just this unique poetics that reveals him an honest, devoted and loyal battler for his fraternal downtrodden and the forgotten people in the lower society. In his eyes and poetry, the common people always struggle to survive each day, but they will live on eternally as a whole.

But how to define Popular Poetics is the first thing before further study. Popular Poetics herein refers to the poetics in poetry which can be widely accepted by and among the masses for its easy understanding in language and form, and resonant theme or topics. In addition, it covers the art of spoken words, performance poetry, hip-hop, rap song, reading aloud and so on.

In the structure of the dissertation, it starts from Chapter One: his common origin, and his early wandering as a hobo, like some from the West and Midwest of America, which played a role in helping him grow into a poet of the people. Then, Chapter Two discusses his political leanings—an ardent socialist and an advocator of democracy. The attitude and his activities concerning this lead to his poetry's approaching the ordinary people and his deep pity on them. And in Chapter Three, some of his important poetry books are analyzed to show his further affinity with the people: *Chicago Poems*, *Cornhuskers*, *Smoke and Steel*, and especially, the most important and popular one—*The People*, *Yes* making him more popularly accepted as the people's poet. Meanwhile, in this part and by the study of his poetry, his notion and understanding of the concept "people" is discussed and concluded. Chapter Four treats Sandburg's poetics and its mass basis in which his mass groundwork decides his people's poetics—popular poetics, including his practice among the commons, the heritage from Walt Whitman, the unique poetic style, the themes about the people, musicality in his poetry, what's more, his "Sense of Nativeness" in grain. The further Chapter Five treats Sandburg as a minstrel, his *The American Songbag* and great influence on modern poetry. At last, the whole dissertation leads to the final Conclusion: Sandburg is worthy of the people's poet who came from the people of his origin, went into the people of his respecters, eulogized the people as his brothers, and conversely, was admired by the people living on eternally. He composed fraternal "songs" in his popular poetics for the eternal people.

Chapter One
Common Origin and Early Wandering

> I was born on a cornhusk mattress. Until I was past ten
> or more years, when we became a family of nine per-
> sons, I remember the mattresses were bedticking filled
> with cornhusks. And we all slept well on cornhusks
> and never knew the feel of feather beds. ...
>
> —Carl Sandburg

Sandburg's origin—the very ordinary family and the bottom of the society
works much to lead to his life long concern for and connection with the ordinary
people, playing a role in the formation and growth of his popular poetics. This
part discusses his family background and his early wanderings in the west as a
hobo and experiences before he came to Chicago to start his career, which resulted in his profound sympathy with the commons and laid a solid foundation for
him to become the people's poet.

Ⅰ. From Midwest and the Common Folk

Sandburg was born in prairie Galesburg, Illinois on January 6, 1878. His
father, Carl August Sandburg, was a Swedish immigrant (his mother, a Swedish
immigrant too, a housewife and once a hotel maid) and one of thousands of semi-
literate immigrants who came to the United States in search of American dream, only
to find he had to endure, like many of his group, inhuman working conditions and
the humiliation from the social system that was oppressive and showed enough indif-

ference to his and their struggles. His father worked ten hours a day, six days each week for 35 years as a blacksmith's helper for a railway company. And Sandburg received stern and sometimes even harsh discipline from his father who worked with unrelenting toil in the pioneering spirit of American workingmen.

As a child, he was mischievous, restless and streetvious, and his school time was happy and poeticized in his memory. At about six, he began his school days. Sandburg recalled, "Many of the boys and girls went in for autograph albums. When they asked me I wrote: When you are old and cannot see / Put on your specs and think of me. Or I wrote an old–time rhyme: Count that day lost whose low descending sun / Views from thy hand no worthy action done" (AYS: 123). As he explained, he had learned these lines from reading autograph albums. We don't care and mind where these words came. At least we can know that at that time when he was very young he could feel rhyme and foot consciously or unconsciously. Maybe most people can do this, but he remembered so clearly.

And even he as well as the children at his age taught themselves to be moral by simple poems; for example: It is a sin / To steal a pin (AYS: 164). It shows though they were naughty, they knew what they should do and what they should not do. For him, "to steal a pin" "is a sin". And he remembered in the late 1880's, on parting of an evening, they would say, "Good night, sleep tight, sleep tight, and don't let the bedbugs bite" (AYS: 164). Anyway, these rhymes helped to ground Sandburg's later poetry creation, for in his school days the memory about poetry seemed more prominent than other things. To instance another, according to his autobiography *Always The Young Strangers*, he still remembered some lines of William Holmes McGuffey① about "Little Things": Little drops of water, / Little grains of sand, / Make the mighty ocean / And the pleasant land··· / Little deeds of kindness, /Little words of love / Help to make earth happy / Like the heaven above (AYS: 177). In this way, Sandburg and the children at his ages educated themselves by some poems and ballads when

---

① American educator who compiled the *McGuffey Eclectic Readers* (1836–1857), schoolbooks that combined reading lessons with moralistic teachings.

they were young.

But the Sandburgs were poor; everybody tried to help the big family. When Sandburg had the first regular job, he was only eleven. He did many odd jobs for earning money. On Saturdays and after school hours he took gunnysacks and went around streets, alleys, barns and houses, hunting in ditches rubbish piles for rags, bones, scrap iron, and bottles, for which cash could be paid to him. His gunnysack could bring him eighteen cents a week. Then with regret in 1891 he left school for good after eighth grade, for the family could not really support two children for school at the same time. From the fall of 1892 Sandburg began to work in a farm as a milk-wagon helper for a small boss who ran a dairy two miles out of town. His mother would wake him up at five-thirty early morning. For a nickel, he could have ridden a trolley car halfway to the farm by paying only one nickel, but he walked two miles each day to save the fare. He worked seven days a week with a salary of twelve dollars a month, with no vacations or holidays all the time.

Late October of that year saw a family disaster coming. He had a sore throat but still continued to work. Then a high fever made him weak enough and he had to stay at home in bed. The illness spread through the Sandburg household quickly, putting his elder brother Mart in bed for several days too. Soon, his two younger brothers, seven-year-old Emil and two-year-old Freddie, suffered the same sore throats that they could not swallow. It turned out to be diphtheria. Several days later Freddie died. Emil, being older, was more rugged. They watched his struggle for breath, hoping he could endure and get it over, but within an hour after Freddie stopped breathing, Emil died too. The family disaster was rooted deeply in his heart, so the portraiture of a cripple in one of Sandburg's poems— "Cripple" can be thought of as an allusion to his two gone brothers:

ONCE when I saw a cripple
Gasping slowly his last days with the white plague,
Looking from hollow eyes, calling for air,
Desperately gesturing with wasted hands

> In the dark and dust of a house down in a slum,
>
> I said to myself
>
> I would rather have been a tall sunflower
>
> Living in a country garden
>
> Lifting a golden-brown face to the summer,
>
> Rain-washed and dew-misted,
>
> Mixed with the poppies and ranking hollyhocks,
>
> And wonderingly watching night after night
>
> The clear silent processionals of stars. (CP: 13 - 14)

Here it seems his two younger brothers suffering diphtheria were "gasping slowly his last days with the white plague," and "looking from hollow eyes, calling for air". Just because of his brothers disaster and shadow, Sandburg could depict the cripple so vividly. And just because of this unhappy experience, he could look "from hollow eyes", and could see into the cripple who was like his gone brothers "calling for air" and wanting to survive and get out of "the dark and dust of a house down in a slum" to live better, to watch "night after night / The clear silent processionals of stars." And "the white plague" can allude to his brothers's uffering-diphtheria. Surely, "white plague" reminds us of tuberculosis; but meanwhile we should learn that the symptom of diphtheria is: the swollen throat first turns pink and red and then "a grayish white" (CSB: 21) . Therefore we can guess in Sandburg's mind, if "plague" stands for only an illness, here "the white plague" can refer to or allude to his brothers´fatal illness-diphtheria.

And things often come not singly but in pairs. In *The People*, *Yes*, he pitied on the illness and the victims again: "A ladder rung breaking and a legbone or armbone with it, layoffs and no paycheck coming, the red diphtheria card on the front door, the price for a child's burial casket, hearse and cemetery lot…" (PY: 157) Apparently, the illness making his family suffer suffered Sandburg much in his lifelong time. And he changed the pain into an extensive pity on the other common people.

Anyhow, the Sandburgs' life had to go on. What Sandburg earned-twelve-dollar salary from the dairy was essential to the family's survival. When winter came, it was savagely cold and bitter with ice and snow. Sandburg walked to cover his daily milk route to save the carfare. His feet were often numb and painful with chilblains. In those frigid days there was no more money for him to spare for shoes. So, when Sandburg worked as a shoeshine boy, he could cherish shoes and could do the job well, and so he said, "I took to my shoeshine stand, where already the first customer had taken the seat and was waiting for me. I shined his shoes, the next, and the next. " (AYS: 367) This is only one of the epitomes of Sandburg's early life, but it roots him profoundly into common people. If shoes can be taken as the foundation of the people's poet, this kind of really hard life in Galesburg is the soles of his supporting him to walk and stand well in his later life.

Though life was hard and Sandburg left school early, he was never unwilling to gain knowledge. In Galesburg there was Lombard College a few blocks away from his home. It had been said people could go in free; so Sandburg often bared feet up to the third-floor chapel and on up the narrow stairs to the little gallery to feel what education was and find something new and fresh to him. He was jealous of the students educated there and wished someday he could go to college. Then as he wished, he applied to the college library to borrow books. "I got my card and began taking out books, one by one, and the date I took the book out got stamped on my card. " He said, " One by one I read all the books in the library by Horatio Alger[1], Oliver Optic, and C. A. Stephens. When all the books by those authors were out, I tried Hans Christian Andersen, and if he was out then some kind of Strange Tales of this and that. " (AYS: 305) So eagerly he read books and gained knowledge.

When bitter ends, sweet then comes. His dream indeed came true after he retired from army as a private in Puerto Rico during Spanish-American War in 1898. He got the chance to be enrolled as a special student in Lombard College in which students came from plain folks mainly, from the working class like

---

[1]　1832–1899, American writer of inspirational adventure books, such as *Ragged Dick* (1867), featuring impoverished boys who through hard work and virtue achieve great wealth and respect. The story and the spirit just encouraged Sandburg to overcome many difficulties in his life and career.

Sandburg, and only some from middle class. During the days of college, sometimes he paid for his tuition by ringing the college bell. In 1900 he began to sell the stereoscopic photographs for money. But in 1902 before graduating he left college to wander over the country to sell Underwood & Underwood stereoscopic photographs for a living.

Young Sandburg became a vagabond who quickly outgrew the boundaries of his hometown. Maybe from his father, he inherited the hunger for travel which led him to make his first trip to Chicago in 1896, and then he joined the vast procession of hoboes, tramps and bums to explore the American frontier, seeking to find or escape work. It is sure that at this time Sandburg embedded himself, at least objectively, into the really common people to some extent.

II. A Hobo in the West

I SHALL foot it Down the roadway in the dusk, Where shapes of hunger wander And the fugitives of pain go by⋯ The dust of the traveled road Shall touch my hands and face.

—Carl Sandburg

As Sandburg's hard life continued in his hometown, a kind of hopelessness was growing in his mind. He wrote, "I had my bitter and lonely hours moving out of boy years into a grown young man. I can remember a winter when the thought came often that it might be best to step out of it all. "What would be the best way?" He thought of "prussic acid", "carbolic acid", "hanging myself", "throw myself into Lake George", "stand in front of Q. ① Fast Mail Train. " (AYS: 375) Indeed, Sandburg felt hopeless since he thought of suicide. Pains

① Standing for Quincy, a city of western Illinois on a bluff above the Mississippi River. It is a trade, industrial, and distributing center.

produce poets. His pain of this time maybe belongs to this kind.

Meanwhile, his admiration for pioneers and old-timers filled him with dreams. When he saw some of them on the street or at the County Fair, at celebrations or at the Old Settlers picnics, they became so real and near to him. It was them that had broken the prairie, built the first roads and streets, set up the first schools and churches, and formed the traditions of the place where Sandburg was born and grew up. These old-timers became part of his mind and memory, working dimly but definitely. And all these encouraged Sandburg to adventure, to try, to explore, to experiment and to exercise himself.

Though he wanted to commit suicide, the pioneers he often saw lit a small glimmer in front of him and he came to realize that the trouble he faced and the reason for his agony was inside himself rather than in other aspects. Then he got to sense and was conscious again; he decided to go to the West to begin his hobo life. That was June of 1897, and at this time he was 19 years old.

When he took to the road, he left Galesburg with his hand free, no bag or bedclothes, wearing "a black-sateen shirt, coat, vest, and pants, a slouch hat, good shoes and socks, no underwear, in my pockets a small bar of soap, a razor, a comb, a pocket mirror, two handkerchiefs, a piece of string, needles and thread, a Waterbury watch, a knife, a pipe and a sack of tobacco, three dollars and twenty-five cents in cast. " (AYS: 381) And the time span of this journey west is from the last week of June of 1897, a bright and cool afternoon, until the afternoon of October 15, 1897.

First he came to Iowa, and this was "my first time off the soil of Illinois, the Sucker State. "① (AYS: 381) He slept on a boat. At Burlington, Quincy, and Keokuk he shouldered kegs of nails. And at Keokuk he "spread newspapers on green grass near a canal, and with coat over shoulders, slept in the open with my left arm for a pillow. " (AYS: 382) Sandburg got a waiter job in a small

---

① Referring to Illinois. In pioneer days, when rivers were the main arteries of travel, all commerce of the entire western country passed by the shores of Illinois on the Ohio and the Mississippi Rivers—to New Orleans, to St. Louis and up the Missouri River to the west and northwest, or up the Mississippi to the north country. Lake Michigan, penetrating deep into the heart of the continent, was another decisive factor.

lunch counter at Keokuk. Next he came to Bean Lake, Missouri. An Irish boss hired him at a dollar and twenty-five cents a day and Sandburg had to pay him three dollars a week for board and room in his four-room one-story house thirty feet from the railroad tracks. Then on a Sunday morning, he hopped a freight for Kansas City. There he worked as dishwasher in a restaurant on Armour Avenue. After a week or so, he got ready to harvest wheat in western Kansas. During this period, he was very economical. For him, an ice cream was a kind of luxury. According to Sandburg, he was ever tempted to spend ten cents for a dish of ice cream and it became the best temptation; after a hard struggle in his mind, he bought one, unfortunately he got a diarrhea as a result.

And even on his way west by hopping freight trains he was once bullied by a bully. Before a train started, a shack① ordered him off an open coal car where Sandburg was crouched hiding. But when the train started, Sandburg again got on the same car again. The hobo came to face Sandburg closely to ask for some money, otherwise he would punish him. Sandburg refused because he thought the hobo was not a passenger-fare collector. Then he was given one fist on his jaw and another fist in his mouth from the rascal hobo.

Sandburg was such a common person; he could endure anything. And he could always survive. This manifests Sandburg was a common one, but equipped with uncommon spirit; one of the common people, bearing what the common people could bear, because the people, like himself, have to live on, and "The people will live on. / The learning and blundering people will live on. / They will be tricked and sold and again sold / And go back to the nourishing earth for ro- othold, / the people so peculiar in renewal and comeback, / You can't laugh off their capacity to take it···/ The people is a tragic and comic two-face: / hero and hoodlum: phantom and gorilla twist-/ ing to moan with a gargoyle mouth: 'They / buy me and sell me··· it's a game··· / sometime I'll break loose···'" (PY: 284) This is Sandburg's people, and this is himself, one of many, living on.

Sandburg went on traveling by boxcar, and experiencing among the com-

---

① In the then American English, a shack refers to a hobo for brakeman on the train in the past.

mon. He came to Hutchinson, Kansas. There he often went hungry for he could not find work for meal. This is just like what he writes in his autobiography Always the Young Stranger: " 'have you got any work I can do for breakfast?' They took one look at me and shut the door. " (AYS: 390) This phenomenon often occurred to hoboes including Sandburg. Hunger went on.

In spite of his common origin, Sandburg would never sink low. In fact he never thought of sinking low. He once met a thief, who asked Sandburg to complot to steal money and jewels through a window, and then split them. Sandburg refused to do it and managed to get away from him. Normally, in this situation, when a common man is difficult to survive and live on, he or she is likely to break his or her base line in morality. Sandburg did not and would not. He had his own firm and solid standard. He would never fall to sin. Never.

Hoboing continued. At Larned, Pawnee, Kansas, Sandburg worked as a carpenter for three days, then worked five days as a thresher on a farm and two days on another, pitchforking bundles of wheat onto the tables of the thresher. Five days later, he again decided to head west to Lakin, because it was said there was more work to do. At Lakin, Kansas, once more he worked with a threshing crew about three weeks. He moved from one farm to another. This really helped him know more people, all kinds of common people working so hard to survive to live on. In Canyon City, Colorado, Sandburg picked pears, earning meals and a few dollars. He went on to Salida, Colorado. Then he took a train heading back east for Denver.

In a hotel of Denver, Sandburg washed dishes for weeks. Heading east on, he stopped in a jungle① three days where he met some hobo friends he communicated much. It was in this way that Sandburg got much first hand information of the people in lower society, the hoboe' language and their stories appearing and retold again in his poems. He had a kind of friendship with these friends, he was even unwilling to leave them, so he mentioned, "I was sorry to leave that friendly jungle. " (AYS: 398) He caught a freight train to Nebraska City, where

---

① A jungle was a place where hoboes camp at that time.

he chopped wood and picked apples. When he chopped woods for a family for meals, a kind lawyer, the man of the house, found his suit was ragged enough and gave him an old suit of his, an iron-gray all-wool suit, "better than any I had had in my life". (AYS: 398). Then Sandburg caught freight for Omaha, Nebraska. In Omaha, he served as dishwasher in Hotel Mercer, but got no payment, because the hotel was closed and the boss vanished.

Till the afternoon of October 15, 1897, Carl Sandburg came back to Galesburg his hometown. "I came to the only house in the United States where I could open a door without knocking and walk in for a kiss from the woman of the house. " (AYS: 400). To make this adventure clear, his route is charted here; within textboxes are the main places where he arrived and worked; inside the arrows, which show his direction of traveling often by free freight or boxcar, is some additional information, with the elliptic labels telling the jobs he did where he went and stayed. (See Table I on next page) .

Looking back, there were some more reasons arousing him to be a hobo. When he lived in Galesburg as a young man, he often went into and talked to the hoboes and tramps that inhabited the "jungles" near the railroad tracks to know that there was a hierarchy of vagabonds. They could be classified into tramps, bums and hoboes. As tramps, they would dream and wander, usually following the lines of the main railroads. There were subspecies of tramps—professionals and amateurs. They were also called "gay-cats", and would break down and work sometimes in hopes of finding regular jobs. Some tramps in fact were runaway boys or dropouts from school who were infected with wanderlust. Bums, who drank and wandered, frequenting houses and saloons; as a principle, bums never worked, and would like to be beggars and sometimes even swindlers. Finally, hoboes, who worked and wandered, usually rode the rails illegally to work on farms at harvest time, or in the cities, the mines or the houses along railroads. And what kind did Sandburg belong to? As discussed, Sandburg hunted for work on the way to the West, sometimes riding the rails illegally, but never being a swindler. So the first traveling west showed he was a hobo.

Table   1   **Carl Sandburg's Hobo Journey**

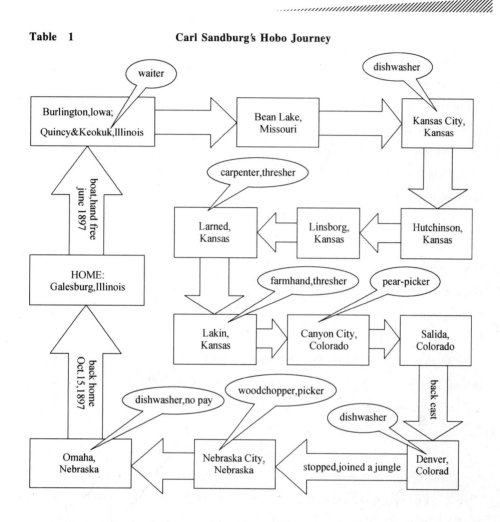

As Sandburg's first west trip, it is important, meaningful and crucial for his later career and poetry creation. As once a farmhand, a thresher, a waiter, a fruit-picker, even a dishwasher and so on, Sandburg experienced so much within half a year. He did so many odd jobs and all were physical. For later Sandburg, this made him realize physical laborers are substantial workers and toilers who are water as the base, while all the others are ships in the water. Sandburg sensed this and insisted on mass line in his subsequent literary creation. And the journey gave him chances to live among all kinds of people including rascals, thieves, etc., who are all under the name of Sandburg's "people". Just by this, he grasped the essential qualities of the people: their life, their hardship, their habits, their thoughts, and their language.

The journey left Sandburg with a permanent wanderlust and affected him profoundly. It reverberated through the rest of his life. What's more, after this Sandburg began to form his habit of meditating which is often requisite to his personal development in poetry creation. It left him with deep emotion to and friendship for hoboes, bums and tramps with their lingo and songs. Meanwhile it deepened his empathy for the common people.

To be further, the hobo journey for Carl Sandburg was an exploration of his own frontier. Being one of the pioneers helping to explore and build a new part of the nation, he pilgrimaged his soul as one of commons for the first time, and shaped his thought and attitudes towards the people and the world. His hobo journey stimulated him to call to mind the stories he experienced and become a storyteller in his poetry.

At this point, Sandburg is similar to Jack London[1] who left school at the age of 14 (Sandburg at 13 years old) and once worked as a seaman and a hobo and adopted socialistic views. London was arrested in Niagara Falls and jailed for vagrancy, and Sandburg was jailed for ten days in the Allegheny County for he didn't buy train ticket, as described in the following Section III. For London, he attributed his success to his hobo experience. He believes, as a writer, "He must create spontaneously and instantaneously—and not upon the theme he reads in the face of the person who opens the door···. I have often thought that to this training of my tramp days is due much of my success as a storywriter. " (CSB: 34) Sandburg did in the similar way. He absorbed and digested the stories his fellow hobos shared, and wove them into his poetry and prose.

In what ways did this journey change Sandburg? Sandburg himself said: "What had the trip done to me? I couldn't say. It had changed me···Away deep in my heart now I had hope as never before. Struggles lay ahead, I was sure,

---

① 1876–1916, American writer of rugged adventure novels, including *The Call of the Wild* (1903) and *The Sea Wolf* (1904) .

but whatever they were I would not be afraid of them. " (AYS: 400) Yes. It changed him to a greater degree in his spirit! It enabled him to face any difficulty in front of him bravely and fearlessly. It gave him self–confidence. He believed he could survive and live on in any case, under any situation, and in any corner. The hobo journey, also a spiritual journey, opened his eyes and ears to the problems of his times. He began to listen to authentic voices from the common people. And with his pen, in his poetry, he started to explore and discover his country, his countrymen, and himself.

Ⅲ. Wanderer–Jailbird's Throes: Predawn Darkness of a Poet

In the summer of 1902, Sandburg went on selling the Underwood & Underwood views with his college classmate Fred Dickinson in some places of Wisconsin. After Dickinson left him for further study, Sandburg went to Vineland, New Jersey, canvassed the town and the Italian fruit farmers. In nearby Philadelphia Sandburg went to visit Independence Hall, and then, Camden, walking along Mickle Street to visit Walt Whitman House for the first time. Then he went to Harleigh Cemetery and worshiped Whitman's tomb, expressing his admiring e-motion to his idol. About Whitman, Sandburg writes: " He didn't know he wouldn't need the tomb and that *Leaves of Grass* would keep his memory greener than any receptacle of granite. " (EWC: 128) And Sandburg didn't know he wouldn't need a tomb either, and his *The People, Yes* "would keep his memory greener than any receptacle of granite. "

On the way of view selling, Sandburg never forgot to study and write. For instance, he bought a book of Shakespeare in Philadelphia. In the meantime, he began to write more and more. He wrote about philosophy and composed poetry.

Unfortunately, in a coal car, on his way to Freeport, Illinois for a job, he was caught and handcuffed by a constable to an office because he did not buy train ticket. In the end he was fined $10. But he could choose to pay the fine or to take ten days in the Allegheny County jail. For lack of money, Sandburg had no choice and was jailed. So, "each morning we were allowed a half hour out of our cell. On a four foot wooden walk with a railing to keep us from falling off, which was called 'the range', we were allowed to walk back and forth." Sandburg records in his autobiography *Ever the Winds of Chance*, "Our cell, holding three prisoners, was meant in the plan of the jail, to hold only one inmate." (EWC: 135) But to tell a later story, fortunately, it was also a good chance for Sandburg to experience another kind of life, probing into every corner of the society, dark or bright. As the title of his autobiography *Ever the Winds of Chance* implies, this adventure and experience should be "Ever the Winds of Chance". It proved to be somewhat the predawn of darkness.

In jail, Sandburg had the chance to communicate with a black. He learned how to understand their language. He came to know the black's words, for example, "Speeshus carrer" means "Suspicious character." The black was in jail for his being a suspect. And when Sandburg asked, "What's your line? What do you do when you are outside?" He answered, "Ah lives wid de hose." Sandburg knew he was saying, "I live with the whores." He and the black related very well sharing the same cell. Even when the black left the jail Sandburg wished him good luck and told him to give his regard to his women. And he wished Sandburg back good luck too.

In Sandburg's eyes, all persons are the people, good or evil. In his opinion, evil comes from inefficient social system, government and society's inability and disorder. The people are passive to live. Ten days' prison life was not long, but Sandburg mentioned it many times in his later life. It gave him something negative, even disgraceful. And undoubtedly, it, too, gave him something positive and active. He used his flashlight and saw clearly many corners of jail and the society. He explored and experienced there.

After that, in Aurora (between Galesburg but near Chicago) Sandburg continued to canvass his views. And he could always get orders any day if he went out. He canvassed from door to door, farm to farm, or office to office. He lived in $1-a-week furnished room with no stove or furnace heat. In the morning he broke the ice in the pitcher and took sponge bath. At that time Sandburg was 27 years old. Certain feeling of monotony was creeping into his mind and life. A-gain just like what he thought of before his westward journey, he thought of sui-cide once more. "I thought of Carlyle's[①] man shaving one morning and what he did with his razor. " He writes in *Ever the Winds of Chance*, "From the west win-dow of my room one evening I watched a clear short winter sunset and found my eyes full of tears; I couldn't get at what the trouble was except that I was sad o-ver how I was doing. " (EWC: 139) Sandburg could be understood. A man, near thirty years old, had nothing stable to do for a living, only traveling from one place to another, let alone starting a career. He could just support himself, or just made ends meet each month. Where could he go? What could he do? "No pains, no gains". This kind of suffering did help much in his later writing. It deepened his writing and poetry to the bottom of the society. It enabled him to see every dead angle of human beings and the very bottom of human feeling. To be brief, he paid to gain, and lost to save.

Timely a kind of dream came to him to hint him a good luck and a success! (Maybe a coincidence, but not superstitious.) During this period, he often dreamt that he was on a horse and the horse was galloping in good time, and Sandburg was riding on the bare back. He could even recall the vivid scene very clearly: "I was doing well to stick on his back as he flew along the road. One night he was a bay, other nights sorrel, black, roan. He was doing his best to get to wherever it was I was going. " (EWC: 139) It's difficult to use psychoa-nalysis of Sigmund Freud (1856–1939) to unscramble the symbol in his dream by rote. But it is sure that Sandburg had been doing his best to get to wherever he had been going and flying "along the road" like a galloping horse, usually with success.

Meanwhile, Sandburg's brother Mart saw that Sandburg needed rest down to think to read and to write for further development. He got him a job at the Brooks Street fire Station in his hometown Galesburg. Mart said to him: "What

---

① Thomas Carlyle, 1795–1881, British historian and essayist whose works, such as *The French Revolution* (1837), are characterized by his trenchant social and political criticism and his complex literary style.

you want is plenty of time to read and write and you can do that in the fire station and you won't have to fuss around and worry about that damn view business. " Sandburg stopped his view business and worked in the fire station. The chief of the station, with a long head like that of his brother Mart, said several times to Sandburg: "I can see, Charlie (Sandburg's infant name), you're trying to make something of yourself. " (EWC: 141-2) He practiced often poetry and article writing. Then, what he had said and Sandburg had dreamed became true.

In December, 1904 he had his first poetry and a few pieces of prose published in a booklet under the title of *In Reckless Ecstasy* by Asgard Press with the help of his respectable college teacher Professor Wright, who was very helpful to Sandburg (to be discussed in Chapter Two in more detail). And to Sandburg's surprise, a reviewer in a journal *Mobile Register* in Alabama reviewed: "There is a vital spirit and an original touch in every word of this little book. " (EWC: 148) The short review encouraged him greatly.

After a fit of "birth" throes, the fireman-author-poet came into being! What an encouragement it should be!! It would lead him to go on, riding his "bay", "sorrel", "black" and "roan" dream-steed, "doing his best to get to wherever it was" and Sandburg was really going to be: a writer, a poet, a people's poet.

Chapter Two
Socialistic Tendency

I am a socialist but not a member of the party. I am an
I. W. W. but I don't carry a red card. I am an anar-
chist but not a member of the organization⋯. If I must
characterize the element I am most often active with I
would say I am with all rebels all the time as against all
people who are satisfied⋯I am for the single tax, for
all the immediate demands of the socialists⋯

—Carl Sandburg

Sandburg's political tendency of socialism actually forms his attitude toward
the common people. And it is determined by the principles and notion of socialism for the masses. Pure and real socialist or not, he was an ardent socialistic
poet caring about the people and serving the people, which later became a part
of footstone of his popular poetics.

Ⅰ. Sandburg's Socialism Concept

What is Socialism? And what socialism is practiced by Sandburg? The definition of Socialism has many editions. But all of them are connected to the following central idea: According to *The Columbia Encyclopedia* (Sixth Edition,
2001), Socialism is a "general term for the political and economic theory that
advocates a system of collective or government ownership and management of the

means of production and distribution of goods. "①

Since "means of production and distribution of goods" are owned and controlled by "collective or government", it means they are not controlled by capitalists, or to be exact, "means of production and distribution of goods" can be owned and controlled by the people. So Socialism is for the people's benefit, not for capitalists'. And here we tend to manifest that Sandburg is the people's poet, and Sandburg's socialism ideal and practice can support this point; then, Sandburg, the socialist is discussed herein.

After the study of materials of or about Sandburg, it is found to be embarrassing to define the socialism conception in Sandburg's mind, or by his understanding, because he would move from the right to the left in practice and his works. But generally speaking, his socialism was rooted in his witness of social and human events, not abstract theory.

Early in 1903 in one of his editorials of *The Lombard Review* of Lombard College, Sandburg began to pay attention to and discuss socialism: "If you think this subject of socialism is easy, and that everybody knows what socialism is. ⋯ You will find that there have been as many varieties of socialists as there are wild birds that fly in the woods and sometimes go up and on through the clouds. These varied socialists do not agree perfectly as to how the money shall be divided, what they shall do when not at work, and what tunes the band shall play as they fling to the breeze the flag of Equality. But on the proposition that there is something pitifully wrong, execrably wrong in the main works of our boasted civilization. ⋯" (EWC: 150). Since he found "These varied socialists do not agree", it is too hard for Sandburg to take advantage of one of the concepts of socialism. And it is unnecessary for him to do so. For Sandburg, all socialisms should take at least the common people's interests into more consideration as *The Columbia Encyclopedia* expresses hereinbefore.

But, what socialism is performed by Sandburg? After some study, simply and centrally speaking, but not so inexactly in science, his Socialism is for-the-

---

① See: http: //www. bartleby. com/65/so/socialis. html. 31 March 2004.

people–ism, "in which workers, the wealth producers are the rulers. " (CSB:
138)

Actually, at this time, Sandburg's socialism was, on the one hand, radical
to some extent, and on the other hand, conservative. When he formally joined
the socialist movement and organization, he showed an attitude of the right wing,
and would like to reform the social system orderly; and in this kind of spirit and
principle, Wisconsin Social–Democrats were highly organized partly by Sandburg; but in some of his poetry, his words suggest a kind of violence, expressing
his eagerness to change the world and society fundamentally; that's the signs of
left wing. The following poem with the title of "Fight" from *Chicago Poems* is
evidence:

RED drips from my chin where I have been eating.
Not all the blood, nowhere near all, is wiped off my mouth.
Clots of red mess my hair
And the tiger, the buffalo, know how.

Here, the poetic "I" is obviously not Sandburg himself, "I" should be one
of the non–proletarian exploiters eating the same kind; "I" am equal to the tiger,
the buffalo. "Clots of red mess my hair" are the aftermath of "fight" . Darwinian
principle of natural selection is: the best survive. But here it seems the fiercest
survive, or the most savage, survive. It's like what he writes in Section 90 of
The People, *Yes*: "The big fish eat the little fish, / the little fish eat shrimps /
and the shrimps eat mud. " (PY: 234) As a matter of fact, it is the live description of capitalism society. Sandburg continues in the poem "Fight":

I was a killer.
Yes, I am a killer.
I come from killing.
I go to more.
I drive red joy ahead of me from killing.
Red gluts and red hungers run in the smears and juices of my inside bones:

The child cries for a suck mother and I cry for war. (CP: 40)

In the second half of the poem, the most prominent is the repetition of "red"; it implies the radical lust of capitalists who will lick up all their interests. Though "The child cries for a suck mother", "I cry for war", for "I was a killer", and "I am a killer." Considering Sandburg's "red" —socialist background, from another angle, "red", the color can imply revolution and socialism to echo with the title "Fight" which doesn't appear in the whole poem at all. The whole poem shows the miserable phenomenon, and the title is the theme of the poem. As a result of such a severe and terrible fact, of course, the people should rise to fight to survive, and to fight to avoid being killed and eaten. "Fight" is a slogan; "Fight" is a call; "Fight" is a summons. This sort of allusion is indicated in another poem from Section 106, *The People, Yes*:

Sleep is a suspension midway

and a conundrum of shadows

lost in the meadows of the moon.

The people sleep.

Ai! Ai! the people sleep.

Yet the sleepers toss in sleep

and an end comes of sleep

and the sleepers wake.

Ai! ai! the sleepers wake! (PY: 283)

In the above poem, the people are from "sleep" to "wake". "Ai" is a surprise, a call, and a joy for hope! After they wake, the people can go to fight for the future, for the life, and for their own hope. The repetition of the interjection "Ai" shows the anxious feeling of the poet when the people are asleep and indicates the poet is eager to urge the people to struggle and fight.

The two poems above are actually some hints of a seduction and an encouragement of violence. Sandburg's leftwing thought is brought forward here clearly. His tendency is to call the people to innovate and reform by "fight" and by violence.

Therefore, there is a contradiction between his poetry and practice. And a concrete definition of socialism from Sandburg can't be made sure in theory and given to support his being an ardent socialist. In spite of this lack and difficulty, materials here can still manifest that Sandburg is an ardent socialist, if not in theory, or both in both theory and practice, but from his zealous enthusiasm for socialistic events, and his sympathy with and support to the common people, the proletarian class.

II. "An Ardent Socialist" [1]

In an essay Conrad Aiken [2] mentions Sandburg is a "Socialist" "with no reservations". (LCS: 243) To be exact, at the first beginning, Sandburg believed in Social Democracy [3], or as we discusses hereinbefore, he had the tendency to belong to the rightwing of socialism (though sometimes leftwing in poetry) . And what an ardent socialist Sandburg once was can be proved by the following discussion: his contacts with socialist friends, his socialistic activities and his poetry.

There is a well-known Chinese saying, "one who stays near vermilion gets stained red, and one who stays near Chinese ink gets stained black" . Simply speaking, one takes on the color of his company or surrounding. Sandburg impossibly hadn't got stained "red", socialism red from his friends, many of whom had the tendency toward, or were socialists.

Among his friends, Professor Green Wright was the most influential to

---

① See *A Quarterly of Language, Literature, and Culture* 31, No. 3 (1983): 237–55.

② Conrad Potter Aiken, 1889–1973, American writer noted primarily for his poetry. He won a 1930 Pulitzer Prize for *Selected Poems*.

③ Social Democracy is a political ideology emerging in the late 19th and early 20th centuries from supporters of Marxism who believed that the transition to a socialist society could be achieved through democratic evolutionary rather than revolutionary means.

Sandburg in writing and political outlook. He was Sandburg's college teacher in Lombard College, Galesburg. They had much "red" communication. As his student, Sandburg even frankly hawked Wright his socialist thought by advising Professor Wright to change the name of his poetry volume into a direct socialistic one: "Do you know tho, I have a little misgiving about the title 'Dreamer' for a volume. The exquisite irony of the poem of that name will be seen only by the elect, and the propriety of the title of the book would appear only after reading the poem. Socialism is pressing forward so strongly before the public that the title 'The Socialist and Other Poems' might be more fetching. " (LCS: 26) But Professor Wright didn't accept his advice. It is difficult for us to judge him as a socialist, but the book conveys a portrayal, the "socialist" through monologue of a moderate revolutionary who wants to change the distribution of wealth. Surely, it is the typical social-democratic view, or the right wing of socialism. No wonder Sandburg tried to persuade him to change the book title directly into "The Socialist and Other Poems". And Professor Wright later became the professor of economics at Harvard University. And the fact is his economics had an inclination to socialism system.

Anyway, Sandburg was always optimistic about socialism with zest as expressed in his writing to Professor Wright on Nov. 22, 1904: "The Political situation is gratifying. The advance of the socialist was pleasing … I am afraid I gloated. It seems to me there are going to be some great times on the political firing-line. There is some splendid blood in the Socialist party, and they are such reckless zealots…" Here it seems the statement is the clear announcement and calling for the people to fight (as the poem "Fight" calls, analyzed in Section II of this chapter); Sandburg goes on and answers: " I shall certainly witness some grand assaults on capitalism, and as sure as our blood is red, there will be a recession of some sort from the present arrogance, and bland, easy assumption of the powers that be. " (LCS: 34) He meant to fight capitalism blood for blood.

And among Sandburg's other friends, John Sjodin was another in his hometown Galesburg. He organized the local Socialist party in Galesburg. And once Sjodin was recommended to Professor Wright by Sandburg passionately in a letter

(Feb. 17, 1904): "Have you ever met one John Sjodin in Galesburg? He is an active socialist, a very earnest 'red'. His father was well acquainted with the Chicago 'anarchists' and John is as violent a non-conformist as a law-abiding man can be. He is a painter by trade, but an agitator by profession. ⋯ If you find the time, look him up and talk with him. He has some eccentricities of genius that you will find interesting, whether there are further results, or not. " (LCS: 24) Apparently, Sandburg recommended to his teacher both "red" and "professional" "expert" in socialism. This is one of his friends, a socialistic one, too. It appears they belong to the same small socialistic circle, a "red" circle.

When he was young Sandburg never lost his enthusiasm about socialism. From his letters, Sandburg was found to contact socialists widely, mainly including writers and critics such as A. M. Simons who was an editor of *International Socialist Review* and mentioned in his letter to Wright on Dec. 8, 1904: " I talked with A. M. Simons this week and he was so sorry that Jack London and Upton Sinclair couldn't flaunt before their readers a more rigid, more Marxian Socialism. " (LCS: 35) The quotation implies Sandburg and A. M. Simons once shared the belief of socialism, which Simons had wished the two writers could have propagandized more about socialism to their readers in their works.

On September 6, 1907, in a letter to his friend Reuben W. Borough, Sandburg talked of Alfred W. Mance, a middle-aged harness maker and ardent worker for the Socialists who was a friend of Borough and Sandburg in Chicago: "Tell Mance that when he dies I will lay a sword on his coffin and say that he was a good soldier in the war for the liberation of mankind. I will do the same for you. I hope you can do as much for me. We are the Three Musketeers. " (LCS: 48) Only by a few words Sandburg's reverence to socialists stands out, in spite of it implying a kind of joke and humor between friends. And these words come from Heinrich Heine's[1] poetic lines:

---

① 1797–1856, German poet. Lived in Paris after 1831. His romantic poems and social essays, containing derision for many modern German institutions, show his love for the German land and people.

When I die, lay a sword on my bier,

For I have been a brave soldier in

Humanity's war for emancipation. (LCS: 48)

What can be affirmed is Sandburg once read Heine's poems, which are revolutionary and full of his yearning towards communism. Here Sandburg can be said to be encouraged and inspired by Heine and his poetry.

And after the study of the closings of letters to his socialistic friends, Sandburg is found to have used intimate and even revolutionary closing words before signature. Maybe after the following study, Sandburg's socialistic ardor can be sensed with his political allies and union friends; and this close friendship resulted from their common belief. It is the socialism belief that bonded them together. Hereby some of Sandburg's chronicled letters to Professor Wright and his compeer Reuben W. Borough are taken as examples:

Table 2　　　　　　Comparison of Letter Closings

Addressee	Date	Words for Signing
Philip Green Wright	May 15, 1904	Yours fraternally
	May 24, 1904	Yours fraternally
	July 4, 1904	Yours for the Better Day
	Nov. 22, 1904	Yours fraternally
Reuben W. Borough	May 30, 1907	Yours in comradeship
	June 9, 1907	Yours fraternally
	Dec. 21, 1907	As ever yours in brotherhood

Here the table shows Sandburg's friendship or brotherhood with Professor Wright and Borough is solid and revolutionary. Words such as "fraternally", "brotherhood" and "comradeship" indicates Sandburg's fraternal brotherhood and comradeship towards his friends with socialistic tendency.

Equally, Sandburg's socialism tendency can be revealed and painted redder by his friends 'or contacts' status, jobs and their political inclinations. They were those whom Sandburg once corresponded with very often. Hereof another table is used to give a further support for it:

Table 3   Status and Political Leanings of Sandburg's Friends

Name	Description
A. M. Simon	Editor of *International Socialist Review* (see LCS: 36)
Alfred W. Mance	A middle-aged harness maker and ardent worker for the Socialist (see LCS: 47)
Chester Wright	Editor of the *Daily Tribune*, Manitowoc, Wisconsin, later became secretary to Samuel Gompers, president of the American Federation of Labor. (see LCS: 54)
Gaylord Wilshire	Publisher of *Wilshire's Magazine* and a socialist. (see LCS: 48)
George Fox	A socialist, a mailman, and later a museum curator.
John Sjodin	Organizer of the Galesburg local of the Socialist party. (see LCS: 24)
Lilian Steichen	A schoolteacher, later became his wife, also a Socialist. Spoke for the Socialists at a large Chautauqua at Marinette. (see LCS: Chronology, x)
Philip Green Wright	Strongly influenced Sandburg's political outlook, having Socialism tendency.
Reuben W. Borough	A reporter for *the Journal-Gazette*, Fort Wayne, Indiana. A Socialist (see LCS: 42)
William Haywood	Helped to found the Industrial Workers of the World (I. W. W.), joined the Socialist party. (see LCS: 51)

In Table 2, Lilian Steichen, with the full name of Lilian Anna Maria Elizabeth Magdalene Steichen, later became Sandburg's wife whom Sandburg called Paula. She translated German socialist literature into English for socialist party's distribution. She had advocated socialism far longer than Sandburg did.

They met in December 1907 and married six months later. At their first dating, Sandburg said he wanted to send her some of his socialist writings, to share ideas in comrade-to-comrade relationship. Then they began to write letters to each other about socialism. She was an active member of the Socialist Party and the Socialist club of Chicago, and an intellectual, theoretical socialist who read the standard socialist literature in German, French and English. But she, as a housewife, later devoted herself to Sandburg's poetry, his socialism practice and his whole career. She helped to shape Sandburg, even urged him to reclaim his given name to affirm his Swedish roots (from American spelling "Charles" or "Charlie" to Swedish "Carl", and "Carl" maybe remind them of Carl Marx). For Sandburg's later life, she was undoubtedly a fundamental force in his creative life. For Sandburg, Lilian Steichen was a devoted wife and a sincere socialistic friend! But his daughter's words are more exact to depict Lilian's influence on Sandburg: "We would probably have had his remembrances of his meeting with and courtship of Lilian Steichen, a fellow socialist, and an appraisal of the influence of this remarkable woman on his poetry and on his life." (EWC: Introduction: xi)

Compared with his attitude towards theoretical socialism, Sandburg liked to practice much more. He told American poet Alice Corbin Henderson[1]: "I like my politics straight and prefer the frank politics of the political world to the politics of the literary world." (CSB: 278) Practically, he really liked concrete activities of socialism, small or big. And he always devoted himself to the actual struggles to defend and protect the people. And the events listed below are only typical ones from the limited materials at hand.

First he actively submitted his articles to some of socialist journals. In a letter to Reuben W. Borough on June 4, 1907 Sandburg wrote, "Here are some things written for *The Daily Socialist* editorial page, if they can be used. If not, will you keep the Mss.? …My good landlady says she see [sic] by the papers that the socialists was likely to break out agin [sic] – aint [sic] it awful?" (LCS: 47) Apparently, he did contribute his article about socialism to The Daily Socialist. And now he was waiting for and expecting socialism revolution to

[1] 1881–1949, associate editor of *Poetry, A Magazine of Verse*, and also co-editor of *The New Poetry*, an anthology of modern English and American poets. She is the author of *Adam's Dream and Two Other Miracle Plays for Children* (in verse), and of a collection of poems called *The Spinning Woman of the Sky*.

"break out" with an extreme high spirit and joy.

On July 13, 1907, Sandburg gave a lecture on Whitman and spoke on Socialism at the Roycroft Chapel. (see LCS: 50)

On October 5, 1907, the paper *Daily Tribune*, which was a workingman's
paper, sponsored Sandburg to lecture at Manitowoc. And the town was a socialist town. And he showed his wish "to learn things there" in the letter to Reuben
W. Borough on October 5, 1907 (See LCS: 53).

When Wisconsin Social–Democrats had gained steady growth in Milwaukee
and other urban places, an urban–rural coalition of socialists was expected to organize to further spread and solidify socialism. Under this situation, with high
zest for socialism, Sandburg wrote to party headquarters in Milwaukee to intro-
duce and recommend himself. Winfield R. Gaylord, a socialist and politician,
admired Sandburg's oratory and enthusiasm for socialism and introduced Sandburg to "a socialist movement that was practical and constructive," and wanted
to recommend him to organize a branch for the Social–Democrats in the Fox River
district of Wisconsin. The prospect appealed to Sandburg very much. "I have
been in pretty close touch with the Wisconsin socialists lately," he wrote to Professor Wright in November 1907, "They have a splendid constructive movement
in Milwaukee, from which socialists all over the country are taking lessons. I
shall probably do some organizing thru the northeastern part of the state this winter, possible making my permanent residence in Manitowoc or Oshkosh." It was
late November of 1907 that the State Executive Board of the Social–democratic
Party of Wisconsin officially appointed Sandburg district organizer for the Lake
Shore and Fox River Valley district.

Immediately Sandburg set to work to perform his socialism practice and ideal, crisscrossing his district, propagandizing socialism with the same fervor with
which he sold stereographs. He talked with people in every village he visited and
built a list of names of subscription of socialist journals.

Inexhaustibly Sandburg explored social problems, which, he thought, have
socialistic solutions. One of his focuses was a national health crisis: tuberculosis
and the White Plague. Sandburg recorded the severe facts in his notebooks. Tu-

berculosis claimed 200,000 lives a year at that time (see CSB: 207). After a survey, they attributed the rampage of the disease to environmental and working conditions. By careful investigation, he wrote an article called "Fighting the White Plague," (published in *La Follette's* in October 1909) discovering that sewing machine operators in sweatshops and garment factories were at great risk, as well as potters, peddlers, seamstresses, wheel-wrights, cigar makers, glass blowers, boilermakers, bartenders, coopers and cabinetmakers. Indeed, Sandburg often went down to working places to explore and study, then made it public to support the working class to struggle for better condition and higher payment.

Sandburg was a careful and mindful person. Before his serious socialism activities, his notebooks were filled with notes about poems and his literary lectures. Once he had been one of the earnest revolutionaries, he began to fill his notebooks with information about politics. In notes for a party speech, he predicted socialism that

No man can name the date in the future when socialism will arrive. All that we can say is that the great change will be a gradual one, that it will come a step at a time, one point gained here and another one gained there until in the end a system of industry is established in which workers, the wealth producers are the rulers. And this change will come about through the action, the education of the workers, the producing class. (CSB: 138)

He was the kind of man who all the time kept himself in high passion to work, to fulfill his ideal, as he did to poetry. And as is mentioned, he tended to use moderate means, "through the action, the education of works, the producing class" to reform and fight against capitalism.

Just because of this, it led to the fact that on the platform of the Wisconsin Social-Democratic Party, Sandburg designed a blueprint to transform the society including "reformed government; the elimination of corrupted power; the prohibition of child labor; protection of rights of women in the labor force; the right of literate women to vote; tax reform, including a graduated income and property tax; urban renewal; free medical care and school textbooks; public works projects to improve the environment and provide work for the unemployed; state farm insurance; pensions; workmen's compensation; municipal ownership of utilities; higher wages and shorter hours for working people; better living and working conditions for everyone. " (CSB: 137) And together with the Wisconsin socialists, Sandburg framed the forum to educate the working people to improve the social system. And this is his typical tendency of right wing of socialism.

The year 1908 saw Sandburg going to Wisconsin as district organizer in the Lake Shore and Fox River Valley district. Also this year, he wrote and published the pamphlet You and Your Job by Social Democratic Publishing Company, Milwaukee. In fact Sandburg put up a socialistic tendency of proletariat, and he was all the time optimistic about socialism future. "These Wisconsin socialists are different from most that I have known. They have very little use for the theory of a social and industrial cataclysm [similar to Sandburg in practice (auctorial)] , the proletariat stepping in and organizing the cooperative commonwealth! They know that a collapse is ultimately inevitable, but they know that a genuine democracy will not follow unless they have been trained and educated by actual participation in political and industrial management before the crisis arrives. [Sandburg never forgot his mass education design for socialism (auctorial)] Ely[1] says, ' Socialism is better than the best presentation of it' " (LCS: 58) Here Sandburg quotes what Ely says, and we believe he himself in his mind would also rather say, "Socialism is better than the best presentation of it", because of the fact that if a person quotes somebody, that means he agrees with the speaker's opinion first.

As a symbol of recognition of his successful socialism career, Sandburg was appointed in 1910 the private secretary of socialist mayor of Milwaukee. But he resigned soon to become a city editor of the Milwaukee Social–Democratic Herald. The same year the Socialist party reprinted Sandburg's pamphlet You and Your Job.

---

[1] Richard Theodore Ely, a scholar, 1854–1943 was one of the prominent proponents of the historical method in America and thus a leading forerunner of the American Institutionalist School. He has work on labor movements and socialism.

In 1911, Victor Berger founded the *Milwaukee Leader*, and Sandburg joined the staff. In the convention of the Wisconsin State Federation of Labor in 1912 Sandburg chaired the resolution committee. Until now, Sandburg had established a sort of fame and a kind of position among the regional socialists. During the later period, he lavished energy on the Milwaukee Leader covering labor and socialist issues. He concluded that opponents of socialism didn't have a clear understanding about that "back of all politics are the conditions of human life, the price of bread and meat, the hours that men stand on their feet and break their backs at productive toil, the terrible power of an employer to take away a man's job and thrust him suddenly into the street, the ever-present threat of a miserable old age without money or work or strength for work. " (CSB: 228) Clearly his words here are so sharp and to the point. He penetrates the nature of politics and points out that the basis of politics is the mass, their life and work condition.

In May 1912, the Socialist Party national convention in Indianapolis nominated Eugene Debs (1855-1926) to run a fourth time for President, who was American labor organizer and socialist leader and was throughout his lifetime the nation's most widely known and eloquent exponent of socialism. Sandburg supported and gave his allegiance to Debs firmly.

During this period, Sandburg had been stimulated by his sporadic dialogues with Charles Kerr, head of the most active socialist press in the Midwest, and by his contact with A. M. Simons, the editor of the International Socialist Review, which came to be the intellectual touchstone of the socialist movement in the United States. Although Professor Wright, as his college teacher, had influenced his political views profoundly, Wright was firstly an economist who framed the idealistic socialism movement as William Morris[1] manifested in England, rather than radical political change, and to some degree Sandburg accepted this mode. So we come to see Sandburg's was an eclectic, even personal and instinctive socialism more than a formal, theoretically political philosophy. Only superficially

---

[1] 1834-1896, British poet, painter, craftsman, and social reformer best remembered for his poetry.

did he know the socialist theories of Marx and Engels, and knew little of the views of scientific socialists. From Sandburg's socialism in practice, we can see that though he was ardent, he was not a thorough socialist.

As a result of his not being an all-sided socialist (both in theory and practice), later in 1912 he left Milwaukee for socialist *Chicago Evening World* in Chicago, a new Socialist paper (but folded by the end of the year). After detachment from socialism organization, he stopped being a formal member of socialists and doing more practical work. But more of his writing and reports spread socialism more widely and brought proletarian into prominence, put forward more social problems for more people to care about and study. This leads us to a famous saying: "All roads lead to Rome", or "Different in approach but equally satisfactory in result". Writing can lead to, too, Sandburg's socialism devotion.

Indeed, after they left Milwaukee, Sandburg and his wife Paula never renewed their membership in the Social-Democratic Party. But Sandburg's political concern was as strong as ever, and he could comment on socialistic events from a more objective angle of the journalist rather than the immediate involvement of the activist and partisan. The Sandburgs never again affiliated with a political party essentially, although they supported liberal and socialism causes all their lives; and meanwhile Sandburg's identity and visibility as a poet and a journalist grew nationally.

During his stay in Chicago from 1912 to 1945 before the family moved to Connemara Farm, *Chicago Poems*, *The People*, *Yes* and many other poems and poetry books were published. These fruitful years stemmed not only from his pre-Chicago experiences but his active activities and deep contact with the working class and common folk. There he used his incisive pen to dig and expose, saw with the naked eyes and to find and express the naked facts, at a literal level, in the language of the common folk, which can be thought of part of the real reasons to draw the people's attention to his poetry and writing.

In 1912 in Chicago there was a strike of pressmen, drivers, and newsboys. Chicago's major newspapers paralyzed. As a sharp contrast, the circulation of the Chicago Daily Socialist (later called the Chicago Daily World) shot up to 600,000 (CSLW: 55) . Sandburg saw it as a great socialist victory and predicted it to have wide influence. So Sandburg hurried to the "Windy City" (Chicago) in August 1912 and was invited to join the staff of the new paper; he was very delighted. But beyond anyone's expectation, the circulation of the *Chicago Daily World* dropped, and by December it was folded.

The year 1915 saw the clothing workers again striking, under the leadership of their president, Sidney Hillman, who, during the struggle, was ill in bed most of the time. Sandburg visited him frequently and felt the strong influence of this active union leader. He studied, analyzed and printed some examples of workers who were adversely affected by the business practices at that time. Sandburg, as one of friends of Hillman, wrote about the strike for his newspaper. He even went to the union offices to sing songs to cheer them up. During that winter and spring of 1916, on the eve of the publication of *Chicago Poems*, Sandburg's work took him in many directions. At *The Day Book*, which later he worked for, he went on digging labor matters as his overriding work for the commons. His writing scope covered the garment workers' strike; working conditions for railroad and hotel workers; Chicago's bus transportation system and so on. At the *International Socialist Review*, sometimes as Sandburg and sometimes as Jack Phillips (his pseudonym), he contributed longer investigative reports on the railroads, and some poems, among which "Child of the Roman", appearing in the January issue, was an ironic one measuring the distances between social classes in American life:

> The dago shovelman sits by the railroad track
> Eating a noon meal of bread and bologna.
> A train whirls by, and men and women at tables
> Alive with red roses and yellow jonquils,
> Eat steaks running with brown gravy,
> Strawberries and cream, éclairs and coffee. (CP: 10)

Now here, "by the railroad track" is a comparison to "at tables" . They are both places for eating. But different place has different food, one is "bread and bologna"; the other is "steaks running with brown gravy, / Strawberries and cream, éclairs and coffee", while "Alive with red roses and yellow jonquils" . And one is on the train; and the other is under the train. The comparison continues:

> The dago shovelman finishes the dry bread and bologna,
> Washes it down with a dipper from the water-boy,
> And goes back to the second half of a ten-hour day's work
> Keeping the road-bed so the roses and jonquils
> Shake hardly at all in the cut glass vases
> Standing slender on the tables in the dining cars. (Ibid.)

The shovelman eats "dry bread" and works to keep "the roses and jonquils/ shake hardly at all" . It is a clear and sharp class contrast! "Train" vs. "track", and "bread" vs. "steak". This is the difference between classes in American life. Sandburg placed the proletarians in his heart. He knew railway workers' life, for his father had worked for a railway company for a long time, and he himself did ever journeywork for railway.

In August 1917 he joined the staff of Chicago Daily News. And it was in the same year that his famous poem "The Four Brothers" was first published in Poetry, then appearing in Chicago *Daily News* in October. Meanwhile he went on submitting socialism articles to some socialism publications. His "The 8-Hour Rail Drive," under the pseudonym of Jack Phillips, was released in The International Socialist Review.

On October 2, 1917, Sandburg published an interview in the Chicago *Daily News* with "Big Bill" Haywood, the Chicago leader of the Industrial Workers of the World. Although the article was sympathetic toward the I. W. W (Industrial Workers of the World), a week later Sandburg made it clear in a story that he disagreed with the efforts of the Socialists to sabotage the war effort. Certainly, it's the manifest of his conservation in socialism.

And it was at this time that Sandburg wrote one of his most quoted poems—"Fog". It contained only twenty-two words, but carried a world of meanings. Carl wrote the poem while sitting in the anteroom of a juvenile court judge, waiting for an interview:

The fog comes
on little cat feet.
It sits looking
over harbor and city
on silent haunches
and then moves on. (CP: 33)

Sandburg used the way, in which he investigated lower class people and social problems with a careful and deep observation, to watch the fog. It is something everyone could understand, but it is the inner melody in a new poetic symphony by Sandburg. In a way, the poem is Sandburg himself—active, floating, and then going on to something new. In it, there is a freedom like that of working on the newspaper The Day Book that carried no advertising: writing what he wanted to write without the consideration for the advertising enterprises of the common journalistic media.

Meanwhile, he was really like the fog, working freely for his belief. So Sandburg had told Romain Rolland① in a letter: "…I am a socialist but not a member of the party. I am an I. W. W. but I don't carry a red card…. I am for the single tax, for all the immediate demands of the socialists…" In spite of this, Sandburg, though not a member of the party any longer, had been and was a socialist; though he didn't carry a red card, he was a real member of I. W. W. In the same letter he continued: "…I would say I am with all rebels everywhere all the time as against all people who are satisfied. I am for any and

---

① 1866–1944, French writer whose varied works include *Jean Christophe* (1904–1912), a series of satirical novels. He won the 1915 Nobel Prize for literature.

all immediate measures that will curb the insanity of any person or institution that is cursed with a thirst for more things, utilities and properties than he, she or it is able to use, occupy and employ to the advantage of the race. " (LCS: 169) Sandburg came from a folk family, a poor and common family. This background helped him understand the situation of the downtrodden people. And also this encouraged him to serve the people and struggle for the people. Forever he was a member of them—the common people.

With the background of this common origin, when he worked for *Daily News* in Chicago, he wrote many labor stories and interviews sometimes without even seeing the persons concerned, because he knew them so well. After writing something, he would telephone the person and read it to him for approval. Sandburg met all kinds of people, especially those from the harsher side of life. He was at home with all sorts of people: bums, job seekers, starving men, and others from the lower class. As E. D. Akers, a former new editor of the *Daily News*, said that Sandburg "was a gentleman and very kind. He said hello to everybody and treated all with great kindness. " (CSLW: 77) Exaggeratedly speaking, he was like an apterous angel moving among all flesh.

Later, Sandburg received a job offer from Sam T. Hughes, the editor–in–chief of NEA (the Newspaper Enterprise Association). Hughes planned to send him to Stockholm as NEA correspondent to Eastern Europe. But he was discouraged and restless, increasingly afraid that his socialist past was impeding his passport. And Sandburg assured Hughes that he had "kept away form the Socialist and I. W. W. bunch" . By in late September of 1918 he had his passport at last. When he came to Stockholm, a series of events brought him to one of the most skillful spies of the Russian revolution, Michael Borodin working in Stockholm for Lenin, who was assigned to transmit Bolshevik propaganda to the United States. Borodin had a special assignment from Lenin himself: to deliver Lenin's *Letter to American Workers* to the United States. For Sandburg, Borodin became one of Sandburg's news sources in Stockholm.

According to some sources, it is sure that Sandburg who introduced Lenin's letter to the United States. He brought back to the United States a published

English translation of Lenin's *A Letter to American Working People from the Socialist Soviet Republic of Russia*. It was printed in English by the socialist Publication Society, and Sandburg hid the copy in his interior pocket of his greatcoat for safe passage back home. And he carried much Bolshevik propaganda in his luggage into America. There, he also gave Sandburg revolutionary literature and $10,000 in drafts for a Finnish agent Santeri Nuortava in the United States.

After he came back to the U. S. , Sandburg was sued for his behavior in Europe. On Jan. 17, 1919, in a letter to Sam T. Hughes, Sandburg offered an explanation (Please pay attention to the underlined words by the author herein) : "The charge against me in case of trial would be that in carrying funds from Norway to the Finnish Information Bureau in the United States I violated the Trading with the Enemy act. This would mean that it is un–American for us to act against the best interests of the present Mannerheim① government in Finland ···. For whom was I carrying funds? For those who fought the Mannerheim government, for the imprisoned and starving whose friends and kinsmen died by tens of thousands under the machine gun and shell fire of Prussian guns···. The farther the matter were carried before a jury the more evident would it become that the prosecution was representing interests alien and inimical to America. The evidence would be overwhelming that the socialists of Finland took a different course from that of the Bolsheviks of Russia in establishing a republic ···. " (LCS: 148) What did Sandburg carry funds for? He said it was for the socialists fighting the Finnish government who pressed the Finnish people, for "the imprisoned and starving", whose "friends and kinsmen " were killed by Prussian soldiers. Apparently Sandburg was against Finnish government, but on the side of Finnish people. And he thought Finnish socialism was different from that of Bolsheviks of Russia. And in a letter of Sam Hughes on May 16, 1919, Hughes wrote back to Sandburg: "I have to tell you frankly that you and NEA are not hitching well together···. You are a great writer your poems are sufficient evidence of that···.

---

① Finnish soldier and politician who fortified the Finnish–Soviet border (1931–1939), led a valiant defense against the Soviet offensive of 1939, and served as president of Finland (1944–1946) .

Nevertheless I don't like to say <u>the word</u> to you <u>that we are through</u>. What do you say?" (LCS: 163) Here "that" and "the word" obviously imply "social-ist". And "that we are through" means "We two understand each other you are a socialist." Then in America, socialists began to work underground for fear of persecution. So Sandburg's place at this time was in a devil of a hole. Though without any result of the charge against him, Sandburg was fired in May by Sam Hughes. Undoubtedly, all this was because of Sandburg's socialist background.

In the Sandburg–Borodin–Spy case, it is sure that Sandburg lied to Ameri-can Government; otherwise it could not be resultless. But his lie was meant to be well–intended, because in his heart what he did was for the people, at least in his own understanding. He would never betray America, especially American people.

After he left Eastern Europe, Sandburg was haunted by the war's savagery he had beheld and heard of. As for the charge, he was puzzled by the assault on his own loyalty and patriotism, and shaken by the official examination about his character. Then he turned to poetry. Soon the poem "The Liars" appeared. It uses a machine–gun repetition to attack powerful political figures who deceive na-tions and the people. He called the poem a sequel to "The Four Brothers". (see Section IV, Chapter Four in detail) He describes a liar in the 44–line po-em like this:

The Liars

(March, 1919)

A LIAR goes in fine clothes.

A liar goes in rags.

A liar is a liar, clothes or no clothes.

A liar is a liar and lives on the lies he tells

and dies in a life of lies.

And the stonecutters earn a living–with lies—

on the tombs of liars.

A liar looks' em in the eye

And lies to a woman,

Lies to a man, a pal, a child, a fool.

And he is an old liar; we know him many years back. (SS: 192–93)

In Sandburg's eyes, a liar can cheat anyone. He disguises himself "in rags" or "fine clothes" to deceive even a fool. After his death, his epigraph will still be full of lies. A liar lies forever, and

A liar lies to nations.

A liar lies to the people.

A liar takes the blood of the people

And drinks this blood with a laugh and a lie,

A laugh in his neck,

A lie in his mouth.

And this liar is an old one; we know him many years.

He is straight as a dog's hind leg.

He is straight as a corkscrew.

He is white as a black cat's foot at midnight. (Ibid)

Being a liar of a nation and the people, he can lie to whomever he wants to lie to. A liar can take "the blood of the people". And this is nothing for him at all; furthermore, he "drinks this blood with a laugh and a lie". The sentence "He is straight as a dog's hind leg" means he runs fast if he needs to lie, or he runs away fast after lying. "He is straight as a corkscrew" implies he is like a corkscrew, by his lies he can open any plug to do whatever he wants to do, and he is as terrible as "a black cat" with white feet at midnight, for

The tongue of a man is tied on this,

On the liar who lies to nations,

The liar who lies to the people.

The tongue of a man is tied on this

And ends: To hell with 'em all.

To hell with 'em all… (Ibid.)

This stanza is the curse on the liars. If you "lies to the people", "to hell with 'em all. " And the repetition of the imperative shows the poet's and the people's deep hatred for the liars. In the whole poem, "liar" is repeated 23 times, toning up the resenting feeling to the liars.

Obviously, in the poem the "Liar" is not a common liar. Sandburg disliked "Liar". The "Liar" must have power, and he would be again any power that abrogated the rights of "the People" . One thing Sandburg curses upon him who lies is: "To hell"! He cannot stand the liar who lies to the people. Sandburg himself once lied to the government, but to the people, he never lied.

Sandburg was such a poet, the people's poet, and a proletarian poet. As a poet and critic, Malcolm Cowley[①] thought that Sandburg's poetry had been disregarded by many critics and academicians during the twenties, because free verse was out of vogue. But Cowley found Sandburg could foresee the resurgence of interest in proletarian poetry because of the Depression, telling him in 1935 "a lot of people are talking about proletarian poetry, and always without mentioning the simple primer-book fact that almost the only good proletarian poetry in this country has been written by a guy named Carl Sandburg. " (CSB: 499) Cowley was also farseeing at this point. Sandburg and his poetry became more and more popular and widely read by more and more common people, more and more proletarians, for his poetry is just about themselves. But all this, whether Sandburg admitted it publicly, or he just kept it secret, to some extent, comes from his socialism ideal. It is an indisputable fact: Sandburg was ever an ardent Socialist.

Ⅲ. Advocator of Democracy

As the years and his prosperity increased, Sandburg became milder and

---

① 1898-1989. American writer, editor, and critic whose works include studies of American expatriate writers of the 1920's and commentaries on William Faulkner.

more moderate. Sometimes he tried to dodge socialism events to avoid arousing suspicion because of the influence of the Sandburg–Borodin–Spy case and more and more serious situation of Socialism in the United States. On the other hand, with Sandburg's tendency toward rightwing of socialism (in spite of leftwing in poetry), and his practice in Social Democracy, his democracy inclination turned into a natural thing. About this, the typical exemplification is Sandburg's communication with Franklin Delano Roosevelt (1882–1945), the 32nd President of the United States (1933–1945).

In 1932 Sandburg received a letter at the *Chicago Daily News*. It was a letter canvassing Sandburg for the Communist candidates in the national election campaign, William Z. Foster and James W. Ford. Part of the letter reads:

> We feel that it is essential at this time for all American intellectuals to express their strong dissatisfaction with conditions as they are, and to give impetus to the only group of workers in the American labor movement who are intelligent and brave enough to fight militantly the powers in control.
>
> The two major parties, we all agree, are hopeless. The Socialist Party, with its present leadership of small businessmen, lawyers, and nice people in general, does not symbolize change, or a leadership feared by the intrenched class. And the Socialists' persistent attacks on the Soviet Union, during its present bitterest years of struggle, deserve sharp rebuke and repudiation. We may not all agree with all the ideas of Communism, but the Communist Party is the only party today feared by the ruling class, and the only party we can vote for that will effectively register our protest against the present economic and political regime. "Will you join us?"
> (CSLW: 116)

And the letter was signed by Sherwood Anderson, Malcolm Cowley, Professor H. W. L. Dana, John Dos Passos, Theodore Dreiser, Waldo Frank, Prof. Sidney Hook, Langston Hughes, Matthew Josephson, and Edmund Wilson. But apparently Sandburg did not give a positive "Yes". Actually at this time Sandburg began to tend to be a Democrat. He voted for President Franklin D. Roosevelt who then was a democratic candidate, thinking "he is a momentous historic character more thoroughly aware of where he is going than most of the commentators. " For further direct encouragement to Roosevelt, on March 29, 1935 Sandburg wrote the President flatly, "Having written for ten years now on ' Abraham Lincoln: the War Years' , starting this year [1935] on the fourth and final volume, I have my eyes and ears in two eras and cannot help drawing parallels. One runs to the effect that you are the best light of democracy that has occupied the White House since Lincoln. You have set in motion trends that to many are banners of dawn. This may be praise to your face but it is also a recording of hope and a prayer that you go on as steadfast as you have in loyalty to the whole people, that in your difficult war with their exploiters your cunning may increase. " (CSLW: 117) Roosevelt was very satisfied with it. And he won the presidential election, while for Sandburg it was also a victory of his supporting democracy. Sandburg admired democracy largely. Roosevelt's democratic administration weighed much in his heart. And Sandburg regarded him as the commander of the nation and the American people in a poem for FDR's death on April 12, 1945. Here in the poem "When Death Came April Twelve 1945", Sandburg expresses the nation's loss and his lament for the president:

...

A bell rings in the heart telling it
and the bell rings again and again
remembering what the first bell told,
the going away, the great heart still—
and they will go on remembering
and they is you and you and me and me. (CPCS: 638)

In the lines, the rings are the memory of Roosevelt. He was "going away", but "the great heart still" lives on. People "will go on remembering" "you". The unconscious repetition of "you" and "me" is the result of Sandburg's sorrow and yearn for the president. He mourns on:

And there will be roses and spring blooms
flung on the moving oblong box, emblems endless
flung from nearby, from faraway earth corners,
from frontline tanks nearing Berlin
unseen flowers of regard to The Commander,
from battle stations over the South Pacific
silent tokens saluting The Commander. (Ibid.)

These lines are the salutation from Sandburg, and from American people, "from faraway earth corners". "Unseen flowers" are deeper "regard to The Commander", the commander of American nation and people, and the commander of American democracy. He continues to question, but with self-confidence:

Can a bell ring proud in the heart
over a voice yet lingering,
over a face past any forgetting,
over a shadow alive and speaking,
over echoes and lights come keener, come deeper? (Ibid.)

What stands out in the stanza is the initial repetition of "over" before each line except the first one. "Over" has duple implication. It can refer to the death of the president, and it can mean President Roosevelt is above all. Though he is "over", he is "over" us, for his "echoes and lights come keener, come deeper". Sandburg wishes him "sweet good night":

Can a bell ring in the heart
in time with the tall headlines,
the high fidelity transmitters,
the somber consoles rolling sorrow,
the choirs in ancient laments—chanting:
"Dreamer, sleep deep,
Toiler, sleep long,

Fighter, be rested now,

Commander, sweet good night. "

[*Woman's Home Companion*, June, 1945] (Ibid.)

The last stanza is the last wishes and send–off singing for the president. With "Commander, sweet good night", the poet ends the whole poem, just like what we often say before going to bed at night to our family members. The feeling thus expressed is so intimate, so gentle, and so warm. The 48–line poem is filled with Sandburg's deep admiration for the democratic president, and for democracy. And the whole poem reminds me of English graveyard school poet Thomas Gray's (1716–1771) . "Elegy Written in a Country Churchyard" : The Curfew tolls the knell of parting day, / The lowing herd winds slowly o'er the lea, / The ploughman homeward plods his weary way, /And leaves the world to darkness and to me···. Apparently, the two poems share a kind of low–key and low spirit, and a kind of sorrowfulness and sadness. We borrow for Sandburg the air of Gray's poem to contribute to his admirer, democratic FDR. But Sandburg's is special for the president and for democracy.

What Sandburg loved about Roosevelt is not only the man as president, but also his democratic thought. Roosevelt's administration was marked by relief programs, measures to increase employment and assist industrial and agricultural recovery from the Depression. He was the only U. S. President to be reelected three times (1936, 1940, and 1944) . This is enough evidence of Roosevelt's being a democratic figure, and he had a wide support from the common people, of course including the people's poet Sandburg. And he was the very person Sandburg supported.

For further discussion, in 1941 when Roosevelt was in his last term of office, under the sponsorship of the Council for Democracy, Sandburg made a speech at a national unity meeting at Madison Square Garden in New York, delivering one of his famous and most frequently quoted interpretations of democracy. He said that the American democratic system " gives more people more chances to think, to speak, to decide on their way of life···than any other system," and "has more give and take, more resilience…and more grand wisdom, than any other system…. Personal freedom, a wide range of individual expression, a complete respect for the human mind and the human personality–this is the ideal of the democratic system. " (CSB: 547) These words are his incisive and penetrating analysis of democracy.

Norman L. Ritchie of the *Chicago Daily News*, in an introductory letter to one of his friends, commented that "Carl…is a man's man. No truer advocate of real democracy, I venture to say, ever lived. " (CSLW: 111) And there are more lines from *The People, Yes* expressing his deep faith in democracy (to be discussed in detail in Chapter Three) .

As an ardent socialist and an active advocator of democracy later, Sandburg always spoke for the people inside and outside his poetry. His common origin made him sympathize with the common people and led to his political inclinations, while his political leanings directed him to "fight" for the common people with his sympathy.

Chapter Three
The People, *Yes*, and "Yes" What?

THE people is Everyman, everybody···
The people is a farmer, a tenant and a share–cropper,
a plowman···
The people is a tall freight–handler and a tough long-
shoreman, a greasy fireman and a gambling oil–well
shooter with a driller and tooler ready···.

—Carl Sandburg

The People, *Yes* was published in 1936. It gathers all Sandburg's emotion
and enthusiasm for the people into ONE book, and is also the high conclusion of
Sandburg as the people's poet. But this everlasting ardor was not collected in a
breath. Before the book, other books of poetry like *Chicago Poems*, *Cornhuskers*
and *Smoke and Steel* had been published. In these previous books, he had dealt
with his fraternal people much more than before. So, to discuss his affinity with
the people, we first speculate on "who and what are the people" by analyzing
his poetic lines of some books and then find out the reasons (especially the local
Universalism in his hometown) guiding him to care for the people so much and
deep, and after this study most of his poetry books chronologically to discover
step by step how he approaches the eternal masses who "will live on" all the way
till into the climax of *The People*, *Yes*.

I. "Who and What Are the People?" ①

First, in Webster's Dictionary of American English②, one of the meanings of "people" is "the ordinary persons of a community, country, etc. , as distinguished from those who have wealth, rank, etc. . " For Sandburg, "Who and what are the people?" Actually, his people cover any common persons good or bad, and noble persons, like his favorite respecter Lincoln, who work and sacrifice for the people. So he had his own understanding and definition. In his poetry we can find his people coming from everywhere, and still in his poetry we can read about and experience all kinds of his people. Here we will, by investigating his poetry from *The People, Yes*, have a close look at who and what are the people of Sandburg.

In Section 14, page 26 of PY, Sandburg writes:
THE people is Everyman, everybody.
Everybody is you and me and all others.
What everybody says is what we all say. (PY: Section 17: 30)

The three lines above are a concise generalization about Sandburg's people. "THE people is Everyman" with the initial letter "E" capitalized showing the emphasis on "everyman". Every "you" and "me" and "all others" belong to people. And he further makes people's voice, democratic voice, stand out by the line: "What everybody says is. what we all say. " The people's voice is the real and democratic voice. Then as he goes on in the book, he continues to unscramble his people concept:

---

① Sandburg, Carl. *The Complete Poems of Carl Sandburg*. San Diego, New York and London: Harcourt Brace & Company. 1990: 456.

② Dalgish, Gerard, ed. *Random House Webster's Dictionary of American English*. Beijing: Foreign Language Teaching and Research Press, 1997.

The common people is a mule
that will do anything you say except
stay hitched (Ibid.)

Like a mule, the people can do and bear any hard work and burden; like a
mule, the people played a part in the development of the West; and like a
mule, the people built the nation up. Here the characteristics of a "mule" are
rented: hard working, painstaking and stubborn enough. The people persist in
their own belief, their own truth; they have their own standard to judge what
they and the others do. And they never "stay hitched", they move on and on,
work and work. Though a question mark ends the lines, the lines are a question
with answer in it: Yes, "the common people" IS "a mule" .

In Section 28, Sandburg describes his people for "those afraid of the people" and those "afraid of sudden massed action of the people":

"Your people, sir, your people is a great beast",
Speaking for those afraid of the people,
Afraid of sudden massed action of the people,
The people being irresponsible with torch, gun and rope,
The people being a child with fire and loose hardware,
The people listening to leather-lunged stump orators
Crying the rich get richer, the poor poorer, and why? (PY: Section 28: 52)

Sandburg compares the people to "a great beast" for those who are afraid of
the people. The reason lies in the fact that the people can have a kind of "sudden massed action" which can overturn "those" people. And we may interpret
"those" into those ruling people, at least those people having great power over
the common people. What are his people? He says once more, the people are
like "a child" who is "irresponsible with torch, gun and rope". They can burn
you, they can shoot you and they can hang you. They have their own leader-

"leather-lunged stump orators", they realize "the rich get richer, the poor poorer. " But "those" are afraid of the people. Why? Because:

> The people undependable as prairie rivers in floodtime,
> The people uncertain as lights on the face of the sea
> Wherefore high and first of all he would write
> God, the Constitution, Property Rights, the Army and the Police,
> After these the rights of the people. (Ibid.)

These are the whys for their fear. They know the people want rights; they know the people are "undependable" and "uncertain" as "prairie rivers in floodtime" and "lights on the face of the sea. " They are weak and powerful, elusive and effective. But Sandburg sees that "those" cannot stand the people to have their own belief and hope. What they do is "trade on these lights of the people", and take advantage of the people:

> THE people is a lighted believer and
>   hoper—and this is to be held against them?
> The panderers and cheaters are to have
>   their way in trading on these lights
>   of the people? (PY: Section 22: 41)

Continuously, in Section 46, Sandburg's people become a child who can make stupid mistakes in school:

> The people is a child at school writing howlers,
> writing answers half wrong and half right:
> The government of England is a limited mockery.
> Gravitation is that which if there were none we would all fly away.
> (PY: Section 46: 96)

The lines mean people have their own understanding about the world. They view

the world from their own visual angle. They apprehend what is practical to them,
like "Gravitation is that which if there were none we would all fly away." Indeed, it is half wrong and half right in science, but a practical thinking for the
common persons living on earth. Further, Sandburg's people appears more:

> In the people is the eternal child,
>
> the wandering gypsy, the pioneer homeseeker,
>
> the singer of home sweet home. (PY: Section 56: 129)
>
> And:
>
> The people is a monolith,
>
> a mover, a dirt farmer,
>
> a desperate hoper…
>
> The people is a trunk of patience, a monolith. (PY: Section 56: 132)

The "eternal child", included in Sandburg's eternal people, is the people.
And a gypsy, a homeseeker and a singer are all the people embracing "a mover,
a dirty farmer, a desperate hoper". "Monolith" is used metaphorically. Originally it means a large block of stone, or something, such as a column or monument made from one large block of stone. Sandburg uses it as a kind of symbol,
the base of nationality, monument of real power of a country. Because of this, it
cannot be moved away and erased, otherwise the whole building and the whole
system would collapse. And due to this, the people will "live on" and be eternal like a monolith. It is obvious that the people's role and position is of such
importance. Though they have "a trunk of patience", their patience is not infinite. As a result, People are what they are / because they have come out of what
was. (PY: Section 71: 187) Sandburg walks on among his people, and again
he finds his "people is a child", you have to please him and feed him, or he
can become "again a hoodlum you have to be tough with":

> Sometimes as though the people is a child to be pleased or fed
>
> Or again a hoodlum you have to be tough with
>
> And seldom as though the people is a caldron and a reservoir

Of the human reserves that shape history,

The river of welcome wherein the broken First Families fade,

The great pool wherein wornout breeds and clans drop for restorative silence. (PY: Section 86: 221)

Though "seldom", the people can still become "a caldron and a reservoir" that can break out and rewrite and "shape history." The river "wherein the broken First Families fade" must be welcomed by dignitaries, because if these original families, which may refer to Indian families, do not exist any longer, the so called dignitaries can do what they want to do on their homeland that have belonged to them from the beginning. The drop of "breeds and clans" may be a temporary silence of restorativeness. As he thinks "The voice of the people is the voice of God". (PY: Section 91: 239), so he depicts people as mysterious:

The people is a long shadow

trembling around the earth,

stepping out of fog gray into smoke red

and back from smoke red into fog gray

and lost on parallels and meridians

learning by shock and wrangling,

by heartbreak so often and loneliness so raw

the laugh comes at least half true,

"My heart was made to be broken." (PY: Section 91: 240)

As mysterious as gray fog, the people are red smoke and a long shadow. Heartbreak and loneliness accompany them so often and rawly. No wonder the people say "My heart was made to be broken." Sandburg continues to use metaphors to picture the attributes of the people:

The people is the grand canyon of humanity

and many many miles across.

The people is pandora's① [sic] box, humpty dumpty,
a clock of doom and an avalanche when it turns loose.
The people rest on land and weather, on time
and the changing winds.
The people have come far and can look back
and say, "We will go farther yet. "
The people is a plucked goose and a shorn
sheep of legalized fraud
And the people is one of those mountain slopes
holding a volcano of retribution,
Slow in all things, slow in its gathered wrath,
slow in its onward heave,
Slow in its asking: " Where are we now? what time is it?"
(PY: Section 97: 253–54)

Here Sandburg generally and always indicates that the people as a whole is like water which can carry a ship now and it can overturn it at other times. And according to Sandburg, the people are like Pandora's box containing all "evils" of human life. He warns the ones over the people not to touch and ruffle the "box", for the people can be "weather", "the changing wind", "a plucked goose and a shorn sheep of legalized fraud" and "one of those mountain slopes holding a volcano of retribution". But this kind of retribution is very dangerous for the regime, for the people are "plucked" and "shorn" as goose and sheep. This trend of power, despite the "slow" speed of gathering, once becoming a kind of wrath, can be "onward heave" and rise to burst out. Sandburg sees clearly "The people is a tragic and comic two–face" in Section 107 of *The People, Yes* in CPC (See the quoted text in Section II, Chapter One). The "tragic" can mean a tragedy for the people themselves, and can mean a tragedy, or to lead a tragedy to the ruling class. So the people are "comic two–face: hero and

---

① "pandora" may be "Pandora" from Greek Mythology, who is the first woman, bestowed upon humankind as a punishment for Prometheus's theft of fire. Entrusted with a box containing all the ills that could plague people, she opened it out of curiosity and thereby released all the evils of human life.

hoodlum". The people are a chessman of their game, bought when useful, sold once useless. But the buyers and venders are afraid the people can sometime "break loose" . It is difficult to guess and see it as a whole, because: The people is a polychrome, / a spectrum and a prism / held in a moving monolith. (Section 107: 286, last page) Once more, the people are a "monolith", but this time it is moving, containing "spectrum and a prism". It implies the uncertainty, powerfulness and unexpectedness of the people.

Now let's go back to the beginning of the section, "THE people is Everyman, everybody. / Everybody is you and me and all others. / What everybody says is what we all say. " This is Sandburg's exploration into his people and study on the people. So after the study of the key lines of some poems from his key book *The People, Yes*, the notion of his "people" is concluded from his poetry; that is to say, his people are "everyman", "you and me"; his people are the common persons, the downtrodden, the forgotten, "a mule", "a plucked goose", "a shorn sheep", who struggle to survive each day; his people are unstable and stable; unstable for the ones above them because they are active; and stable still for the ones over them, because they are sometimes passive.

But widely speaking, Sandburg's people include more. As a Polish philosopher says, humanity should consist of mob on the top and mob on the bottom; on this end they are ignorant, idle and incompetent leisure class; on the other end they are the "vags, bums, down-and-outs, the rickety, mal-nourished, tubercular and anemic men, women and children of the slums". (see LCS: 171) But Sandburg thinks the philosopher neglects the middle people, and he responds, "Our Polish philosopher neglected taking account of the vast section of people between these two mobs. I have a theory-with no authenticated facts to support it-that Jesus of Nazareth was crucified by the lower mob through a conspiracy organized by the secret diplomacy of the upper mob and therefore, the mercy of the Russian mob toward its former czar should stand as the classic instance rather than the crucifixion of Christ and the ride of humiliation on the rump of a jackass round about the walls of Jerusalem. " (LCS: 171-2) What does Sandburg mean? For him, the mob on the top and the mob on the bottom are part of the

people, but top ones are the same as the bottom ones, for, for example, Jesus
was "crucified by the lower mob through a conspiracy" but organized by the upper mob. So sometimes the top mobs are more evil. And clearly, Sandburg never
neglects mob, he forms mobs into his line of people; and in a sense, the people
equals the mob. "Mob" is what top ones call the people in another way. In all
his poetry, two of them treat mob directly; one is from *Chicago Poems*, the other
is from *Cornhuskers*:

I Am the People, the Mob
I AM the people the mob the crowd the mass.
Do you know that all the great work of the world is done through me?
I am the workingman, the inventor, the maker of the world's food and clothes.
I am the audience that witnesses history. The Napoleons come from me and the
Lincolns. They die. And then I send forth more Napoleons and Lincolns.
I am the seed ground. I am a prairie that will stand for much plowing. Terrible
storms pass over me. I forget. The best of me is sucked out and wasted. I forget.
Everything but Death comes to me and makes me work and give up what I have.
And I forget. (CP: 75)

In the first line, "I" does not refer to the poet. It refers to anyone of the people, the mob, the crowd, and the masses. They are many-sided. "I" am everybody
and anybody, and "the great work of the world is done through me". "I" am the
food-clothes-maker and inventor of the world. Persons like Napoleon come from
the people, the mob. The people also produce and can make more Lincolns.
Only "Death" can stop "me" from working and giving up "what I have." But
anyway, people will "live on", for "I am seed ground" where more people can
rise and grow up. And why do "I forget"? Do "I" really "forget"? No. For the
toughness and endurance of the people, no matter what has happened, and regardless of natural or man-made disaster, they will live on. "You" cut "me"
down, and then the new "I" grow out. In the poem Sandburg continues:

Sometimes I growl, shake myself and spatter a few red drops for history to remember. Then I forget.

When I, the People, learn to remember, when I, the People, use the lessons of
yesterday and no longer forget who robbed me last year, who played me for a fool
then there will be no speaker in all the world say the name: "The People," with
any fleck of a sneer in his voice or any far-off smile of derision.

The mob the crowd the mass will arrive then. (Ibid.)

When "I" am in a high oppression that "I" cannot stand, "I" will
"growl", and will "spatter a few drops for history to remember. " In the following line, when he frankly says "When I, the People…" he implies that "I"
stands for "the People", and "I" am the speaker of the People, expressing his
own wish and determination to speak for the People, because someone "robbed
me (the People) yesterday" and "played me (the People) while no one could
think of the name of "The People" any longer.

In "Always the Mob", *Cornhuskers*, Sandburg this time rents the power
and holiness of Jesus to start his mob analysis:

Jesus emptied the devils of one man into forty hogs and the hogs took the edge of
a high rock and dropped off and down into the sea: a mob…
Stones of a circle of hills at Athens, staircases of a mountain in Peru, scattered
clans of marble dragons in China: each a mob on the rim of a sunrise: hammers
and wagons have them now.
Locks and gates of Panama? The Union Pacific crossing deserts and tunneling
mountains? The Woolworth on land and the Titanic at sea? Lighthouses blinking a
coast line from Labrador to Key West? Pigiron bars piled on a barge whistling in a
fog off Sheboygan? A mob: hammers and wagons have them tomorrow. (C: 34)

In the beginning, "forty hogs" got "the devils of one man" by Jesus, and
then they became mobs; they are a kind of mob. Those who build "the stones of
a circle of hills at Athens, staircases of a mountain in Peru", and the "scattered
clans of marble dragons in China", are another kind of mob; and this group of
mob belong to the mass of common people working hard for others and living dif-

ficultly. Sandburg widens his people into wider scope, from Athens to Peru and then to China and Panama: "Hammers and wagons have them." They are doomed to use these tools to work. They do not have "hammers and wagons"; reversely, they are owned and controlled by "hammers and wagons". To use the tools is their must and their lot. The work on the ships by Panama Canal, and the work from Woolworth[①] shops and Titanic[②] and pig iron bars, all need them—the mobs to do. And mobs are more:

> The mob? A jag of lightning, a geyser, a gravel mass loosening⋯ The mob⋯⋯
> kills or builds⋯ the mob is Attila or Genghis Khan, the mob is Napoleon, Lin-
> coln.
> I am born in the mob—I die in the mob—the same goes for you—I dont care who
> you are.
> I cross the sheets of fire in No Man's Land for you, my brother—I slip a steel
> tooth into your throat, you my brother—I die for you and I kill you—It is a twis-
> ted and gnarled thing, a crimson wool:
> One more arch of stars,
> In the night of our mist,
> In the night of our tears. (Ibid.)

The mob is the people including Attila, Genghis Khan, Napoleon, Lincoln and so on. Even Sandburg "am born in the mob" and will "die in the mob." You "are" my brother, also a mob. "I" can "slip a steel tooth into your throat" to "kill you", and while "I" can "die for you". But when night comes, when stars lighten, when mist falls, tears can be seen. It's such a contradiction, "twisted and gnarled"; so much sheep "wool" has been stained with the color of blood crimson. "Wool" is the symbol of common people who are stained by some of the upper class.

But here one thing must be mentioned in advance, that is Sandburg nar-

---

① American merchant. From 1879, he built a successful national chain of five-and-tens shops.
② It should be the Titanic Ship and the tragedy of the ship.

rowed his concept of "people". He seldom widened his "people" into a world-wide "people" (though sometimes he did as the above). This shows his limitation in his belief, his mind and his politics, and reflects the parochialism of his native sense. Just because of this, he was an ardent, but not a firm and constant socialist, which has been analyzed in Chapter Two. And his native sense is to be discussed in Section IV, Chapter Four of the thesis herein. In spite of this, he was caritative enough to love universal people, which can be revealed in some ways by the influence of his hometown religion Universalism.

II. Universalism: His Guide to Universal People

Why was he concerned about the people so much? Firstly, Sandburg came from one of the common folk's families, the working class, which aroused him (but not always arouse all the commons) to sympathize with them and this has been talked about in Chapter One hereinbefore; secondly, he worked with and widely approached and stepped into the common people's life, including their mind and their work, and he knew the hardship of the people, which in the same way aroused his sympathy for the ordinary persons; thirdly, he was greatly influenced by Walt Whitman's democratic thought, free verse as a style, common folk's language, and sincere attention for the people in terms of poetic theme (and this will be analyzed in detail in Chapter Four). But here, fourthly, the point chosen to be discussed is about Universalism's influence on Sandburg, which was a necessary reason and influenced him much and certainly.

Universalism, a kind and gentle religious tradition, was once dynamic in Galesburg, Sandburg's hometown. It has gone through the complete cycle from germination to extinction there. The first Universalist Church was built in Galesburg in 1895. In the town, the Lombard College, where Sandburg studied for a few years and left without completing his degree requirements, was founded and sponsored by the Universalist Church. In the early 1930s, when Sandburg was in his fifties, the college was merged with Knox College and the campus became

the location of a public school. In 1963 it was damaged four years before Sandburg's death in 1967. Comparing its history from 1895 to 1963 with Sandburg's
life span from 1878 to 1967, we can regard the Church as just a service for Sandburg, and maybe it would be doomed to influence Sandburg.

Though the Church building was built in 1895, the Universalism, according
to an American writer Rex Cherrington, a researcher of Knox County history, began to appear and influence the natives in 1856. [1] It has worked on and served
the native people more than 100 years. But gradually after 1950s it melted into
the Unitarian Universalist Association (UUA) growing out of the consolidation in
1961, of two religious denominations: the Universalists, organized in 1793, and
the Unitarians, organized in 1825.

What is Universalism on earth? There are many definitions. But generally,
Universalism is a kind of religion with the teaching that through the atonement of
Jesus, every person can ultimately be saved. However, traditional Christianity
tells that heaven is reserved for the selective—a small minority of people, while
the vast majority will go to Hell to be tortured eternally without mercy. In Universalism, God is regarded as a love that permeates all things in the world.

And what is Galesburg Universalist? In the 1950s in a pamphlet issued by
the Universalist Church in Galesburg the mention of Universalist is made:
"What is a Universalist? A Universalist is one who believes that in religion, as
in everything, each individual should be free to seek the truth for himself, un-
hampered by official creeds. He regards creeds as negative: they say 'No' to
new truth. The mind can only honestly affirm what actually persuades it and this
often can be in conflict with the creeds. To a Universalist, it is therefore a sacred obligation to accept whatever he finds to be the truth, and to follow it wherever it leads him. " [2] It says a Universalist is free to pursue what he / she thinks
right and go wherever it leads him. Sandburg did so; he loves the people,
rhymes the people and cries a battle cry for the people till his death in his poetry

---

[1] See the article "Universalism: A Kind and Gentle Religious Tradition was Once Dynamic in Galesburg" by
Rex Cherrington from http: //www. thezephyr. com/archives/universm. htm. 6 Mar. 2004.

[2] Ibid.

and many essays. This is just a universalist's essence and spirit and it also meets the covenant of later UUA:

1. The inherent worth and dignity of every person;

2. Justice, equity and compassion in human relations;

3. Acceptance of one another and encouragement to spiritual growth in our congregations;

4. A free and responsible search for truth and meaning;

5. The right of conscience and the use of the democratic process within our congregations and in society at large;

6. The goal of world community with peace, liberty, and justice for all;

7. Respect for the interdependent web of all existence of which we are a part. [1]

A detailed study of Universalist history and UUA is beyond the scope of this thesis. But a study of relationship between Universalism and Sandburg is a must. When Sandburg was young, his father believed in no religion except for the Swedish Lutheran. And Sandburg sometimes attended the Swedish Lutheran Church with his family. In his autobiography *Always the Young Stranger*, in the Chapter of "Judgment Day" he describes a memory that illustrates the theology preached in the church and the impact it had on his family. He writes:

> (After dinner) Slowly and not suddenly the talk shifted to the sermon of the day. Slowly the talk got around to where the preacher had so solemnly told us nobody knows for sure who will be among the saved on that last day. It might be you, it might be him or me. There would be loved ones separated, some going to the blessed happiness of heaven, others to the everlasting fire.
>
> And then, not slowly but suddenly, everyone at the table was in tears. Down our cheeks the tears ran and we looked at each other. It had never happened before in our house···. So we wept, in unison we wept. Slowly we gulped and choked down the sorrow that had come suddenly, the sorrow that arose out of that mystery of what the judgment will be on us in the last day. (AYS: 64)

---

① See: http: //www. uua. org/aboutuua/principles. html. 17 Mar. 2004.

From the text, the family, including the tough father, did not like the idea of God's selecting only some, with the majority going to the Hell. But in the town of Galesburg there was only one religious group that digressed from the traditional theology of the Lutherans, Baptists and Methodists. It was Universalism. The religious group in 1851 established a school called Lombard College in Galesburg. Within the school was a seminary to train Universalist ministers. Its members rejected the view that only a few were elected for salvation and believed that God would save everyone. The fear of Hell from Lutherans and the salvation of Universalism led Sandburg to the tendency toward Universalism, and the spirit of intellectual and religious freedom at Lombard was important later for Sandburg to develop into a writer.

And about Universalism's impact on the family, in the chapter of "Father and Mother", in Always the Young Stranger, Sandburg mentions about the religion:

> Mama spoke in hushed tones about the Universalists. I was eight or nine years old when I asked her about them. She shook her head with a grave face. She gave her ideas about the Universalists in two short sentences. "They say there is no hell," and "They believe in dancing in the church." On the first point I found out she was correct and that Universalists were saying there is no hell. On the second point I learned that she had been listening to gabmouths [sic] . I came to see later that most of the preachers in town spoke from their pulpits against dancing, either square or round, while the Universalists said little or nothing about dancing, either in church or out, claiming only that since there is no hell you couldn't dance your way to hell. (AYS: 93)

His sense of religion was impressed very deeply in his heart. There must have been a kind of struggle in his mind about which salvation was right. Clearly Sandburg and his family tended to believe in Universalism in order to be saved. The following story from a hobo, which he heard when he hoboed in the West, can also show his understanding about religion:

> A hobo (knocked) at a back door, asking a hatchet–faced woman for some-

thing to eat because he had not had a bite to eat for two days. The woman said she would get him something. He waited. The door opened and the women's skinny hand went toward him with a thin dry crust of bread in it as she said, "I give you this not for your sake nor for my sake but for Christ's sake. " As he took the crust of bread and looked at it he turned his face toward the woman and said, "Lady, listen to me. I beg of you not for my sake nor for your sake but for Christ's sake, put some butter on it!" (AYS: 389)

Though it is funny, humorous and full of wit, it indicates the existence of God in each person's mind. And for God's sake, the people can do many good deeds for the future salvation. The very short story went into Sandburg's heart so deep, and it is just because it is superficially humorous, but on the other hand, he wished everyone to be saved by God, to be cared by each other and by God. And this is the core spirit of Universalism.

The school (Lombard College), which Sandburg entered in 1899, had been originally founded to accept Universalists' children, because other schools tried to teach the children of Universalists against the beliefs of their parents. When children returned home they would denounce their parents for their belief in universal salvation and told that they would go into Hell after death. In fact, many schools of this kind were founded then, among which those of Universalists did not require religious courses and did not attempt to indoctrinate students religious doctrines. Schools established by Universalists that are still in existence today include Tufts University, St. Lawrence University, the University of Akron, and California Institute of Technology. So when Sandburg studied in the college, he felt free to develop.

Like other Universalist schools, the faculty in Lombard College did not require students to attend Lombard College to study the Universalist religion. Students like Sandburg could receive a good dose of liberal religion.

One thing must be talked of. When Sandburg was in the college, to earn part of his tuition, he got a part-time job to ring the bell for class at school. He worked in the bell tower. It so happened that the school used the bell tower as storage place to hold some books from the college library. The books stored in the tower consisted primarily of books about Universalism; so when Sandburg was waiting between classes to ring the bell in the tower, he would read Universalist theology. Harry Golden depicts Sandburg's Universalism reading in these words when Sandburg was still alive, "When Sandburg didn't have a class immediately after his bell-pulling stint, he would stand reading these theological works and to this day he is perfect in all the arguments that God is good and will not send us to hell. " (CS: 63) Who will read books he does not like if not for class or examination? It is sure Sandburg enjoyed reading the Universalism books. And he was more or less influenced by the leisure reading about Universalism.

As a son of a railroad worker, Sandburg found it easy in Universalism to identify with his origin and dream, because the then Universalists mostly came from farmers and laborers. They had no grace and sophistication of the upper class. And Universalism is just a more loving and inclusive religion than others. At least it is a humane religion for all people living in the secular world. They no longer fear the vindictive God and all people would go to heaven in the end while God became loving and kind.

Although Sandburg did not join the Universalist Church, its theology became his theology. He developed a Universalist belief into the goodness and dignity of every human being—all of his people. About religion, when Harry Golden, the author of Carl Sandburg, once asked him directly about his belief in religion, he answered: "I am a Christian, a Quaker, a Moslem, a Buddhist, a Confucian and maybe a Catholic pantheist or a Joan of Arc① who hears voices. I am all these and more. Definitely I have more religions than I have time or zeal to practice in true faith. " Although here he did not mention Universalism from the appearance, this was just the spirit of Universalism (CS: 64) .

And also as he describes his seventeen-month-old daughter in a poem, in

---

① French military leader and heroine. The "voices" refers to she was inspired and directed by religious visions. She organized the French resistance that forced the English to end their siege of Orleans (1429) .

spite of a kind of children's efforts at learning to talk, it soaks the credo of Universalism:

"Spoon" for spoon or cup or anything to be handled, all instruments, tools, paraphernalia of utility and convenience are SPOONS.
Mama is her only epithet and synonym for God and the Government and the one force of majesty and intelligence obeying the call of pity, hunger, pain, cold, dark—MAMA, MAMA, MAMA. (GMA: 198)

In the poem, the last line should be touched upon. "Mama is…God" is a child's interpretation of God. "Mama" can give, just like God can offer and bless. The "call of pity, hunger, pain, cold, dark" is the majesty and intelligence of "Mama", just like those of God. God will save all as "Mama" will save her child. The repetition of "Mama" is the repetition of the call to God to eliminate "hunger, pain, cold, dark". Children and the elective will all be saved by "Mama" and God. And this is what Universalism preaches.

In 1967, when Sandburg died, although he was not a member of any church, his wife, who knew very well Sandburg's religion tendency, invited a minister—a Unitarian Universalist for the memorial service. From the choice of his family, the great influence of Universalism from Sandburg's childhood to his death can be deeply felt.

In all his life, Universalism really consciously or unconsciously influenced him, more or less dominated his philosophy, here and there penetrated poetry, and steered his activities this way or that. By this he loved the people, cared about the people, sang of the people, and served the people. The people in God's eyes in Universalism are just the people in Sandburg's eyes. So, since in Universalism God is regarded as a love that permeates all things in the world, this just helped him approach and believe in socialism and develop into an ardent socialist as treated in Section II, Chapter Two. Now, several lines containing the teaching of Universalism from *The People, Yes* are extracted to end and summarize this part—Universalism as one of the reasons influencing Sandburg to care for the ordinary people so much , whom he thinks of as his brethens , and more or less worked to make him believe in socialism :

> The best preacher is the heart ⋯
> The best teacher is time.
> The best book is the world.
> The best friend is God. (PY : 117)

Amen !

Ⅲ. *Chicago Poems*

After moving to Chicago with his wife , Sandburg worked as journalist for several newspapers , meanwhile writing poems and receiving rejections. He had come to make Chicago his city , and began to write about the city , understood the city , loved the city , and carped at the city , but never disliked and avoided the people there.

The poem "Chicago" was at first submitted as an entry for a poetry competition organized by the Chicago Town Hall in 1910 ; it won the first prize , and with it , Sandburg's career as a poet really began. Then for the first time Sandburg brought some of Chicago poems to Harriet Monroe[①] at Poetry magazine. Then and there , when the staff opened the envelope from the unknown Sandburg , they shared an instant enthusiasm for the unconventional poems. Eunice Tietjen , an assistant editor , immediately urged Harriet Monroe to publish them. She chose nine ones for the March 1914 issue of *Poetry* , calling them "Chicago Poems". Sandburg had expected one more rejection ; but what he was rewarded was not only publication , but also an award for the best of *Poetry's* poems that year. Ti-

---

① 1885–1977 , American poet who founded and edited (1912–1936) Poetry , an influential magazine in which works of Marianne Moore , Wallace Stevens , William Carlos Williams and Carl Sandburg were first published. Later he became Sandburg's good friend.

etjen in an article described the poet–to–be as "lanky, warm and human, slow–spoken and witty. " "I was not prepared," she wrote, "for the sweep and vitality of the Chicago Poems which he brought into the office the first day I met him. They quite took us off our feet and it was with much pride that we introduced this new star in the firmament···. We adopted Carl at once and loved him. "[1] And later Harriet Monroe wrote "Carl was a typical Swedish peasant of proletarian sympathies in those days, with a massive frame and a face cut out of stone. His delicate–featured very American wife told me that ours was the first acceptance of Carl's poems, although for two years she had been collecting rejection slips. " (CSLW: 57)

After this, it was Theodore Dreiser who first advised Sandburg to collect his Chicago poems for a book. Sandburg admired Dreiser's work, especially The Titan, second of the controversial trilogy of novels based on the life of Chicago's street–railway tycoon Charles Yerkes. And it was their mutual friend Edgar Lee Masters that had brought the two men together at Dreiser's request. Dreiser once wrote to Sandburg in August 1915:

> Sometime ago I asked Mr. Masters to get you to gather your poems together and let me see them. Last Monday he came in bringing them and I have since had the pleasure of examining them. They are beautiful. There is a fine, hard, able paganism about them that delights me–and they are tender and wistful as only the lonely, wist–ful [sic], dreaming pagan can be. Do I need to congratulate you? Let me envy you instead. I would I could do things as lovely···.
>
> My idea is that if as many as a hundred and twenty–five or a hundred and fifty poems can be gotten together a publisher can be found for them. I sincerely hope so–I mean now···.
>
> My sincerest compliments. When I next get to Chicago I will look you up.
> (CSB: 268)

Sandburg accepted his sincere suggestion. In 1916, *Chicago Poems* as a

---

[1]   Sandburg, Helga. *A Great and Glorious Romance*. New York: Harcourt, 1978: 193.

book was published by Henry Holt and Company, New York. But no one would think that it became Sandburg's one of his representative works and it got into the symbol of Sandburg from one of visual angles.

And then, when "Chicago" as the theme poem appeared in the book of *Chicago Poems*, it unveiled a new poetic idiom in America. It begins with:

Hog Butcher for the World,
Tool Maker, Stacker of Wheat,
Player with Railroads and the Nation's Freight Handler;
Stormy, husky, brawling,
City of the Big Shoulders: (CP: 1)

How musical and rhymed it is!! Fresh, strong, concise, clangorous, and sonorous, each word is! These are the live people: butcher, maker, stacker, player, handler, shoulder. The repetition of [ə] can give us a sense of beauty, music, and kindness, because vowels bear the nature of being full, smooth, sweet and suave. These are just the qualities of the people. "Stormy" and "husky" remind us of Chicagoan's hoarse and high voice; in the meantime there is the rhythm of rhyming "stormy and husky". Especially when we hear and see "Big Shoulders", we see statue groups of Chicagoans with big and broad shoulders. It was such "Big Shoulders" that built Chicago's greatness and mightiness. The hog butcher, tool maker, wheat stacker (Sandburg himself once was), railroad player, freight handler and Big Shoulders, though they are "stormy, husky, brawling", are all the people, the real people. Even

They tell me you are wicked and I believe them, for I have seen your painted women under the gas lamps luring the farm boys.
And they tell me you are crooked and I answer: Yes, it is true I have seen the gunman kill and go free to kill again.
And they tell me you are brutal and my reply is: On the faces of women and children I have seen the marks of wanton hunger. (Ibid.)

The three "they tell me" are like the refrain of a song laying emphasis on the people's dark side: wicked, crooked, and brutal. The "painted women" under the gas lamps luring the farm boys "are part of the people;" the gunman "killing and going free to kill again is a member of the people; the" women and children "with" marks of wanton hunger "belong to the people. Yes. They are all the People, part of the People, even though they are wicked, crooked and brutal. They are what they are. But Sandburg cannot stand "those who sneer at this my city" and the people:

And having answered so I turn once more to those who sneer at this my city, and I give them back the sneer and say to them:
Come and show me another city with lifted head singing so proud to be alive and coarse and strong and cunning.
Flinging magnetic curses amid the toil of piling job on job, here is a tall bold slugger set vivid against the little soft cities;
Fierce as a dog with tongue lapping for action, cunning as a savage pitted against the wilderness, (Ibid.)

Sandburg here sneers at those "who sneer at this my city", and he is very proud of the city of Chicago. He is calling: who have this kind of city? Who dare to "come and show me another city" with head raised so high, and "singing so proud"? Which city can be so "alive and coarse and strong", and even "cunning"? Who can spit and fling the "magnetic curses? Who is the " bold slugger "looking down at the" little soft cities? What is "fierce as a dog lapping for action"? And who can be" cunning as a savage pitted against the wilderness It is the city–Chicago. But what's and who are in Chicago? Who make and made it so fierce, proud, bold, cunning and strong? Sandburg has the answer: they are the People, yes, the People,

Bareheaded,
Shoveling,
Wrecking,

Planning,

Building, breaking, rebuilding,

Under the smoke, dust all over his mouth, laughing with white teeth,

Under the terrible burden of destiny laughing as a young man laughs,

Laughing even as an ignorant fighter laughs who has never lost a battle,

Bragging and laughing that under his wrist is the pulse, and under his

ribs the heart of the people,

Laughing!

Laughing the stormy, husky, brawling laughter of Youth, half-naked,

sweating, proud to be Hog Butcher, Tool Maker, Stacker of Wheat,

Player with Railroads and Freight Handler to the Nation. (Ibid.)

In the last part of the poem, there are fifteen present participles: shoveling, wrecking, planning, building, breaking, rebuilding, laughing (six times), bragging, brawling and sweating. After reading we were really encouraged to move. It seems we could see the people are doing and laughing. So vivid and musical the sense is. On the surface, it is the city that is "bareheaded, building and rebuilding". Can a city do so? Of course, it cannot. Behind, inside and under it, it's the working class who are bareheaded, building and rebuilding. It's the working people who are under the smoke with dust all over their mouths and laughing with white teeth. They work and laugh again and again. They laugh to the "heart of the people".

Really the poem shocked many readers accustomed to more elegant poems. Sandburg uses the slang and the earthy idioms of the common people. So the people like to read it. Sandburg comes from the People. Sandburg writes about the People. The People who read his poems are to read themselves. With his increase in output of poems there also came acceptance by more readers; and more readers, more common people go into his poetry to read the people themselves.

Generally, "Chicago" contains symmetry clear to the eye by its arrangement of some parallels and some refrains as discussed, and to the ear for its sweeping cadences. It is meant to be spoken and heard. His vivid similes and metaphors were original: the city of "Big Shoulders", "tall, bold slugger,"

"Fierce as a dog," and "cunning as a savage." In a unifying personification, the city was a brawny and bareheaded young man, alive, coarse, strong, cunning, shoveling, wrecking, building, and laughing; and a bold, sweating young man under whose wrist is his pulse, and under whose ribs is his heart— "the heart of the people". There is a closing unity and symmetry in the repetition of the opening lines: "Hog Butcher, Tool Maker, Stacker of Wheat, Player with Railroads and Freight Handler to the Nation"

Chicago Poems, regarded as a whole, contains 260 pieces of poems, which can be found that it centers around the People and the city—Chicago. Sandburg arranges it into seven sections. The first section, *Chicago Poems*, with "Chicago" as the leading poem of this section and the whole book, includes vivid and often harsh portraits of the city and its people— "the Poor, millions of the Poor, patient and toiling; more patient than crags, tides, and stars; innumerable, patient as the darkness of night–and all broken, humble ruins of nations", containing the children working in factories and children (the word appears in the book nineteen times) "who tumble barefooted and bareheaded in the summer grass"; women of the night with "their hunger–deep eyes"; factory girls "who wasn't lucky in making the jump when the fire broke" and died; cabaret dancers, policemen, a Jewish fish crier, Hungarian immigrants relaxing with music and beer on a Sunday afternoon; "long lines" of working girls and men and children; anarchists and ice handlers; black workingmen, and refugees from the South, "brooding and muttering with memories of shackles"; "mockers" digging ditches for the city; millionaires and cash girls; a stockyards hunky burying his child with sorrow; and an Indiana girl who lost herself in the city where she had come to search "romance / and big things / and real dreams / that never go smash." (CPCS: 17)

As to the city, Sandburg chooses Chicago's skyscraper as the symbol of the city, which can nearly reflect all aspects of the city and the people in it. In this way, he both praises the city— "this my city", exposes the people in and around it, and mixes the two together, and neither one can be separated from the other one, for the city is the production, success and result of the people's toil, sweat, blood and life:

Skyscraper

BY day the skyscraper looms in the smoke and sun and has a soul.

Prairie and valley, streets of the city, pour people into it and they mingle among its twenty floors and are poured out again back to the streets, prairies and valleys.

It is the men and women, boys and girls so poured in and out all day that give the building a soul of dreams and thoughts and memories.

(Dumped in the sea or fixed in a desert, who would care for the building or speak its name or ask a policeman the way to it?)

Elevators slide on their cables and tubes catch letters and parcels and iron pipes carry gas and water in and sewage out. (CP: 29)

In the beginning, it outlines the city's life. The skyscraper is the symbol of the city. The people going in and out of it are the ones going in and out of the city. And it is the men and women, boys and girls–the people that build "a soul of dreams and thoughts and memories." Skyscraper's greatness is actually that of these "men and women, boys and girls." And it is complicated and somewhat mysterious:

Wires climb with secrets, carry light and carry words, and tell terrors and profits and loves—curses of men grappling plans of business and questions of women in plots of love.

Hour by hour the caissons reach down to the rock of the earth and hold the building to a turning planet.

Hour by hour the girders play as ribs and reach out and hold together the stone walls and floors.

Hour by hour the hand of the mason and the stuff of the mortar clinch the pieces and parts to the shape an architect voted.

Hour by hour the sun and the rain, the air and the rust, and the press of time running into centuries, play on the building inside and out and use it. (Ibid.)

It is "hour by hour", all the time, that the people knit the wires climbing "with secrets" into each corner of the building and of the city with "light and words", holding the building to "turning the planet"; it is "hour by hour", all the while, that the girders, the people "play as ribs" of the building, of the city, and "hold together the stone walls and floors" with the "hand of the mason and the stuff of the mortar" to run it "into centuries". And the following people are the ones from the common building the skyscraper with blood, sweat, life and soul:

> Men who sunk the pilings and mixed the mortar are laid in graves where the wind whistles a wild song without words
> And so are men who strung the wires and fixed the pipes and tubes and those who saw it rise floor by floor.
> Souls of them all are here, even the hod carrier begging at back doors hundreds of miles away and the brick-layer who went to state's prison for shooting another man while drunk.
> (One man fell from a girder and broke his neck at the end of a straight plunge—he is here—his soul has gone into the stones of the building.) (Ibid.)

The Skyscraper, remembers the builders of the building and the city. The men "who sunk the pilings" and "mixed the mortar", and the men "who strung the wires" and "fixed the pipes and tubes", have been dead, with only souls left and fixed into the building and the city. A hod carrier now lost his job, begging at many back doors. A bricklayer went to prison for crime. While another man fell down from a girder, with the other builders, his soul has gone "into the stones of the building" forever. These are the People. Unmistakably, the People. The dead have been dead. But the alive have to live on:

> On the office doors from tier to tier—hundreds of names and each name standing for a face written across with a dead child, a passionate lover, a driving ambition for a million dollar business or a lobster's ease of life.
> Behind the signs on the doors they work and the walls tell nothing from room to room.

Ten–dollar–a–week stenographers take letters from corporation officers, lawyers, efficiency engineers, and tons of letters go bundled from the building to all ends of the earth.

Smiles and tears of each office girl go into the soul of the building just the same as the master—men who rule the building.

Hands of clocks turn to noon hours and each floor empties its men and women who go away and eat and come back to work.

Toward the end of the afternoon all work slackens and all jobs go slower as the people feel day closing on them. (Ibid.)

These living people show varied faces. Some are the "dead" children, while some have lost their simplicity and puerility, and now they become "a passionate lover, a driving ambition for a million dollar business" or are living "a lobster's ease of life". In the Skyscraper, in the city, the real drudgeries are the stenographers, the office girls with "smiles and tears" . Their souls, like any one in the building, like any builder in the city, go into the building, and go into the city. After work, people leave from work and leave the building:

One by one the floors are emptied··· The uniformed elevator men are gone····.

Spelled in electric fire on the roof are words telling miles of houses and people where to buy a thing for money. The sign speaks till midnight.

Darkness on the hallways. Voices echo. Silence holds··· Watchmen walk slow from floor to floor and try the doors····.

A young watchman leans at a window and sees the lights of barges butting their way across a harbor···

By night the skyscraper looms in the smoke and the stars and has a soul. (Ibid.)

The Skyscraper is the epitome of Chicago City. After work the people in the building and the city go to another life. Each goes to his or her self and fate. Elevator men, scrubbers, like the others, are doing the commonest work. But, though they leave, they become part of the building as a soul. The vision of the tall building is the reduction of the city.

In the poem, Sandburg gives prominence to the common things and the people's common life. Under the greatness of the Skyscraper is the common. It's made of the common things and by the common folk. That is: commonness brings up greatness! And who is the commonness? The People are! In the section, the first poem is "Chicago"; the last one is "Skyscraper". It emphasizes the theme: Chicago and the greatness of the common people. Chicago is the Skyscraper. The people made the Skyscraper and the city—Chicago.

The second section, *Handfuls*, is a gentle counterpoint to the brutal reality of *War Poems* (1914-1915) (Section Three). Section Four is a contemplative section called *The Road and the End*. The three sections gather some of Sandburg's early poems, each containing exact eleven (totally thirty–three) short poems, covering in all only 19 pages. It explores pensive reflections on the commoners' attitudes towards death and loss, the meaning of the past and the possibility of the future as in follows:

<table>
<tr><td>**Love**</td><td>**Troth**</td></tr>
<tr><td>I HAVE love</td><td>YELLOW dust a bumble</td></tr>
<tr><td>And a child,</td><td>Bee's wing</td></tr>
<tr><td>A banjo</td><td>Grey lights in a woman's</td></tr>
<tr><td>And shadows.</td><td>asking eyes,</td></tr>
<tr><td>(Losses of God,</td><td>Red ruins in the changing</td></tr>
<tr><td>All will go</td><td>sunset embers:</td></tr>
<tr><td>And one day</td><td>I take you and pole high</td></tr>
<tr><td>We will hold</td><td>the memories</td></tr>
<tr><td>Only the shadows.)</td><td>Death will break ger claws</td></tr>
<tr><td>(CP: 35)</td><td>on some I keep.   (CP: 35)</td></tr>
</table>

Both are short but deep contemplations about common life. Sandburg recognizes in the poems the essence of life. Everything will become "shadows". People have no choice; people have to face "Death". But "Grey lights in a woman's asking eyes" is a struggle before the inevitable death. It is the poor people's resistance and it is so weak.

In *Fogs and Fires*, the poems are lyrical, and sometimes imagistic with themes of love and memory and a restless search for self and meaning by probing into the daily things and gentle sentiment from day-to-day life. This section is the intended part of *Handfuls*, *War Poems*, and *The Road and the End*. By Sandburg, the common folk's life is not always hard and difficult. "Back Yard" tells us part of ordinary people's quiet, happy and lovely life:

Shine on, O moon of summer.

Shine to the leaves of grass, catalpa and oak,

All silver under your rain to-night.

An Italian boy is sending songs to you to-night from an accordion.

A Polish boy is out with his best girl; they marry next month; to-night they are throwing you kisses.

An old man next door is dreaming over a sheen that sits in a cherry tree in his back yard.

The clocks say I must go—I stay here sitting on the back porch drinking white thoughts you rain down.

Shine on, O moon,

Shake out more and more silver changes. (CP: 57)

The poem is like a serenade, like an Italian boy's song "from an accordion". And it is like the love of Polish boy and his best girl. The poem is the people's sweet life. What is the common people's happy life? The Italian boy's songs are happy; the Polish boy's love is happy; the old man's dreaming way is happy; and "I", "sitting on the back porch drinking white thoughts you rain down", am happy, too. Sandburg wishes "you" — "moon of summer" could "shake out more and more silver changes" —in other words, bless us ordinary people with more and more happiness.

The last second part Shadows paints haunting vignettes of the city, "Lines based on certain regrets that come with rumination upon the painted faces of women on North Clark Street, Chicago." Here are bold indictments against the exploitation of women by men and by the society as revealed in the poems such as "Used Up" and "It Is Much".

In "Used Up", women are compared to "roses" which are so easy to be trampled and damaged:

Roses,

Red roses,

Crushed

In the rain and wind

Like mouths of women

Beaten by the fists of

Men using them.

O little roses

And broken leaves

And petal wisps:

You that so flung your crimson

To the sun

Only yesterday. (CP: 65)

Sandburg expresses deep sympathy for women in the lower class. Women look like "broken leaves" and are so weak under "the fists of Men using them"; their beauty and value have been "used up", which is implied by the title "Used Up". (Even now, such bad situation of women exists in some areas and countries.)

In "It Is Much", women are the ones of "night life amid the lights" and "along the shadows" and have become so "gaunt" that they look like "a bitch worn to the bone". "Bitch" is often regarded as offensive, but here who would offend a gaunt bitch worn to the bone? None! It only invites profound compassion:

Women of night life amid the lights

Where the line of your full, round throats

Matches in gleam the glint of your eyes

And the ring of your heart—deep laughter:

It is much to be warm and sure of to—morrow.

Women of night life along the shadows,

Lean at your throats and skulking the walls,

Gaunt as a bitch worn to the bone,

Under the paint of your smiling faces:

It is much to be warm and sure of to—morrow. (CP: 66)

In the poems of "Trafficker" (See CPCS: 62) and "Harrison Street Court" (See CPCS: 62) women encounter the same fate. They are scorned as degraded women. Things are the same as is exposed in "Soiled Dove" in which Sandburg explores the reality of a woman and a prostitute in certain marriage:

LET us be honest; the lady was not a harlot until she married a corporation lawyer who picked her from a Ziefeld chorus.

Before then she never took anybody's money and paid for her silk stockings out of what she earned singing and dancing.

She loved one man and he loved six women and the game was changing her looks, calling for more and more massage money and high coin for the beauty doctors.

Now she drives a long, underslung motor car all by herself, reads in the day's papers what her husband is doing to the inter—state commerce commission, requires a larger corsage from year to year, and wonders sometimes how one man is coming a—long with six women.

The poem describes the typical image pressed by men and by society. A man has six women, but each woman in this situation should endure six times of pressure from a man. Prostitution is what she is forced to do. This section of poems with special subject on lost women concluded with a poignant portrait of Chick Lorimer, "a wild girl keeping a hold / on a dream she wants. " Nobody knows, Sandburg writes, where and why she has " Gone with her little chin / Thrust ahead of her / And her soft hair blowing careless / From under a wide hat, / Dancer, singer, a laughing passionate lover ⋯ / Nobody knows where she's gone. (CP: 68) Indeed, nobody knows, nobody can predict and nobody can be sure of her fate. They are the weak group in the society. But they are part of the people, and he never forgot their wretched fate and never forgot to write them into his poetry. Shortly, in a certain way, it reveals Sandburg's sense of feminism and his true solicitude for the women oppressed by the society.

Other Days (1900–1910) is the last section of the book and a soft-spoken denouement. In the final section Sandburg arranges some of his earlier poems, including "Dream Girl" who "will come one day in a waver of love, /Tender as dew, impetuous as rain, "and with " a film of hope and a memoried day". These gentle ones just juxtapose the sharp city portraits. And the finale, "Gypsy" ends the last section and the whole book: "Tell no man anything for no man listens, /Yet hold thy lips ready to speak. " (CP: 80), telling the people to voice at emergency, and keep silent when "no man listens".

What did the people say about *Chicago Poems*? In Poetry magazine, Harriet Monroe praised the powerfulness and honesty of these poems, some of them appeared first in the publication of *Poetry*. She thought of it as "verse of massive gait," In agreement with her was Amy Lowell①, who in the New York Times stated the following attitudes towards Chicago Poems:

> Chicago Poems is one of the most original books this age produced. The impression one gets on reading this book is of a heavy steel grey sky rent open here and there, and through the rents, shining pools of clear pale blue. It is a rare and beautiful combination which we find in this volume, under whatsoever simile we describe it. Seldom does such virility go with such tenderness···. Try as he will, Mr. Sandburg cannot help feeling that virtue resides with the people who earn their daily bread with their hands rather than with those who do so with their brains. (CSLW: 72)

After the publication of Chicago Poems, a wide audience began to listen to Sandburg. His poems spoke in new ways to readers who still equated rhyme and

---

① 1874–1925, American poet. A leader of the imagists, she wrote several volumes of poetry, including *Sword Blades* and *Poppy Seed* (1914) .

romanticism with poetry. Amy Lowell characterized Sandburg and Masters as the two revolutionary American poets. And the focus of revolution was their using free verse and realistic subjects about the universal human experience, especially about the common themes of the varied American experiences. Sandburg would continue to speak to and from the heart of ordinary American people and American life, and when Louis Untermeyer[①] pronounced him as the emotional democrat of American poetry, Sandburg was well on his way to becoming the People's poet. An investigation on the titles of the whole book can be used as an example to support the point in a way: In the book, there are two hundred pieces of poems. The titles directly referring to specific persons are 43. These titles involve such persons as "Mag", "Anna Imroth", "Margaret" and so on, or nouns or pronouns referring to persons like "Old Woman", "Plowboy", "To Certain Journeyman", "Passers-by", "Working Girls" and many others. Some or most of the others, not referring to particular common persons, in fact, discuss peoples' daily life and their situation. Chicago Poems is his first book making his name, and it began to lead him to the way of becoming a great People's poet. What he does in poetry is reflect the real life and deep thoughts of the people, make the people's needs known, support the people movement, and speak for the interests of the people.

After reading the book, Gay Wilson Allen, an editor and critic, found in Chicago Poems the longing of ordinary people for the beauty and happiness, which he did not know and could not find much before:

This clutching of dreams was not a creation of Sandburg's fantasy, but a social phenomenon which he accurately observed···. A more cheerful theme is the laughter and joy workmen manage to find in spite of their toil and poverty. The face of the Jewish fish crier on Maxwell Street is the face "of a man terribly glad to be selling fish, terribly glad that God made fish, and customers to whom he may call his wares from a pushcart." The poet searches for happiness and finds it one Sun-

---

① 1885–1977, American writer and editor of poetry anthologies, including *Modern American Poetry* (first published 1919), which provided a medium for both established and emerging poets.

day afternoon on the banks of the Desplaines River in "a crowd of Hungarians under the trees with their women and children and a keg of beer and an
accordion. " ①

Gay Allen's words are right. But on the other hand, Sandburg never ig-
nored the potentials of the mass. This connotation can be seen and revealed in
paeans to the people such as "Masses":

MASSES

Among the mountains I wandered and saw blue haze and red crag and was amazed:
On the beach where the long push under the endless tide maneuvers, I stood si-
lent;
Under the stars on the prairie watching the Dippers slant over the horizon's grass,
I was full of thoughts.
Great men, pageants of war and labor, soldiers and workers, mothers lifting their
children—these all I touched, and felt the solemn thrill of them.
And then one day I got a true look at the Poor, millions of the Poor, patient and
toiling; more patient than crags, tides, and stars; innumerable, patient as the
darkness of night—and all broken, humble ruins of nations. (CP: 2)

After the concrete investigation on the people, Sandburg gives an abstract
percipience about them. So he felt "the solemn thrill of them". In the poem he
sees the power in depth from the patient people who are "more patient than
crags, tides, and stars" and patient as the darkness of night". In essence, he is
warning the dignitaries of the current of potential from the people. He tells them
not to overlook this group of people, "millions of the Poor", and reminds the
people themselves of the fact that they can be powerful and they can be strong e-
nough to vindicate and release themselves.

Chicago Poems deals with the people positively. Sandburg lightens Chicago
city with the people's fire. He erects the city's greatness with the people's support

---

① See the poem "Happiness" in *Chicago Poems* on page 8. (CSLW: 82) and powerfulness. He speaks out what the people want, think and feel. He exposes the reality of the people's life, no matter how hard and happy, dark and bright. As the people's poet, he melts a big and heavy "YES" into the People.

IV. *Cornhuskers*

Chicago Poems and Cornhuskers established him as a poet of national stature. At last, he had unified his free-verse style and his realistic subject matter into a powerful, compelling poetic voice.

—Penelope Niven

When Sandburg worked for Newspaper Enterprise Association (NEA) abroad in Europe, *Cornhuskers* was published by Henry Holt and Company at the very end of 1918. The 103 poems in it that form this early collection earned for Sandburg the Pulitzer Prize for Poetry of 1919. And before this, Sandburg shared with Margaret Widdemer the $500 prize of the Poetry Society of America for 1919 for Cornhuskers.

As he himself recommended it to Alfred Harcourt[1] On May 3, 1918: "The book will be a real and honest singing book···and is a bigger conceived and all round better worked-out book than *Chicago Poems.*" (CSLW: 85) Indeed, on the whole it is more refined and includes more diverse subjects (though less optimistic) than *Chicago Poems.* If we say *Chicago Poems* celebrates the people in the city, we can say *Cornhuskers* rhymes the people in the country. In the book, he turns his major attention away from urban Chicago toward the broad Midwest countryside in which he had grown to manhood. Or in other words, some poems from the second half of the book convey in particular his kind of Romanticism not to be discussed here, now that it is not the focus of the dissertation. Though it

---

[1]   One of Sandburg's main publishers and good friends, who published Sandburg's many books and poems.

contains a few urban poems of his traditional realism, their subjects were not so often about Chicago as cities like Omaha or Buffalo. He continued to experience and explore among the people as an American people's poet. So his poems in the book are still about America and her people, only painting some romantic color on the landscape of the Midwest.

The whole book includes the following five parts in file: "Cornhuskers", "Persons Half Known", "Leather Leggings", "Haunts" and "Shenandoah". The first two parts treat more materials about working people and their life in the countryside. Among the poems, some concern the harvesting happiness; some are about the poet's meditation on and observation about working people's life, especially in the country. The poem "Autumn Movement" is a case in point:

> I cried over beautiful things knowing no beautiful thing lasts
> The field of cornflower yellow is a scarf at the neck of the copper sunburned woman, the mother of the year, the taker of seeds.
> The northwest wind comes and the yellow is torn full of holes, new beautiful things come in the first spit of snow on the northwest wind, and the old things go, not one lasts. (C: 10)

The first line is the poet's speculation on beauty after seeing the yellow cornflower in the field. Since "no beautiful thing lasts", he "cried over beautiful things". And he connects the flower beauty with woman, "the copper sunburned woman". Then "the old things go, not one lasts", the beauty goes, and new beauty begins to grow, like the cycle of life. The title "Autumn Movement" implies the beauty movement. It is also the life movement, or wheel of life. Here Sandburg treats of the philosophy of human life. In "Autumn Movement", though no farmer can be found, many farmers seem to be able to be seen in the vague feelings and mind. They are quiet in heart. They have their own understanding about life. Comparatively, the poem "Village in Late Summer" conveys a sense of the people's impulsion of life to us:

Lips half–willing in a doorway.

Lips half–singing at a window.

Eyes half–dreaming in the walls.

Feet half–dancing in a kitchen.

Even the clocks half–yawn the hours

And the farmers make half–answers. (C: 11)

Again, no person can be seen as a whole, but it seems we could see lips speaking, eyes winking and feet tapping, which expresses the people's enjoyment of late summer's good crop and expectation of coming autumn harvesting. They are too happy to stay still. The personification of clocks, for example, the clocks' half–yawn, increases the satisfaction of farmers. And farmers' "half an-swers" suggest to us farmers' proud self–confidence about autumn crop.

In another poem, "A Million Young Workmen, 1915"[1] [as in "Grass" (see Section II, Chapter Four.), "Old Timers" (See CPCS: 137), and "Smoke" (See CPCS: 142)], Sandburg is in league with many American peo-ple, and in tune with their profound suspicion of war's motivations and far–reac-hing effects:

A Million Young Workmen, 1915

A MILLION young workmen straight and strong lay stiff on the grass and roads,

And the million are now under soil and their rottening flesh will in the years feed

roots of blood–red roses.

Yes, this million of young workmen slaughtered one another and never saw their

red hands.

And oh, it would have been a great job of killing and a new and beautiful thing un-

der the sun if the million knew why they hacked and tore each other to death.

The kings are grinning, the kaiser and the czar–they are alive riding in leather–

seated motor cars, and they have their women and roses for ease, and they eat fresh

–poached eggs for breakfast, new butter on toast, sitting in tall water–tight houses

---

① 1915 is the second year of World War I (1914–1918) .

reading the news of war.

I dreamed a million ghosts of the young workmen rose in their shirts all soaked in crimson… and yelled:

God damn the grinning kings, God damn the kaiser and the czar.

Chicago, 1915. (C: 65)

In the poem Sandburg shows that his first reaction to World War I is that of most Socialists throughout the world then. He exposes the miserable phenomenon to the public that "millions of young workmen straight and strong lay stiff on the grass and road," and "under soil and their rotten flesh will in the years feed roots of blood-red roses". Some of the dead young men here are and come from Sandburg's "Cornhuskers", belonging to part of the people. They killed each other in the way Cain[①] did to Abel in Holy Bible. In a way they were killing themselves; they are fanned and used by "grinning kings", "the Kaiser and the czar", the starters of WWI, and the oppressors of the people. This is the aftermath of WWI. And at last the victims are forever the common people. "A million ghosts of young workmen" yelled at the kings, Kaisers and czar for they felt the people themselves were undeserved to be killed. Of course it is, too, the roaring of Sandburg for the people from the heart.

However, in Cornhuskers' last poem "The Four Brothers", (for more discussion, see Section II, Chapter Four) with the subtitle of "Notes for War Songs (November, 1917)", Sandburg's attitude changes to that of Whitman in the poem "Beat! Beat! Drums!" [②]. In it, Sandburg says:

…

I say now, by God, only fighters today will save the world, nothing but fighters will keep alive the names of those who left red prints of bleeding feet at Valley Forge in Christmas snow.

---

①   In the Old Testament, Cain is the eldest son of Adam and Eve, who murdered his brother Abel out of jealousy and was condemned to be a fugitive.

②   About the text of "Beat! Beat! Drum!" see: Ferguson, M. M. Salter & J. Stallworthy. The Norton Anthology of Poetry. New York: W. W. Norton & Company, 1996: 971.

On the cross of Jesus, the sword of Napoleon, the skull of Shakespeare, the pen of
Tom Jefferson, the ashes of Abraham Lincoln, or any sign of the red and running
life poured out by the mothers of the world⋯ (C: 68)

Who are "fighters"? The people are. The sentence "Only fighters today will
save the world" frankly tells us only the people can save the world. But he only
found the strength of the "sword of Napoleon, the skull of Shakespeare, the pen of
Tom Jefferson, the ashes of Abraham Lincoln", and he could not find the bitterness
of victims made by the war starters, he could not see the same people of the same
kind oppressed by the war hawks. Hence, Sandburg's another side appears: more or
less parochial native sense (which will be discussed in detail in Section IV "His
'Sense of Nativeness'in American Grain", Chapter Four).

But, in spite of its unevenness and Sandburg's mutable, and even uncon-
stant (as his socialism tendency) mood, Cornhuskers is one of his finest volumes of poems. The uneven mood was probably due to the turbulence of the period in which these poems were written: the time from 1915 to 1918, which
nearly completely covers WWI. No matter how he changed his mood, he never
lightened the weight of the people in his heart. The tall man in the poem "A Tall
Man" is an attestation:

THE MOUTH of this man is a gaunt strong mouth.
The head of this man is a gaunt strong head.
The jaws of this man are bone of the Rocky Mountains, the Appalachians.
The eyes of this man are chlorine of two sobbing oceans, Foam, salt, green, wind,
the changing unknown.
The neck of this man is pith of buffalo prairie, old longing and new beckoning of
corn belt or cotton belt, Either a proud Sequoia trunk of the wilderness or huddling
lumber of a sawmill waiting to be a roof⋯ (C: 66)

The lines immediately remind us of Abraham Lincoln. Yes, it is about Lincoln. Sandburg, as a biographer of Lincoln, highly values Lincoln. Why did he
do so? It is because Lincoln valued the people very much and he put the people

in a special place in his heart, and because Sandburg also prized the people. He praised Lincoln to praise the people. And the poem is selected here also because Lincoln is the representative of the people. The mouth, the head, the eyes, and the neck are all gauntly strong. That's Lincoln's unyielding, that's the people's doughtiness. Lincoln is the symbol of the people, and representative of the people:

> ···he is white sky of sun, he is the head of the people.
> The heart of him the red drops of the people,
> The wish of him the steady gray-eagle crag-hunting flights of the people···
> (Ibid.)

As the head of the people, he is like "white sky of sun". His heart is the heart of the people. The blood running in his body is the "red drops of the people", and "the wish of him" is that of the people. The weight of Lincoln weighs equally the weight of the people. This kind of "cult of personality", not like that of Saddam Hussein of former Iraqi dictator, is "cult of the people".

Cornhuskers from *Cornhuskers* are of the same importance as that of those people from the city of Chicago in *Chicago Poems*. They are part of the people, building the nation, tilling the land, and writing the history. They are of great value, forever for Sandburg!

V. *Smoke and Steel*

> Smoke into steel and blood into steel···
> Smoke and blood is the mix of steel···
> Five men swim in a pot of red steel.
> Their bones are kneaded into the bread of steel:
> Their bones are knocked into coils and anvils···
> So ghosts hide in steel like heavy-armed men in mirrors···
>
> —Carl Sandburg

In the year of 1920, Harcourt, Brace and Howe published Smoke and Steel by Sandburg. In Harcourt's office, there was such an excitement when Sandburg's manuscript arrived that all other work was suspended for "This office has been on a complete bat today;—no one has done a lick of work. Mr. Harcourt came upstairs at ten this morning with the ms—I could not get a word out of him until 11: 30 when he began to read from the ms to Mr. Spingarn; then Mr. Spingarn took part of it and read it back to him and me—they went out to lunch and when Mr. Spingarn got back at 2: 30 he started on it—at 3: 30 Mr. Untermeyer came in; then he and Mr. Spingarn started reading it—and now here comes Mr. Harcourt again and all four of us have begun all over again—Really—see what you have done—" (CSB: 353) And Sandburg was told by Harcourt the colleagues in the company "spent most of the day gloating over your manuscript⋯ are very proud of it already and are going to be more so. " (CSB: 354)

Sandburg's third book of poetry, *Smoke and Steel* was in many ways the culmination of his work, revealing his interior life as well as the emotional and social milieu of his times. Till this time, the three anthologies *Chicago Poems*, *Cornhuskers and Smoke and Steel* were highly original and forceful, reflecting a typical common person's soul and experience, revealing in varied portraits of working people the problems of contemporary life and the universal themes—love, loss, joy, pain, death, war and so on.

What is the most striking theme of *Smoke and Steel*? One step after another, Sandburg came from *Chicago Poems* with a kind of pride, and then *Cornhuskers* with an air of romanticism, to *Smoke and Steel* with a theme of disillusionment of the world war and the society and soulful sympathy with the people. With the pivotal book, Sandburg began to turn his readers toward their shared history, collective fate and joint future.

In the book, the leading poem is "Smoke and Steel" in which images of "Smoke and Steel" came from his travels to steel towns. One of them is Gary, Indiana, which he most frequently visited when he was a reporter. The city was founded on land and purchased by the U. S. Steel Corporation in 1905; it was a real and highly industrialized steel city. In the poem Sandburg gives us a mixed vision:

> The smoke changes its shadow
>
> And men change their shadow;
>
> A nigger, a wop, a bohunk changes.
>
> A bar of steel—it is only
>
> Smoke at the heart of it, smoke and the blood of a man.
>
> A runner of fire ran in it, ran out, ran somewhere else,
>
> And left—smoke and the blood of a man
>
> And the finished steel, chilled and blue. (SS: 3–10)

In fact, smoke and steel and steel workers are a combined mixture. A "nigger", a "wop" or a "bohunk", no matter which he is, they are part of steel. A bar of steel is made of "smoke and the blood of a man". The industrialized product—steel has been infused with human energy, flesh and spirit. And it has not only been a kind of material. If we go back to the producing process, we will feel shocked at "the finished steel, chilled and blue" wresting the blood of steel workers like a blue bloodsucker ghost. In the following lines, Sandburg unmasks this open secret to us:

> And always dark in the heart and through it,
>
> Smoke and the blood of a man.
>
> Pittsburg [sic], Youngstown, Gary—they make their steel with men.
>
> In the blood of men and the ink of chimneys
>
> The smoke nights write their oaths:
>
> Smoke into steel and blood into steel;
>
> Homestead, Braddock, Birmingham, they make their steel with men.
>
> Smoke and blood is the mix of steel. (Ibid.)

Usually what we can see is the only shining steel from appearance. Seldom can we find it agglomerates "the blood of a man". The blood was left in the steel; the soul of workers was gone with the wind in the smoke, for "they make

their steel with men" in places such as Pittsburgh, Youngstown, Gary, Home-
stead, Braddock and Birmingham. He leads people to see clearly that "smoke
and blood is the mix of steel". Sandburg chose "Smoke and Steel" as the title;
however, if it could be changed into "Soul and Steel", it would be better and
direct. The smoke is the soul of steel workers and the steel is also the blood of
them. These are part of the people and these are where the people's contribution
and sacrifice lies. Meanwhile, this blood–consuming fate is doomed if they do
not want to go hungry:

> The anthem learned by the steel is:
> Do this or go hungry
> Look for our rust on a plow.
> Listen to us in a threshing–engine razz.
> Look at our job in the running wagon wheat. (Ibid.)

What can they do, if they don't want to go hungry? The "rust on a plow" is
part of the workers; the "threshing–engine razz" contains the workers' mourn-
ing; "the running wagon" rolls and winds the workers' soul.

At the end of it, Sandburg reflects on the transience of the lives of men,
and permanence of the people forged into a steel bar they leave behind:

> A pool of steel sleeps and looks slant–eyed
> on the pearl cobwebs, the pools of moonshine;
> sleeps slant–eyed a million years,
> sleeps with a coat of rust, a vest of moths,
> a shirt of gathering sod and loam.
> The wind never bothers… a bar of steel.
> The wind picks only… pearl cobwebs…pools of moonshine. (Ibid.)

The poem shows workmen wresting steel from fire, with some even dying in
the process. Men and steel are simultaneously tools and symbols of the industrial
society, for "Their bones are kneaded into the bread of steel / Their bones are

knocked into coils and anvils" as is expressed in the quotation under the sub-head of this section. And many people's death accompanies modern civilization like that of Chicago.

The theme and the sprawling formal symmetry in "Smoke and Steel" repeat the pattern that Sandburg established in "Chicago" in *Chicago Poems* and "Prairie" in *Cornhuskers*. In each of the previous three, the leading poem is all followed by a series of dark portraits of working people under the burden of and overwhelmed by the society and their lives.

Similarly, in the poem "Crimson Changes People" (see more detailed discussion in Section I, Chapter Four.), there is the despair of "a crucifix in your eyes," and the "dusk Golgotha":

DID I see a crucifix in your eyes
and nails and Roman soldiers
and a dusk Golgotha? ··· (SS: 42)

The crimson color in the title apparently implies Jesus' tribulation and blood. Sandburg uses biblical quotation to show his disillusionment from the severe society. He is disappointed with the doomed fate of the ordinary people. Though he uses a question mark, he made sure that he saw "a crucifix", "nails" and "Golgotha" in "your eyes". Actually under the high pressure from the society, the people have no alternative, and they can but bear this suffering just like Jesus suffered. "Crimson Changes People" indicates suffering changes the people. The crucifixion on earth changes the people's life attitude into a passive and tolerant one. And he wishes in heart "crimson" could urge the people into action instead of tolerance. Or we can regard it as a lament for the people's tribulation. In "Cahoots", however, the poem contains a sense of cynicism with disillusionment:

Play it across the table.
What if we steal this city blind?

If they want anything let ' em nail it down.
Harness bulls, dicks, front office men,
And the high goats up on the bench,
Ain't they all in cahoots? (SS: 45)

It is sure they are playing a game " in cahoots ". The mood of " Harness
bulls, dicks, front office men ", especially " dicks ", produces an insulting
effect on these persons. By the way, " goat " can mean lecherous man. On the
one hand, Sandburg regards them as "bulls, dicks" and " goats " ; on the other
hand, he 'd like to put harness on them. By all appearances he looks them down
as the animals and the indecent for they are carving up the people 's benefits :

Ain't it fifty–fifty all down the line,
Petemen, dips, boosters, stick–ups and guns–
what's to hinder?
Go fifty–fifty.
If they nail you call in a mouthpiece.
Fix it, you gazump, you slant–head, fix it.
Feed 'em⋯.
Nothin'ever sticks to my fingers, nah, nah,
notin'like that,
But there ain't no law we got to wear mittens–
huh–is there?
Mittens, that's a good one – mittens!
There oughta be a law everybody wear mittens. (Ibid.)

They are brazenly and openly partitioning the city, the people 's benefits
" fifty–fifty ", half–and–half, and completely with " guns ". " What's to hinder?"
Nothing! That's because they have guns shamelessly. But they realize " mitten "
is good for them to wear to insure " Nothing' ever sticks to my fingers " . The
poem is full of scorns and bitter mocks, putting up Sandburg 's deep hatred for
the upper class oppressing the lower class. " Bulls ", " dicks ", " goats " are

their images; and "mittens" are their veils and instrument to hide evils and crimes. Like many other common people, and as one of them, Sandburg takes the guys as disgustful. But he takes himself as a fighter for the people, a champion for the interests of the people like John Brown①in the poem "Finish":

> Death comes once, let it be easy.
> Ring one bell for me once, let it go at that.
> Or ring no bell at all, better yet.
> Sing one song if I die.
> Sing John Brown's Body or Shout All Over God's Heaven.
> Death comes once, let it be easy. (SS: 266)

And thereupon, he his life approached the finish in 1967, there were songs and poems, as outlined in the poem, and one bell for the eighty-nine-year singer and seeker to make his last wish and dream of dying like John Brown come true. Yes, death came only once and easily for him. But as we know, his whole life, like John Brown too, fighting and speaking for the people, was not a piece of cake, containing a spirit of backbone and perseverance.

Sandburg was forty-one when he had *Smoke and Steel* published, standing professionally and emotionally near the midway of his life and climax of his career and with his thought, philosophy and poetry having grown mature. In the book his most remarkable statement of disillusionment of the world war is in *Four Preludes on Playthings of the Wind* including four cantos:

FOUR PRELUDES ON PLAYTHINGS OF THE WIND
"The past is a bucket of ashes."
THE WOMAN named To-morrow
sits with a hairpin in her teeth

---

① A famous American abolitionist. In 1859 he and his 21 followers captured the U. S. arsenal at Harper's Ferry as part of an effort to liberate Southern slaves. But his group was defeated, and Brown was hanged after a trial winning sympathy as an abolitionist martyr.

and takes her time

and does her hair the way she wants it

and fastens at last the last braid and coil

and puts the hairpin where it belongs

and turns and drawls: Well, what of it?

My grandmother, Yesterday, is gone.

What of it? Let the dead be dead. (C: 7)

Tomorrow comes in the form of a woman taking her time. What does the woman symbolize? "The woman named To-morrow" symbolizes a society. "My grandmother, Yesterday, is gone," she says, "What of it? Let the dead be dead". And what does Yesterday mean? It represents social history. Since "My Grandmother, Yesterday, is gone", "Let the dead be dead": Let history be history and past. That has become lessons. This just makes the epigraph of the poem clear: "The past is a bucket of ashes" echoing Sandburg's "Prairie" in *Cornhuskers*:

I speak of new cities and new people.

I tell you the past is a bucket of ashes.

I tell you yesterday is a wind gone down,

a sun dropped in the west.

I tell you there is nothing in the world

only an ocean of tomorrows,

a sky of tomorrow···. (Ibid.)

He leaves promise for tomorrow, calling the people to leave the past behind, seeing tomorrow beautiful. But whatever tomorrow is, Sandburg cannot conceal the mood of disillusionment, and disillusionment is the keynote in the poem and in the book. Anyway he, as a member of the ordinary people, never forgets to remind his fraternal people of "Tomorrow is a day" and will be beautiful.

In the second prelude, doors twisted on broken hinges suggest the spiritual and moral degeneration of societies smashed by war and some upper people's greed, and imply the destroyed relationship of the people and the society, and the inharmony between the people and society, morality and social system:

> The doors were cedar
> and the panels strips of gold
> and the girls were golden girls
> and the panels read and the girls chanted:
> We are the greatest city,
> the greatest nation:
> nothing like us ever was.
> The doors are twisted on broken hinges.
> Sheets of rain swish through on the wind
> where the golden girls ran and the panels read:
> We are the greatest city,
> the greatest nation,
> nothing like us ever was. (SS: 75-77)

In the prelude, it describes doors of cedar and panels of gold bearing the inscription: "We are the greatest city, the greatest nation, nothing like us ever was." It is chanted by golden girls with pride, and it is repeated four times including the following part in the third prelude. The haunting refrain, as in a song, highlights a feeling of tension and unifies the tightly organized poem. When "Sheets of rain swish through on the wind, / "Strong men put up a city and got / a nation together":

> It has happened before.
> Strong men put up a city and got
> a nation together,
> And paid singers to sing and women
> to warble: We are the greatest city,
> the greatest nation,
> nothing like us ever was.
> And while the singers sang

and the strong men listened

and paid the singers well

and felt good about it all,

there were rats and lizards who listened

···and the only listeners left now

···are···the rats···and the lizards. (Ibid.)

Is the nation really so great and strong in Sandburg's eyes? Why are the singers paid well to sing? Why were there only rats and lizards listening? Sure e-nough, Sandburg doesn't think so here. And the reason that the singers and women were paid to sing, but were unwilling to sing, is that an illusive and un-real prosperity lies in the country. To pay to sing is to satisfy the strong men" themselves and satisfy the vanity of them. Here Sandburg's cynicism is shown a-gain by theemployment, for example, of "rats" and "lizards". The "rats" and "lizards" belong to the same group— "the strong men" :

And there are black crows

crying, "Caw, caw,"

bringing mud and sticks

building a nest

over the words carved

on the doors where the panels were cedar

and the strips on the panels were gold

and the golden girls came singing:

We are the greatest city,

the greatest nation:

nothing like us ever was.

The only singers now are crows crying, "Caw, caw,"

And the sheets of rain whine in the wind and doorways.

And the only listeners now are···the rats···and the lizards. (Ibid.)

The second half of the third prelude denotes the fate of the nation after war that sang of their own greatness. Black crows, always hinting misfortune, begin to nest over the doors made of cedar and gold. Singers have been substituted. "The only singers now are crows crying", "Caw, caw," and "the only listeners left are⋯ the rats⋯ and the lizards." Black crows and rats predict the degeneration of civilization. And "sheets of rain" do not "swish" any more like before, but begin to "whine in the wind and doorways", echoing the cawing of crows.

And the fourth prelude of the quartet depicts the symbolic dominance of the rats scrambling over the civilization of the nation:

> The feet of the rats
> scribble on the door sills;
> the hieroglyphs of the rat footprints
> chatter the pedigrees of the rats
> and babble of the blood
> and gabble of the breed
> of the grandfathers and the great-grandfathers
> of the rats.
> And the wind shifts
> and the dust on a door sill shifts
> and even the writing of the rat footprints
> tells us nothing, nothing at all
> about the greatest city, the greatest nation
> where the strong men listened
> and the women warbled: Nothing like us ever was. (Ibid.)

According to Webster's Dictionary[①] again, a rat can refer to a scoundrel, or untrustworthy person. Sandburg should have used the word in this sense. It was these "rats", the scoundrels, the untrustworthy persons that disordered the society and civilization. "Rats" are the starters of war. "Rats" are the destroyer of peace. "Rats" are the destructor of civilization. Sandburg's "Four Preludes" captures the emptiness and fragility of the people's contemporary life, and the

---

① Dalgish, Gerard, ed. Random House Webster's Dictionary of American English. Beijing: Foreign Language Teaching and Research Press, 1997.

abatement of hope, reflecting WWI's deep negative influence on the people. But who made the people lost? Who were the chief criminals? They were these "rats". And these "rats" were the killers and misleaders of the people.

Right off, "The Four Preludes" will easily remind us of T. S. Eliot's[1] *The Waste Land* which was published two years later and which is a symbol of stark disillusionment presaging the spirit of modernist disenchantment. The poem contains five cantos: I. The Burial of the Dead; II. A Game of Chess; III. The Fire Sermons; IV. Death by Water; and V. What the Thunder Said. Here are some lines of "The Fire Sermon" listed for illustration and comparison:

"On Margate Sands. [2]

I can connect

Nothing with nothing.

The broken fingernails of dirty hands.

My people humble people who expect

Nothing. "

la la

To Carthage then I came[3]

Burning burning burning burning[4]

O Lord Thou pluckest me out!

O Lord Thou pluckest

burning [5]

---

[1] Thomas Stearns Eliot, 1888–1965, American-born British critic and writer whose poems "The Love Song of J. Alfred Prufrock" (1915) and *The Waste Land* (1922) established him as a major literary figure. He also wrote dramas, such as *Murder in the Cathedral* (1935), and works of criticism. He won the 1948 Nobel Prize for literature.

[2] A tongue of land extending into the Thames opposite Greenwich, a borough of London.

[3] "V. St. Augustine's Confessions: 'to Carthage then I came, where a cauldron of unholy loves sang all about mine ears'" [Eliot's note]. Augustine is recounting his licentious youth.

[4] "Taking from the complete text of the Buddha's Fire Sermon (which corresponds in importance to the Sermon on the Mount)" [Eliot's note].

[5] Ferguson, M. & Mary Salter, etc. *The Norton Anthology of Poetry*. New York, London: W. W. Norton & Company, 1996, pp. 1244–1245.

Eliot probed the personal meditation and social decline in civilization in the context of postwar Europe in depth. In the poem he says "I can connect / nothing with nothing", because the postwar civilization was broken by world war. "People who expect nothing" feel hopeless. Then Eliot exclaims: "la la" with surprise. "Carthage" is the representation of civilization, but he finds it "burning". Meanwhile in the United States Sandburg, too, chronicled social changes, emptiness in the people's mind, the people's disillusion from war and conflict in civilization, stepping into an embarrassment and vortex as a war correspondent in Europe with mission given by NEA. It was Sandburg's self-imposed social responsibility for the people, and ternary view angle as journalist, social advocate and poet that produced finally the "Four Preludes."

In detail, as Sandburg did at the very beginning of "Four Preludes", Eliot, too, offered the evocative image of a woman arranging her hair (quotation omitted. about more detail, see the text of *The Waster Land*: Ferguson, M. M. Salter & J. Stallworthy. *The Norton Anthology of Poetry*. New York: W. W. Norton & Company, 1996: 1236–1248). But, why could "The Waste Land" by Eliot catch the attention of the literary world when it was first published in the *Dial* and then in 1922 was published in book form? In my opinion, this involves two reasons. Firstly, Sandburg's "Four Preludes on Playthings of the Wind" was then embedded in the wider text of *Smoke and Steel* in 1920, and overshadowed by other poems in the book. Secondly, its title is too long and hence it is difficult to guess the meaning by the formal words before readers read through the whole poem; that is to say, the title can not stir readers' interest to read on; while the three-word title "The Waste Land" with only three words can immediately draw the readers' attention. Anyway in my eyes, Sandburg's "Four Preludes on Playthings of the Wind" is not in the shade of *The Waste Land*, in spite of the fact that it is superficially a little second or condescension to *The Waste Land* for several reasons.

With an overview of *Smoke and Steel* from other people's standpoints, it brought Sandburg many acclamations, congratulatory letters and critical reviews.

Maxwell Bodenheim[1] wrote to him: "I consider *Smoke and Steel* to be ten hundred and ninety three miles above your other books. It is like a dirty giant tearing a sunset into strips and patching the rents in his clothes." (CSB: 360) And Sara Teasdale[2] wrote: "how it seems to me more real in its tenderness and sympathy than any other poetry being written in our language today." (CSB: 360) And from his mother in Galesburg came a letter full of pride in her son's work, though she could not comprehend all of it: "The book of poems has come with its spicy words and deep thought it will take more than a life time to learn what it all means and is impossible for plain simple workingmen to understand." (CSB: 361) The poet Amy Lowell reviewed in *The New York Times* positively, saying: "Reading these poems gives me more of a patriotic emotion than ever 'The starspangled banner' has been able to do." (CSB: 361) The famous editor and critic Louis Untermeyer claimed Smoke and Steel as "an epic of modern industrialism and a might paean to modern beauty." He regarded Sandburg and Frost the nation's two living major poets. (CSB: 361)

As is mentioned above, different people have different appreciations. But generally speaking, the tone of disillusionment of "Smoke and Steel" came from Sandburg's disillusionment about World War One. It was Sandburg's consideration and contemplation on the side of the people. And it was Sandburg's sense of social responsibility sense that threw him into such a deep speculation. It is sure, Sandburg, as the people's poet, never unburdened the people's weight from his back and his heart. "Smoke" is the soul of the working class gone with the wind and in the history. "Steel" is forged with the flesh and bone of the working people. The "Four Preludes" is the music accompaniment to "Smoke and Steel". All those compose a symphony of modern industry and modern society, and a symphony of suffering and tribulation of the common folk, with the composer is as Mr. Sandburg.

---

① Maxwell Bodenheim (1893–1954), American writer of cynical, sometimes grotesque poetry and realistic novels, such as Crazy Man (1924).

② 1884–1933, American poet whose classically styled lyrical works appeared in *Love Songs* (1917) and other collections.

After the publication of *Smoke and Steel*, Sandburg gradually became a defender and celebrant of the common people. And he began to hold more and more readers at arm's length, making them find more and more of their own images in the mirrors of his poems, and probing more and more about their common experience rather than the particulars of his own.

Ⅵ. *Slabs of Sunburnt West*

Among his other poems, the representatives are his *Slabs of the Sunburnt West*, then *Good Morning, America* (which will not be treated in the thesis for its less connection with the purpose herein). The first appeared in 1922, with the text covering 76 pages.

Slabs of the Sunburnt West covers a broader panorama than before. He began to view the past in the light of a pageant of history instead of his individual past. And he began to shape the people's character in the westward movement and discuss its significance to American development and civilization. Sandburg in the book interprets the experience which the western pioneers underwent in their struggle with the natural environments trying them in the crucible of the frontier.

"The Windy City" is the first one, regarded as the recapitulation of Sandburg's earlier themes speaking for the people. In the long poem, he, in fact, recreated Chicago and its history, and it is evident in the ten long free-verse stanzas Sandburg merges fascination with history, myth and legend:

THE WINDY CITY

The lean hands of wagon men

put out pointing fingers here,

picked this crossway, put it on a map,

set up their sawbucks, fixed their shotguns,

found a hitching place for the pony express,

made a hitching place for the iron horse,

the one–eyed horse with the fire–spit head,

found a homelike spot and said, "Make a home,"

saw this corner with a mesh of rails, shuttling

people, shunting cars, shaping the junk of

the earth to a new city. (STSW: 3)

Sandburg traced the quest of the pioneers, the wagon men who "found a home—like spot, and said, ' Make a home ' " (which is similar with God's words in "Genesis", showing the pioneers' greatness and holiness), recording the sounds of industrial Chicago, the language and songs of the modern city, and packing the poem with slang and slogans. He borrows a means of myth to depict the building process of Chicago city. The poem is like a legend, painting Chicago with a mysterious color. He continues:

The hands of men took hold and tugged

And the breaths of men went into the junk

And the junk stood up into skyscrapers and asked:

Who am I? Am I a city? And if I am what is my name?

And once while the time whistles blew and blew again

The men answered: Long ago we gave you a name,

Long ago we laughed and said: You? Your name is Chicago. (Ibid.)

The "breath" is like God's breath to create man. "Junk" seems to be a mysterious thing; it should (not mean discarded material) refer to man's power to collect common things into a big and mysterious Skyscraper and a big city– Chicago. Indeed it is like a legend, but in faith it is a fact! It is the people that built the great city up, which Sandburg sees clearly all the time.

The other poems (no more examples to be given) like "The Windy City" take the same mood, discussing the common people's contribution to American development. *Shortly and essentially*, *Slabs of the Sunburnt West* is "the People of the Sunburt West. "

VII. *The People, Yes*

The people will live on.

The learning and blundering people will live on.

They will be tricked and sold and again sold

And go back to the nourishing earth for rootholds,

The people so peculiar in renewal and comeback,

You can't laugh off their capacity to take it.

The mammoth rests between his cyclonic dramas.

—Carl Sandburg

In November 1935, Sandburg sent Alfred Harcourt, publisher, a final draft, telling him he would have a "large intelligent horselaugh". And in August of the second year, *The People, Yes* was published by Harcourt Brace & Company. As we mentioned at the beginning of this chapter, it is the most valuable book revealing Sandburg's affinity with the ordinary persons.

Of all 107 sections of the book, some are on the death of those who sacrifice their lives for the society's development and for the people themselves, or some common folk as workers and builders; and some of the others are about assembling the collective wisdom of the common people about war, property, justice, and the law. In one word, the whole book is about only one theme: the people, the common ones. And it was published as one single poem with a prefatory poem "*The People, Yes*" as foreword of the book defying the accustomed preface:

Being several stories and psalms nobody would

want to laugh at

interspersed with memoranda variations worth a

second look

along with sayings and yarns traveling on grief and

laughter

running sometimes as a fugitive air in the classic
manner
breaking into jig time and tap dancing nohow
classical
and further broken by plain and irregular sounds
and echoes from
the roar and whirl of street crowds, work gangs,
sidewalk clamor,
with interludes of midnight cool blue and inviolable
stars
over the phantom frames of skyscrapers. (*PY: Preface*)

As a preface, the poem covers the themes and subjects of the book. It is "memoranda variations worth a second look" full of "sayings and yarns", "plain and irregular sounds", "roar and whirl of street crowds, work gangs, sidewalk clamor" and with "midnight cool blue and inviolable stars" as interludes. Indeed it is a book filled with the people's stories, sounds, echoes, and a memorandum of the people's life and work, thought and spirit.

Sandburg, as a member of the people and a poet of conscience, was deeply affected by the people's suffering from the Great Depression spanning the years from 1929 to 1941, which was just a severe reality. At this time, the people needed encouragement, and the book of Sandburg was on the beam purporting the voice of the long-suffering Americans. Section 16 of *The People, Yes* hints someway the background of the society when the long poem was written and published, and the hope of Sandburg, also that of the people during the Great Depression. Here is Sandburg's "tattered" hope flag:

Hope is a tattered flag and a dream out of time.
Hope is a heartspun word, the rainbow, the shadblow in white,
The evening star inviolable over the coal mines,
The shimmer of northern lights across a bitter winter night,
The blue hills beyond the smoke of the steel works.

The birds who go on singing to their mates in peace, war, peace,

The ten-cent crocus bulb blooming in a used car salesroom,

The horseshoe over the door, the luckpiece in the pocket,

The kiss and the comforting laugh and resolve—

Hope is an echo, hope ties itself yonder, yonder.

The spring grass showing itself where least expected,

The rolling fluff of white clouds on a changeable sky,

The broadcast of strings from Japan, bells from Moscow,

Of the voice of the prime minister of Sweden carried

Across the sea in behalf of a world family of nations

And children singing chorals of the Christ child

And Bach being broadcast from Bethlehem, Pennsylvania

And tall skyscrapers practically empty of tenants

And the hands of strong men groping for handholds

And the Salvation Army singing God loves us····. (PY: 29)

Under the high pressure of the Great Depression, Sandburg by poem gave the people the looming hope, and so Sandburg says here "Hope is a tattered flag". Or, in other words, Sandburg is encouraging the people not to lose hearts. He gives the people "the evening star", "the shimmer of northern lights" to dream, to expect the recovery of economy— "the coal mines", "the steel works". Sandburg compares hopes to many things as "heartspun word", birds singing, star twinkling, "ten-cent crocus bulb", a gentle "kiss", a "laugh" to heart, "the spring grass", "fluff of white clouds" and so on. Meanwhile, the stagnancy and the sense of the desolation as a result of the Great Depression are everywhere: the "coal mines", "bitter winter night", "used-car salesroom", a "changeable sky" and "tall skyscrapers practically empty of tenants". Here Sandburg even borrows music of foreign musician as a kind of mental treatment, and "God", "Christ Child", "the Salvation Army" as a kind of spiritual support to excite, embrave and encourage the people to tide over the sufferings of the Great Depression. The last suspensive points hint the continuity of the Great Depression and no one knows when it comes to an end, though the "Salvation Army" are "singing God loves us" .

In structure, as mentioned in the upper part, the book is divided into 107 sections consisting of dialogues, folk–wisdom, character sketches, legends, biographies, yarns, anecdotes, proverbs, and even clichés. But it is not easy and even difficult to divide 107 sections into several subtopics, for the transition from one part to another is not so clear and Sandburg sometimes tends to have a changeable attitude to something. Here the poems are roughly cut it into several parts for analytical convenience only.

Section 1–5 can be taken as the opening part, describing Babel Tower from *Old Testament* (the whole text's so long, see PY: 3) . The Babel building was unsuccessful due to God's interference, and the people were baffled by many problems: What is their identity? What is next move? And what is their ultimate destiny? They seemed to be refrains hovering in the people's mind:

Five hundred ways to say, "Who are you?"
Changed ways of asking, "Where do we go from here?"
Or of saying, "Being born is only the beginning" ⋯ (PY: 4)

And these even confuse children:

"What is the east? Have you been in the east?" ⋯
"Papa,
what is the moon
supposed to advertise?" ⋯
"Has anybody ever given the ocean a medal?
Who of the poets equals the music of the sea?
And where is a symbol of the people
Unless it is the sea?" (PY: 8–9)

In fact, it is Sandburg himself, including the people, that is finding the origin of the people and symbol of the people. For Sandburg, ocean is just the symbol of the people. So wide, open, strong, deep, and voluminous, while so fearful and "dangerous", are ocean and the people. But the people are less powerful than God who stopped people from building Babel. Who does God refer to? It refers to the ruler of the people, who "was a whimsical fixer" "with another plan in mind", "And suddenly shuffled all the languages", "changed the tongues of men", messed the people and squashed the people's dreams, or simply, stultified the masses.

Sections 6–8 go into the second part with concentration on people's dreams and ideals making the world running. Eastman, the Kodak man in Section 7, is a good example. Eastman accomplished his dream, as we know, and his final words were "My work is finished. Why wait?" To discuss the life significance and the meaning and causes of his death is beyond the purpose here. At least, the powerfulness of dreaming is shown clearly. Dream leads to success. Dreamlessness can mean and even lead to suicide. It is dream that runs the world, the society and each person. In the last lines of Section 8, the great mother supports his child for he has a dream "ahead and beyond":

"I love you",
said a great mother.
"I love you for what you are
knowing so well what you are.
And I love you more yet, child,
deeper yet than ever, child,
for what you are going to be,
knowing so well you are going far,
knowing your great works are ahead,
ahead and beyond,
yonder and far over yet. " (PY: 17)

What is on earth going far? What is "ahead, ahead and beyond / yonder and far over yet"? The answer is simple: dream; nobly speaking, ideal, which were and are leading and driving many people to move forward, to run the world and to operate the society.

The third part can include section 11–19. It tells us the people should not forget history, and should learn to remember, for only by this can they profit from the past. In the past, it was them that the civilization depended upon; it was they that formed and form the army; it was they that died for the country, for the people themselves, and mostly for the war starters meaninglessly; and it is they that build the social economy. In Section 11, he writes, "The cry of the child wrongfully punished stays in the air." (PY: 22) Who is the child "wrongfully published"? The people are. The child is the symbol of the people who were treated unjustly in history. Why does the "cry" of the people stay in the air? It is because they were wronged and became ghosts wandering above the present society and because they remind the people of historical lessons. So "The people move / in a fine thin smoke, / *the people, yes.*" (PY: 22) At the same time, Sandburg jacks the people that history is really "a fine thin smoke"; so fine, so thin, and so trivial. Today's everything will right away turn into yesterday. He describes that people are still suffering from the Great Depression: "Streetwalking jobhunters, walkers alive and keen, / sleepwalkers drifting along, the stupefied and / hopeless down–and–outs, the game fighters / who will die fighting" . (PY: 34) While many people are "driving their cars, stop and go, red light, green / light, and the law of the traffic cop's fingers, / on their way, loans and mortgages, margins to cover". (PY: 35) In spite of the Great Depression, the people had to live on with hardship and bitterness.

The fourth part of the book involves Section 20–31. At the very beginning of it, Sandburg comes up with his theme of this stanza:

20

WHO shall speak for the people?
Who knows the works from A to Z
so he can say, "I know what the
people want"? Who is this phenom?
where did he come from? ⋯ (PY: 38)

Here the first line "Who shall speak for the people?" is the main idea of this part. Sandburg continues to question in Section 24: "WHO shall speak for the people? / who has the answers? / where is the sure interpreter? / who knows what to say?" (PY: 44) To answer these questions, he offers us Section 26 telling us who is the qualified spokesman for the people:

26

You can drum on immense drums
the monotonous daily motions of the people
taking from earth and air
their morsels of bread and love,
a carryover from yesterday into tomorrow.
You can blow on great brass horns
the awful clamors of war and revolution
when swarming anonymous shadowshapes
obliterate old names Big Names
and cross out what was
and offer what is on a fresh blank page. (PY: 48)

But who are "you"? The one who must be able to express "the monotonous daily motions of the people", the people's daily deeds and their great dreams. The one who must be able to teach them how to draw the lessons "from yesterday to tomorrow". The one who must be able to record the people into history with his ability to "obliterate old names Big Names / and cross out what was" and write a fresh page of history. Apparently, Sandburg tends to express that sociologically it is the people that create the history. But who are "you" again? Personally speaking, it is the poet Sandburg. He takes, as we do, himself indeed the people's poet speaking for the people and writing for the people. And he thinks history should record the tortures and the contributions of the people; and the people, whether a "great beast" (see PY: 53) or not, have done the work of creating the history of the country.

But how do the people grow? Section 32 – 68 report to us that the people

learn and grow through painful experience, through work, through disappointment, and through being deceived. The very beginning of Section 32 lets us see
Sandburg talk of the process of people's learning:

32

What the people learn out of lifting and hauling and waiting and losing and laughing
Goes into a scroll, an almanac, a record folding and unfolding, and the music goes
down and around:
The story goes on and on, happens, forgets to happen, goes out and meets itself
coming in, puts on disguises and drops them.
"Yes yes, go on, go on, I'm listening." You hear that in one doorway.
And in the next, "Aw shut up, close your trap, button your tongue, you
talk too much."
The people, yes, the people⋯ (PY: 61)

But the trouble lies in that the people can be very easily cheated. They are
honest and loyal to what they do and think, not like "the chameleon":

33

Remember the chameleon. He was a well-behaved chameleon and nothing could be
brought against his record. As a chameleon he had done the things that should have
been done and left undone the things that should have been left undone. He was a
first-class unimpeachable chameleon and nobody had any-thing on him. But he came
to a Scotch plaid and tried to cross it. In order to cross he had to imitate six different
yarn colors, first one and then another and back to the first or second. He was a brave
chameleon and died at the cross-roads true to his chameleon instincts. (PY: 67)

The chameleon did not have a lucky end. Before the "Scotch plaid" with
variant colors, he was at the end of his wits. Though "he was a brave chameleon", he "died at the cross-roads true to his chameleon instincts." Why did
the chameleon lie? What's the difference between the chameleon and the people? Sandburg writes on:

What kind of a liar are you?

People lie because they don't remember clear what they saw.

People lie because they can't help making a story better than it
was the way it happened.

People tell "white lies" so as to be decent to others.

People lie in a pinch, hating to do it, but lying on because it
might be worse.

And people lie just to be liars for a crooked personal gain.

What sort of a liar are you?

Which of these liars are you? (Ibid.)

We see the people's lies are "white lies so as to be decent to others" . But
Sandburg does not answer his own questions here: "What sort of a liar are you?"
and "Which of these liars are you?" In spite of this, readers can be very clear a-
bout the answers and know who they are. At least they are not the common people; and at least their lies are not so well-intended as the people's "white lies"
. And it is just these liars that are befooling the people:

67

...

"Do you make your newspaper for yourself or the public?" was asked a New York
    founder who replied, "For the public, of course. "

"Why isn't your newspaper more intelligent?" was asked a Chicago publisher who
    laughed, "We make our newspaper for boobs. "

"Secret influence is the greatest evil of our time," testified a Harvard president
    from a birthmarked anxious face.

"And," added another world-renowned educator, "the crookedest crooks in the
    United States government have been well educated. " ... (PY: 171)

What the publisher said— "we make our newspaper for boobs" makes us
feel bitterly disappointed. Upon that, a Harvard president said: "Secret influence is the greatest evil of our time" . Newspapers sometimes play a role of this

evil. Since they "have been well educated", the people easily become their playthings. And this just accords with what Chinese former Chairman Mao Zedong said: "The more knowledge you have, the more reactive you are" (Though mostly it is wrong, we borrow it to scold those befooling the people).

To return to *The People*, *Yes*, equity is found to haunt Section 69–85. Firstly in Section 69, law as the weapon of equity is discussed:

69

"A LAWYER," hiccuped a disbarred member of the bar, "is a man who gets two
    other men to take off their clothes and then he runs away with them."
"If the law is against you, talk about the evidence", said a battered barrister. "If
    the evidence is against you, talk about the law, and, since you ask me, if
    the law and the evidence are both against you, then pound on the table and
    yell like hell."
"The law," said the Acme Sucker Rod manufacturer who was an early Christian
    mayor of Toledo, Ohio, "the law is what the people will back up."
"You haven't climbed very high," said a Wall Street operator who was quoted in
    the press "unless you own a judge or two." ⋯ (PY: 181)

By law the necessity of equity is a must; and still by law, inequality is found. If you have "climbed very high", you can have chances to unbalance the law. For them, equity is relative; inequality is a common occurrence. The dialogue at the end of Section 73 is interesting to prove this:

"Do you solemnly swear before the everliving God that the testimony you are about
    to give in this cause shall be the truth, the whole truth, and nothing but the
    truth?"
"No, I don't. I can tell you what I saw and what I heard and I'll swear to that by
    the everliving God but the more I study about it the more sure I am that no-
    body but the everliving God knows the whole truth and if you summoned
    Christ as a witness in this case what He would tell you would burn your in-
    sides with the pity and the mystery of it." (PY: 191)

Equity is obviously difficult to arrive at. People, Judges and lawyers have to ask God for help in the poem, though mostly or all the time it is useless. Why is the person asked to swear to tell the truth "before the everliving God"? That's because the people need equity and do not want a raw deal. And Sandburg's statement "The flowing of the stream clears it of pollution" (PY: 198), which is repeated two times in Section 76, says that history will prove everything, time will say anything clear and is sure to be on the side of the people, implying equity will be the eventual victor. And Section 77 announces that the people are magnanimous enough to forgive and tolerate many things, and the sea again becomes the symbol of the power of the people to absorb everything and to overcome the inequality:

THE bottom of the sea accommodates mountain ranges.
This is how deep the sea is
And the toss and drip of the mystery of the people And the sting of sea-drip.
In the long catacombs of moss fish linger and move. ··· (PY: 199)

But Section 85 reminds us of the existence of injustice appealing to the world for equity:

85

One memorial stone reads:
"We, near whose bones you stand, were Iroquois.
The wide land which is now yours, was ours.
Friendly hands have given us back enough for a tomb. " ··· (PY: 219)

In fact, whether it is now or in history, in America, for example, time can give the people the equity; and history can not balance everything, though the people are magnanimous enough like a sea to absorb anything. Can Americans return the land to Iroquois? No! Sure enough! Equity is after all only Sandburg's good wish and beautiful dream.

In the last second section—Section 86-101, the threat motif appears. The second half of Section 86 contains the feeling of the powerfulness of the people, and the weakness of the kingship. The people are like a sea that "accommodates mountain of ranges" and everything, but this kind of inclusion and tolerance is not limitless:

"The czar has eight million men with guns and bayonets.

Nothing can happen to the czar.

The czar is the voice of God and shall live forever. (PY: 222)

Really? "The czar is the voice of God and shall live forever"? Well, what's the voice of the masses, the people? And really "Nothing can happen to the czar"? But, even the Chinese Foolish Old Man removed the mountain in front of his house①!

Turn and look at the forest of steel and cannon

Where the czar is guarded by eight million soldiers.

Nothing can happen to the czar. " (Ibid.)

No matter how many times and how long in time "Nothing can happen to the czar" was repeated, the "eight million soldiers", and even "the forest of steel and cannon" could not and can not stop the running history and press and weaken the strength of the people:

They said that for years and in the summer of 1914

In the Year of Our Lord Nineteen Hundred and Fourteen

As a portent and an assurance they said with owl faces:

"Nothing can happen to the czar. "

Yet the czar and his bodyguard of eight million vanished

And the czar stood in a cellar before a little firing squad

And the command of fire was given

And the czar stepped into regions of mist and ice

The czar travelled into an ethereal uncharted siberia

While two kaisers also vanished from thrones

---

① It's a Chinese allegory saying an old man in the past was very strong – willed, he removed the mountain, which blocked his way out.

Ancient and established in blood and iron—

Two kaisers backed by ten million bayonets

Had their crowns in a gutter, their palaces mobbed.

In fire, chaos, shadows,

In hurricanes beyond foretelling of probabilities,

In the shove and whirl of unforeseen combustions

The people, yes, the people,

Move eternally in the dements of surprise,

Changing from hammer to bayonet and back to hammer,

The hallelujah chorus forever shifting its star soloists. ··· (Ibid.)

The people, yes, it was the people that overturned the czar at last, while "two Kaisers also vanished from the thrones". "Changing from hammer to bayonet and back to hammer" implies that the people come from working, they could not stand the oppression, and then they uprose; after victory, they came back to their work and common life again. The people as a whole are really a threat to the upper class, but not a threat to the people themselves. Anyway, forever the people "will live on" and "move eternally" on.

What leads to the people's final intolerance? It is the oppression and inequity. Equity is the second and sub-motif of this section, and it actually serves as the potential reason leading to the people's "threatening" situation:

101

THE unemployed

without a stake in the country

without jobs or nest eggs

marching they don't know where

marching north south west—

and the deserts ?

marching east with dust

deserts out of howling dust-bowls

deserts with winds moving them. ··· (PY: 270)

They are marching and they are going to fight; they are going for food because of their unemployment without "jobs" to do, and without "nest eggs" to eat. The end line of Section 101 is the best explanation for all wonders, "Do this or go hungry"? (PY: 272) This is Sandburg's most classical statement to show the embarrassing situation of the people in the society. People cannot wait to get "equity". Equity needs fighting for, for it is never a natural balance if it were not in primitive society or the future idealized Communism.

The last part, Sections 102-7, is the poet's prophecy: the people will live on; the people will win, though it is somewhat vague. First, Sandburg warns the liars of their potential defeat in Section :

102

Can you bewilder men by the millions

with transfusions of your own passions,

mixed with lies and half-lies,

texts torn from contexts,

and then look for peace, quiet, good will

between nation and nation, race and race,

between class and class? (PY: 273)

It is a forceful question without the necessity to answer. "Lies and half-lies" are only covered by a thin fog. Sun will anyway come out. Nobody can garble the facts forever. Honesty is the only choice to win the people and the peace. And according to a Chinese saying, "The wisdom of three cobblers exceeds that of Zhuge Liang the mastermind"①, the aftermath can be anticipated if only one "you" is brought to front "millions" of people.

Section 107 is the end of whole book, and the last lines of this section are the coda of Section 107 and the whole epic, *The People*, *Yes*:

---

①   Zhuge Liang, a statesman and strategist in the period of the Three Kingdoms (220-265) in Chinese history, who later became a symbol of resourcefulness and wisdom in Chinese folklore.

This old anvil laughs at many broken hammers.

There are men who can't be bought.

The fireborn are at home in fire.

The stars make no noise.

You can't hinder the wind from blowing.

Time is a great teacher.

Who can live without hope?

In the darkness with a great bundle of grief

the people march.

In the night, and overhead a shovel of stars for

keeps, the people march:

"Where to? what next?" (PY: 286.)

In it, the "old anvil" symbolizes the people, the everlasting people. The "hammers", stand for the upper class, working on the people as the "anvil"; but "hammers" are all temporary; the "old anvil" anyhow can outlive the "hammers". The "hammers" being broken one by one is a good proof. You cannot stop the people from marching on just as "you can't hinder the wind from blowing". Though sometimes the people are like "the stars" making "no noise", they plod on and on. Though they move on "in the darkness" and "in the night", they cherish their hopes and grief. Though their future is vague and they don't know "Where to? what next?" they march on with aspirations, because the people know they can outlast all the others in history.

Next, after the analysis of each part of the book, another angle can be shown to study the great book and see how some celebrities'and his own words are embodied about *The People, Yes*.

Hazel Durnell, who is the author of *The America of Carl Sandburg*, commented on it as follows: "Into *The People, Yes* went the failure and the strength, the chaos and the achievement, the mediocrity and the ambition, the good and the bad that make up America. Sandburg has been among the men of character whom Emerson would designate as the conscience of the society to which they belong; as such, he understands why America is what she is and at the same time, as the prophets of old, he reminds her of her true role in the context of her past history. " (CSLW: 94) She enjoyed the book so much that later she wrote a book about Sandburg—*The America of Carl Sandburg*. To confirm what Hazel Durnell mentioned of about the book, the first lines of Section 50 can be a proof:

FROM what graveyards and sepulchers have they come,
these given the public eye and ear
who chatter idly of their personal success
as though they flowered by themselves alone
saying "I," "I," "I,"
crediting themselves with advances and gains,
"I did this, I did that,"
and hither and thither, "It was me, Me,"
the people, yes, the people, being omitted
or being mentioned as incidental
or failing completely of honorable mention,
as though what each did was by him alone. (PY: 108)

Sandburg treats "success" as Hazel found. He thinks in the poem success should not be personal; it belongs to the collective people. But individuals over-emphasize personal success by saying "I did this, I did that", while with "the people, yes, the people, being omitted", "as though what each did was by him alone". Clearly Sandburg values the people's strength as collectivity: and there is a realm of personal achievement wherein he was the boss, the big boy, and it wasn't luck nor the breaks nor a convenient public but it was him, "I", "Me", and the idea and the inference is the pay and the praise should be his— from what graveyards have they strolled and do they realize their sepulchral manners and what are the farther backgrounds? (Ibid.)

Sandburg thinks "the pay and the praise" should not fall into an individual. Or Sandburg means history is written by the people collectively, not by individuals.

Oscar Cargill who came from New York University regarded the book as "Diffuse, occasionally rambling and sometimes long-winded, *The People*, *Yes* is still a splendid organic growth. Nowhere else in poetry is there such a survey of the people's businesses, their routine affairs, their employments, their concern. " (CSLW: 95) Section 19 depicts what Cargill commented concisely:

> THE people, yes, the people,
> Everyone who got a letter today
> And women at the cookstoves oreparing meals,
> in a sewing corner mending, in a basement
> The women at the factory tending a stitching
> machine, some of them the mainstay of the
> Streetwalking jobhunters, walkers alive and keen,
> hopeless down—and—outs, the game fighters
> who will die fighting
> Walkers reading sings and stopping to study
> windows, the signs and windows aimed
> straight at their eyes, their wants,
> Wonem in and out of doors to look and feel , to
> tyr on, to buy and take away, to order and
> have it charged and delivered, to pass by on
> account of price and conditions… (PY: 34)

These lines are enough to test Cargill's description about Sandburg's *The People, Yes*. The people have their greatness, and the people have their daily affairs and trivia to care about. Sandburg's all—around picturing is the real reflection of the really common people. The people have their own advantages as well as their own disadvantages. Since they have to live on, of course they have to live their trifling routine life.

What did Sandburg himself say about the book? He remarked about *The People, Yes* in this way: " Parts of it are superb: the creations of free imagination operating among the people. The rest of it may or may not be a songswept [sic] footnote to the stride of democracy in our era. " (See CSB: 501) And he told Malcolm Cowley about *The People, Yes* that it was "a ballad pamphlet harangue sonata and fugue···an almanac, a scroll, a palimpsest, the last will and testament of Mr. John Public, John Doe, Richard Roe, and the autobiography of whoever it was the alfalfaland governor meant in saying, 'The common people will do anything you say except stay hitched. '" (CSB: 501) In 1936, Sandburg, as fervently as in 1908 when he went to Wisconsin as district organizer of socialism organization, believed that they failed to realize that "the roots and sources of their holdings are in the people, the workers, the consumers, the customers, the traveling public!" He told Oliver Barrett, who was a fan of Lincoln and collected many things about Lincoln, helping Sandburg much, he had never seen "greed, fear, brutality among the masses to surpass what may be seen among the rich. " (CSB: 502) That means the people all through the ages have been and are forever very easy to be satisfied.

And Barrett suggested to Sandburg that some lines of *The People*, *Yes* were intended "to convey the thought that the laboring class are exploited by wealthy malefactors and should be made to feel hate and resentment against their employers," Sandburg argued that "if Sam Adam, Tom Jefferson and Patrick Henry[①] had kept silence on the exploitation of other American colonists by the imbecile British crown there would have been no American revolution. " (CSLW: 96) In the society, from Sandburg, only by revolution can people liberate themselves. And he thinks the rich, whatever they are and however they do, are afraid of the poor, the people:

In the days of the cockade and the brass pistol Fear of the people brought the debtors' jail. The creditor said, "Pay me or go to prison," And men lacking property lacked ballots and citizenship. Into the Constitution of the United States they wrote a fear In the form of "checks and balances," "proper restraints" On the people so whimsical and changeable, So variable in mood and weather. (PY: 52)

The debtees were afraid of the debtors who had no money. What did they actually fear? They feared the people's poverty. They feared the debtors were not a-

---

①　1736–1799, American Revolutionary leader and orator. A member of the House of Burgesses (1765) and the Continental Congress (1774–1776), he spurred the creation of the Virginia militia with his words "Give me liberty, or give me death" (1775). He also served as governor of Virginia (1776–1790) .

ble to pay back. And where did and does the property go? It went and goes to the
rich who often got and get fortune by plundering and exploiting this way or
that. What the Constitution protects is just this movement. This situation is like
"Golden Trumpet", the one who is rich enough to be able to buy a golden trumpet can use the trumpet to voice aloud "their ballots and citizenship". Can't the
people be "variable in mood and weather"? Who can stay quiet under this situation? Who will be so silent under this situation? Nobody. So the people are "so
whimsical and changeable":

> Lights of tallow candles fell on lawbooks by night.
> The woolspun clothes came from sheep near by.
> Men of "solid substance" wore velvet knickerbockers.
> And shared snuff with one another in greetings.
> One of these made a name for himself with saying.
> You could never tell what was coming next from the people:
>
> ...
>
> The people undependable as prairie rivers in floodtime,
> The people uncertain as lights on the face of the sea
> Wherefore high and first of all he would write
> God, the Constitution, Property Rights, the Army and the Police,
> After these the rights of the people. (Ibid.)

In Sandburg's opinion, the people are "undependable as prairie rivers in
floodtime," and "uncertain as lights on the face of the sea". Sandburg here e-
quals God with Constitution, Property Rights, the Army and the Police, and this
is a kind of satire. God, in reality cannot protect the people. Constitution and
the others cannot do better than God. People believe in Constitution, Property
Rights, the Army and Police as they believe in God. And Sandburg himself explains why the rich are afraid of the people:

> The meaning was:

The people having nothing to lose take chances.

The people having nothing to take care of are careless.

The people lacking property are slack about property.

Having no taxes to pay how can they consider taxes?

"And the poor have they not themselves to blame for their poverty?" ···

(PY: 52–53)

Sandburg's friend, American poet and writer Stephen Vincent Benet (1898–1943) also agreed with the "*The People, Yes*" and said: "···it is the memoranda of the people. And every line of it says '*The People, Yes.*'" (CSB: 504) Sandburg also takes it as a memorandum outspeaking on many issues. He even thought many of their fellow journalists had "luxuriated in the power of their rostrums, petted their passions, wreaked their whims. They think the people lap it up." (CSB: 504) And he thinks in poetry:

The public has a mind?

Yes.

And men can follow a method

and a calculated procedure

for drugging and debauching it?

Yes.

And the whirlwind comes later?

Yes.

Sandburg concluded the above lines actually from Abraham Lincoln's July 4th Message to Congress[1] (July 4, 1861) for starting the Civil War[2] liberating American blacks. He here sees through those who are drugging and debauching the people by "a calculated procedure". But Sandburg is sure that "the whirlwind comes later". The "whirlwind" should refer to the people's "massed ac-

---

① See: http: //millercenter. virginia. edu/scripps/diglibrary/prezspeeches/lincoln/al_ 1861_ 0704. html. 26 March 2005.

② It refers to the war in the United States between the Union and the Confederacy from 1861 to 1865.

tion". He does not believe at all that those guys can really "bewilder men by millions" with "lies", then "look for peace, quiet, good will" forever.

To sum up *The People, Yes*, it is the culmination of Sandburg's career as a poet. From its style, scope, and contents, *The People, Yes* is an epic celebrating the feats of traditional hero, in which the traditional hero is the People. When the book was published he was 48 years old. Sandburg had put up the scaffolding of the poem nearly half a century and more than half of his lifetime of experience and observation on the American society and listening respectively to the people. So the poem was a profound affirmation of the American people and a singular public document. Since book after 1936, there was little significant growth in his poetic style and theme change. *The People, Yes* is a poem but more than a poem. It is unprecedented and very modern, an articulation of the American Dream and struggle built with native spirit and materials. And it is for the first time that Sandburg expands his vision beyond America to the world, the universal, embracing all human beings on the earth. His affidavit of hope, forged out of myth and realism, heartened many of his fellow people during the Great Depression. While some regarded *The People, Yes* as a poem about America, but when Norman Corwin, a writer at CBS Radio, worked with composer Earl Robinson working on an operatic setting of *The People, Yes*, he looked upon it as universal. "The way I see it," he told Robinson, "TPY (*The People, Yes*) should be the kind of music-drama which, if translated into the French or the Persian or the Portuguese could play without a single change···. Examine the original TPY and see if CS (Carl Sandburg) is writing about an American, or even a country. The thing that makes it great is that he is writing about all people everywhere. " (See CSB: 542) And it is a gift Sandburg gave to the American people and those all over the world; it is also a hope he gave to the American people when the Great Depression had smashed the hope of life. In the book, Sandburg immits optimism into the people. He is sure that the people can get equity only by struggle. He sees that the people are a threat to the upper class. He believes that in history the people will live on and win out. As the people's poet, he says again and again: "The people, yes, the people. " And Sandburg, the people's poet, yes, indeed!

VIII. "Yes" What?

What is the significance of "Yes" repeated so many times in the long poem *The People*, *Yes* and in *The Complete Poems of Carl Sandburg*? Totally, there are 181 "yes" in all of his poems, and in *The People*, *Yes*, there are 88 "yes" . Now here the essence of "Yes" in terms of his comprehension about his "people" is to be concentrated for discussion.

First of all, the people, yes! Yes, "they are what they are!" [①]:

THE people, yes—
Born with bones and heart fused in deep and violent secrets
Mixed from a bowl of sky blue dreams and sea slime facts—
A seething of saints and sinners, toilers, loafers, oxen, apes
In a Womb of superstition, faith, genius, crime, sacrifice—
The one and only source of armies, navies, work gangs,
The living flowing breath of the history of nations,
Of the little Family of Man hugging the little ball of Earth,
And a long hall of mirrors, straight, convex and concave,
Moving and endless with scrolls of the living,
Shimmering with phantoms flung from the past,
Shot over with lights of babies to come, not yet here···. (PY: 55)

Sandburg uses romantic measures to define "the people" . The people are the common persons "born with bones and heart" . "A bowl of sky blue dreams" is a bowl of the people's hopes. And the people contain "saints and sinners, toilers, loafers···. " "They are what they are" . They are "the one and only source of armies, navies, work–gangs" . And in "a long hall of mirrors,

---

① It refers to the war in the United States between the Union and the Confederacy from 1861 to 1865.

straight, convex and concave", the "straight" mirror stands for the people in the present society, the "convex" mirror implies the people in the future, and the "concave" mirror symbolizes the people in the past. They consist of all the people. And "the people will live on" "moving and endless with scrolls of the living".

From more of his poetic lines, what Sandburg "yeses" can be found clearly. In "A Million Young Workmen, 1915" (see the text of the poem in Section III, Chapter Three above), *Cornhuskers*, Sandburg yeses the victims of so many young men in battlefield who even did not know they were slaughtering each other, their own fellowmen on the earth. *The people, yes*, are yessing the millions of young men cheated and fooled by war hawks.

"YES, the Dead speak to us. / This town belongs to the Dead, to the Dead and to the Wilderness." (SS: 109) Sandburg here yeses the dead who built the city; he yeses the role and contribution of the people in the history. And he yeses the people with "dreams" and hopes: "There are dreams stronger than death. / Men and women die holding these dreams. / Yes, 'stronger than death': let the hammers beat on this slogan." (PY: 17) Maybe for a person dying, he or she is still dreaming. And it is just this kind of dream "stronger than death" that drives the society forward and advances the development of history. He also yeses the people from every walk of life:

> WHO knows the people, the migratory harvest hands and berry pickers, the loan
> shark victims, the installment house wolves,
> The jugglers in sand and wood who smooth their hands along the mold that casts the
> frame of your motorcar engine,
> The metal polishers, solderers, and paint-spray hands who put the final finish on
> the car,
> The riveters and bolt-catchers, the cowboys of the air in the big city, the cowhands
> of the Great Plains, the ex-convicts, the bellhops, redcaps, lavatory men—
> ··· (PY: 40)

The people, yes, they all belong to the people: the migratory harvest hands, the berry pickers, jugglers, metal polishers, solderers····. They are all laborers and are all like Sandburg himself who did some of the jobs. He yeses all the work the people did and do, promoting together the society's progress, and similarly in the following quotation Sandburg looks down upon the excessively proud persons neglecting the dedication of the people as he discusses in Section 50 of the The People, Yes. (See text quoted in Section VII, Chapter Three) . The poet hates the kind of persons who are too egoistic and never see the role of the people. When they show off their success, they omit the people, or unwillingly and flatly mention the people "as incidental", "as though what each did was by him alone". The people, yes. Yes, they are omitted and seldom mentioned. Yes, they are not included in "a realm of personal achievement" of these swaggers. This is typically and precisely what a Chinese idiom says: "Kill the donkey the moment it unburdens the millstone". In their eyes, the people are just used as a machine:

> The machine yes the machine
> never wastes anybody's time
> never watches the foreman
> never talks back··· (PY: 109)

Again, the people, yes, but yes what? Yes, the people work like a machine, only knowing to work on and on, and they are only the victims and games-flesh of some "animals":

> Here is a moving colossal show,
> a vast dazzling aggregation of stars and hams
> selling things, selling ideas, selling faiths,
> selling air, slogans, passions, selling history.
> The target is who and what?
> The people, yes——··· (PY: 218)

The people have to buy what they hawk: things, ideas, faiths, slogans, passions, history and even air to breathe. The people are just their targets of selling. The people, yes, victims are they. But they forget and cannot realize that " the people are a caldron and a reservoir". Once the people really become a "threat" to them someday, it will mean the end of their powerfulness. So Sandburg wish "Lady Luck" could accompany the people forever:

> Yes, get Lady Luck with you and you're made: some fortunes were tumbled into
> and the tumblers at first said, Who would have believed it? and later, I
> knew just how to do it.
>
> Yes, Lady Luck counts: before you're born pick the right papa and mama and the
> newsreel boys will be on the premises early for a shot of you with your big toe
> in your mouth…. (PY: 165-6)

The people, yes! Yes, they are "Lady Luck", being able to survive all the time, at least in the end. The people, yes, "they are what they are": vulnerable, simple, kind, omitted, painstaking, "frightening", powerful, and meaningful.

Secondly, Yes, "I" (Sandburg) am for the People!

As the people's poet, Sandburg valued the people all the time, in his poetry, in his action and in other places. He was an ardent socialist embracing the socialist ideal with the dream of serving the people more. In October 1919, in a letter to Romain Rolland he writes: "Any steps, measures, methods or experiences that will help give the people this requisite strength and wisdom, **I am for** (auctorial emphasis). I can not see where the people have ever won anything worth keeping and having but it cost something and I am willing to pay this cost as we go along—rather let the people suffer and be lean, sick and dirty through the blunders of democracy than to be fat, clean, and happy under the efficient arrangements of autocrats, Kaisers, kings, czars, whether feudal and dynastic or financial and industrial. I can not understand how the people are going to learn except by trying and I do not know any other way to honestly conduct the experiment of democracy than to let the people have the same opportunities of self-determination that belong of right to nations small and large, the same opportunities of self determination that are the heritage of a healthy child. In their exercise of the right of self determination I expect the people to pass through bitter experiences and I am aware it is even possible that the people shall fail in the future as they have failed in the past. " (LCS: 170–171) This quotation can be regarded as his manifesto of his speaking for the people. He thinks all social activities should take the people as the basis, and consider the people's interests, and even laws are not exception: "I am against all laws that the people are against and I respect no decisions of courts /and judges which are rejected by the people. " (LCS: 170) So uncompromisingly and resolutely, when more than eight hundred men, women and children were drowned in the capsizing of the ship Eastland in the Chicago River in the summer of 1915, Sandburg denounced both the Western Electric company sponsoring the outing for its employees and their families on the ship, and the U. S. Secretary of Commerce, who was responsible for the safety of such ships. He condemned why there was no one to "stop a cranky unstable ancient hoo–doo–tub like the excursion boat Eastland from capsizing with twenty--five hundred human lives within a few hundred yards off shore in plain view of parents and relatives of the children who were drowning?" He said that "Business required it. " And his article appeared in the International Socialist Review. He also mounted an even more violent assault in an unpublished poem Eastland. He concluded that the disaster was the roots of all the social "disasters" inflicted on the American working class by callous government and business interests (See CSB: 263). Here is the poem partially quoted from Carl Sandburg, A Biography by Penelope Niven:

The Eastland

···It was a hell of a job, of course

To dump 2, 500 people in their clean picnic clothes

All ready for a whole lot of real fun

Down into the dirty Chicago river without any warning···.

Women and kids, wet hair and scared faces,

The coroner hauling truckloads of the dripping dead···.

···Yes, the Eastland was a dirty bloody job–bah!

I see a dozen Eastlands

Every morning on my way to work

And a dozen more going home at night. (CSB: 264)

Eastland Incident was only one of many. Sandburg exposed it to the sun only to warn some upper persons of the safety of the working class. And he expressed that the government involved should be responsible for the disaster.

Surely, Sandburg cherishes the spirit of the people, he is concerned about the severe situation of the people, and he provides hope to the people. All these are worthy for Sandburg to devote himself to. And from Chicago Poems to The People, Yes, he yeses the people with his identity as one of the people and as the people's poet; he yeses the people from time to time in the refrain "the people, yes", coming over through part of his life; he yeses the people in morality and in class, good or bad, high or low; he yeses the people as "what they are"; he yeses the people who "will live on"; he yeses the people who are his brethens; he yeses the people that "move eternally" without retreating. And he yeses "I", Sandburg, AM FOR THE PEOPLE! And therefore, he yeses his popular poetics in his poetic practice for the people.

Chapter Four
The Popular Poetics on the
Basis of the Commons

Poetics here is chosen to mean literary criticism that deals with the nature, forms, and laws of poetry. A poet's poetics often has his or her own background and unique traits. Sandburg is one of many, insisting on his own basic principle of poetry all the way in his creation, showing fully his own poetic style, particular versification and dominant common subjects. That is to say, his poetics has its origin and basis. To trace, find and demonstrate it, this part treats how the people act as his foundation stone in his poetics, how he behaved as a realistic poet, how his "Sense of Nativeness" determined his scope of poetry, how his poetics works in his poetry, and how his principle of poetry–to function in society runs through his poetics and concrete poetic lines. And all these elements of his poetics and its basis play a role in leading Sandburg onto the way of becoming the people's poet.

I. His Poetic Theory and Social Function of Poetry

In "Notes for a Preface" of his *The Complete Poems of Carl Sandburg* (1970), Sandburg's poetic theory is revealed and unfolded on some level. First, for the definition of poetry, Sandburg has his own understanding: "A poet explains for us what for him is poetry by what he presents to us in his poems" just like "A painter makes definitions of what for him is art by the kind of paintings his brush puts on canvas. An actor defines dramatic art as best he can by the way he plays his parts···" (CPCS: xxvi–xxvii). Sandburg did not define poetry in a scientific way, but it is enough for us to have a very clear and exact understanding about poetry from him, generally he thinks poetry is just what a poet writes.

But on the other hand, though it is not strictly academic, the following poem of Sandburg to some extent can help us understand what poetry is by Sandburg:

TENTATIVE (FIRST MODEL) DEFINITIONS OF POETRY

1　*Poetry is a projection across silence of cadences arranged to break that silence with definite intentions of echoes, syllables, wave lengths.*

2　*Poetry is an art practiced with the terribly plastic material of human language…*

4　*Poetry is the tracing of the trajectories of a finite sound to the infinite points of its echoes…*

8　*Poetry is a slipknot tightened around a time–beat of one thought, two thoughts, and a last interweaving thought there is not yet a number for…*

11　*Poetry is a series of explanations of life, fading off into horizons too swift for explanations.*

12　*Poetry is a fossil rock–print of a fin and a wing, with an illegible oath between…*

15　*Poetry is a search for syllables to shoot at the barriers of the unknown and the unknowable…*

17　*Poetry is a type–font design for an alphabet of fun, hate, love, death…*

24　*Poetry is the harnessing of the paradox of earth cradling life and then entombing it.*

25　*Poetry is the opening and closing of a door, leaving those who look through to guess about what is seen during a moment…*

27　*Poetry is a statement of a series of equations, with numbers and*

symbols changing like the changes of mirrors, pools, skies, the on-
ly never–changing sigh being the sign of infinity.

28   *Poetry is a packsack of invisible keepsakes.*

30   *Poetry is a kinetic arrangement of static syllables···*

33   *Poetry is an enumerations of birds, bees, babies, butterflies, bugs,*
      bambinos, babayagas, and bipeds, beating their way up bewilder-
      ing bastions···

35   *Poetry is the establishment of a metaphorical link between white*
      butterfly–wings and the scraps of torn–up love–letters.

37   *Poetry is a mystic, sensuous mathematics of fire, smoke–stacks,*
      waffles, pansies, people, and purple sunsets.

38   *Poetry is the capture of a picture, a song, or a flair, in a deliber-*
      ate prism of words. (CPCS: 317–19)

However, Sandburg's greatness lies in another aspect—his expounding a-
bout the relationship between readers and writers (though it concerns not much
with the theme of the dissertation herein, it is one of his key points about literary
criticism.): "There stands the work of the man, the woman who wrought it. We
go to it, read it, look at it, perhaps go back to it many a time and it is for each
of us what we make of it. The creator of it can say it means this or that-or it
means for you whatever you take it to mean. He can say it happened, it came into being and it now exists apart form him and nothing can be done about it. "
(CPCS: xxvi–xxvii. The underlined words serve as authorial emphasis.) This
theory just meets Roland Barthes' ①theory—"The Death of Author". And to our
surprise, the unsystematized theory was put forward by Sandburg in about 1950,
or even earlier; ② while, Barthes' theory appeared in his essay–selected book
Image, Music, Text, in 1977 (London: Fotana, 1977). It was 27 years later.

Roland Barthes' (1977) "The Death of Author", demonstrates that an author is not simply a "person" but a socially and historically constituted subject.

---

①   French critic who applied semiology, the study of signs and symbols, to literary and social criticism.

②   "Notes for a Preface" in *The Complete Poems of Carl Sandburg* was copyrighted 1950 by Carl Sandburg.

Carl Marx demonstrated that it is history that makes man, and not, as Hegel supposed, man makes history. Here Barthes, in the way of Sandburg, emphasizes it is writing that makes an author and not vice versa. The writer can only imitate a gesture that is always anterior, but never original. Thus the author cannot claim any absolute authority over his or her text, because, in some ways, his only power is to mix writings. That is to say, a text's unity lies not in its origin, but in its destination. It is the reader who "produces" a text on his or her own terms, gaining meanings from what has already been read, and hence the reader is no longer the consumer but the producer of the text. This has no difference from what Sandburg adheres to "it (the poem, the text) means for you whatever you take it to mean. He (the poet, the author) can say it happened, it came into being and it now exists apart from him and nothing can be done about it. " But there is no evidence to prove Roland Barthes once read about Sandburg. And it is a pity for Sandburg not to systemize his raw theory about the relationship between readers and writers.

Actually, Sandburg the poet was not always deeply interested in pure theory and poetics (including his socialism opinion); comparatively, he emphasized the responsibility of a poet in society, which encouraged him to be a poet of the people, and so he was more interested in a poet's function, his relationship to society, his role in the society and his down-to-earth common theme from and for the ordinary people. What relationship is there between poets and society? And what part should politics play? Sandburg thinks the theme is worth discussing: "Poetry and politics, the relation of the poets to society, to democracy, to monarchy, to dictatorships—we have here a theme whose classic is yet to be written" (CPCS: xxvi). As a poet, he chose the raw materials of human existence, trying to synthesize his own experiences and the universal experiences of the people's life. Being both a poet and a journalist, he derived inspiration, essence of life and society by stepping into society to fulfill his adherence to poet's functioning and responsibility in society, while his journalism and social practice could feed his poetry. So his poetry was deeply rooted in his passion for social justice, and became a kind of reflection of his participation in his times. This is the result of his emphasizing the social function of poetry, and this is the embodiment of his responsibility for the society. To read through his poems is to read in chronology and context and a man's autobiography, not exaggeratedly, and even a nation's biography of his time. (See Penelope Niven 1991: 362) Naturally, his poetic theory impenetrates his poetry practice as to be discussed in the following.

Ⅱ. The People as the Foundation Stone

Sandburg's social function of poetry and his sense of responsibility for the society determines his choice of people, who are the main body of a society, to step into his poetry. So naturally, the people play a part and even are the foundation stone in Sandburg's poetics, and his poetic subjects are extracted from the people who are the basis of his practice and become a backbone in his poetic lines.

How Many "People" are there in His Poetry?

In order to show how Sandburg puts the people in his poems and how much the people weigh in his poetry, investigation of the number of the word "people" used in the whole book of *The Complete Poems of Carl Sandburg* is one of good ways. The statistics of the word frequency of "people" in his poems can be one of many illustrations to support Sandburg as a people's poet:

Table 4   **Word Frequency of "people" in CPCS**

No.	Sections in CPCS	Frequency (times)	Percentage
1	Introduction and Notes	13	2.4
2	Chicago Poems	23	4.3
3	Cornhuskers	30	5.6
4	Smoke and Steel	63	11.8
5	Slabs of Sunburnt West	20	3.7
6	Good Morning, America	38	7.1

Continued

No.	Sections in CPCS	Frequency (times)	Percentage
7	The People, Yes	322	60. 2
8	New Section	19	3. 6
9	1950–1967	7	1. 3
Total		535	100

Apparently, it is a surprise that the word "people" appears so many times in a book of less than 800 pages. Totally there are 535 times for the "people" in it. And averagely, each page contains about 0. 7 "people". Among all the sections, *The People, Yes* contains 322 "people", covering 60. 2%, or more than half of the total number. Then in turn, from more to less, the percentage of each section is: *Smoke and Steel*, 11. 8%; *Good Morning, America*, 7. 1%; *Cornhuskers*, 5. 6%; *Chicago Poems*, 4. 3%; *Slabs of Sunburnt West*, 3. 7%; New Section, 3. 6%; Introduction and Notes, 2. 4%; and the last and the least, the section of poems of 1950–1967, 1. 3%. Since *The People, Yes* concentratedly discusses the people, it naturally owns and is worthy of having the highest frequency.

To carry out a comparison, the word frequency of the "people" in Walt Whitman's *Leaves of Grass*[①] is investigated too. The "people" is repeated only 45 times in the 365–page book. Averagely, each page has only about 0. 12 "people"; while in Sandburg's *The Complete Poem of Carl Sandburg*, each page contains 0. 7 "people". It is obvious that Sandburg's emotion and affection for the people is warm and high enough.

And as we know, Walt Whitman was the first people's poet in America. Here, I do not mean Sandburg deserves the title of the people's poet more than Walt Whitman. Counting the frequency of "people" is only one of many ways to prove a poet the people's poet. That is to say, to investigate the word frequency

①　Whitman, Walt. *Leaves of Grass*. New York: Caxton House, 1900.

of the "people" is among many means to do it. In fact, other words like "man", "women", "human", and any other word referring to a member of the people can expound something about the people's poet to some degree. Anyway, this sort of investigation is somewhat unilateral, and but also anyway, this investigation can prove Sandburg's qualification as the people's poet from one angle of view.

Going into the People

Theory comes from practice. Sandburg's poetics is based on his practice among the people. He cared about the people, worked for the people, and spoke for the people.

Sandburg was as common as the common folk. Though he had associated with celebrities, he never lost the common touch. For example, he could treat with equal deference an inglorious editor of a little railroad magazine. He admired his views. Even a nameless workman weighs equally in his mind; the poem "Child of the Romans" in *Chicago Poems* is a good example (about the poem text, see Section II, Chapter Two).

Just by this spirit and attitude towards the common people and his common origin, remembering what a role a poet should play, Sandburg could easily step into the common people, their world and their life. Even this became his preference. In his railway travels on the lecture circuit, Sandburg liked to spend his time in the smoking car with ordinary salesmen and businessmen instead of with other writers and celebrities. (See CSLW: 114)

Additionally, in mass education, Sandburg contributed something to American citizens' civilization. During the influx of blacks from the South to Chicago City, Sandburg reported much about the racial problems considered his best reporting. One of his reports involved the Chicago Urban League issued a creed to promote cleanliness for women:

For me! I am an American citizen. I am proud of our boys "over there", who have contributed soldier service. I desire to render citizen service. I realize that our soldiers have learned new habits of self-respect and cleanliness. I desire to help bring about a new order of living in this community. I will attend to the neatness of my personal appearance on the street or when sitting in the front doorway. I will refrain from wearing dustcaps, bungalow aprons, house clothing and bedroom shoes when out of doors. I will arrange my toilet within doors and not on the front porch. I will insist upon the use of rear entrances for coal dealers and hucksters. I will refrain from loud talking and objectionable deportment on street cars and in public places. I will do my best to prevent defacement of property, either by children or adults. (CSLW: 75)

Sandburg did not dislike and avoid the blacks. As is mentioned above, he helped much in blacks' education showing his care for them. But unfortunately, Sandburg could not find the causes behind the bad or uncivilized behaviors (but later he realized it). It is the worse economic condition than that of the whites that led to their "wearing dustcaps, bungalow aprons, house clothing and bedroom shoes when out of doors". Anyhow, he went into the people and the blacks further. In 1919, Sandburg spent some days roaming the Black Belt to investigate shopkeepers, housewives, factory workers, preachers, gamblers and many others including pimps for facts of racial strife rampant in Chicago and other cities across the nation such as Washington, New York, Omaha and so on. For example, the story of black war veteran Private William Little appeared as the subject of one of Sandburg's articles in the *Chicago Daily News* in July: When the black wearing his army uniform returned home to Blakely, Georgia, a hostile crowd of whites ordered him to take off his army uniform and walk home only in his underwear. Bystanders persuaded the men not to torture and shame him. And he continued to wear his uniform for he really had no other clothes to wear. Unfortunately he was "found dead, his body badly beaten, on the outskirts of town. He was wearing his uniform." (See CSB: 337) What he found and reported draw many people's attention and caused much sympathy with blacks.

Also after studying the plight of black women, Sandburg discovered that "At the time of the greatest labor shortage in the history of this country, colored women were the last to be employed. They did the most menial and by far the most underpaid work". (CSB: 338) Whereas they often tolerated abominable working conditions that white women refused to accept. For him, it is unfair and a serious problem. He found it, reported and made it known to the world, functioning a poet's role as he persisted in.

All the time in this way, reporting the incontrovertible facts, Sandburg kept a tight focus on the blacks' life in Chicago's Black Belt, trying to find the roots of racial problems. For this, he put himself into real practice and experience. Another example is on a Sunday afternoon of July in 1919, Sandburg stood together with nearly two thousand people for three hours under the hot sun at a meeting of American Federation of Labor to support the workers and get the first-hand materials and experience. (See CSB: 338)

Believing economics and education could eliminate the racial problems across the country, Sandburg printed the "radical" platform of the National Association for the Advancement of Colored People, calling for an equal service to acquire an education; an equal service on trains and other public carriers; equal rights to use parks, libraries and other community services for blacks; equal chance for employment. He also analyzed race conflict in other cities in the country, studied crime rates involving blacks, reported on the realities of poverty–truancy, dilapidated homes, homelessness, families broken by "death, desertion, divorce, drink, promiscuous living or degeneracy. " (See CSB: 339) He stepped into such a depth into the people, the blacks, and the society.

And by such a practice he fed his poetry, some of which are just the reflection of his social practice of going deep into the masses. "Hoodlums" is a bitter poem he conceived during the turbulence of the 1919 riots in America. Later it was revised and published in Smoke and Steel. It reads:

I am a hoodlum, you are a hoodlum, we and all of us are a world of hoodlums–maybe so.

I hate and kill better men than I am, so do you, so do all of us–maybe–maybe so.

In the ends of my fingers the itch for another man's neck, I want to see him hanging, one of dusk's cartoons against the sunset.

This is the hate my father gave me, this was in my mother's milk, this is you and me and all of us in a world of hoodlums–maybe so.

Let us go on, brother hoodlums, let us kill and kill, it has always been so, it will always be so, there is nothing more to it.

Let us go on, sister hoodlums, kill, kill, and kill, the torsos of the world's mothers are tireless and the loins of the world's fathers are strong–so go on–kill, kill, kill.

Lay them deep in the dirt, the stiffs we fixed, the cadavers bumped off, lay them deep and let the night winds of winter blizzards howl their burial service.

The night winds and the winter, the great white sheets of northern blizzards, who can sing better for the lost hoodlums the old requiem, "Kill him! Kill him…"

Today my son, tomorrow yours, the day after your next door neighbor's—it is all in the wrists of the gods who shoot craps—it is anybody's guess whose eyes shut next.

Being a hoodlum now, you and I, being all of us a world of hoodlums, let us take up the cry when the mob sluffs by on a thousand shoe soles, let us too yammer, "Kill him! kill him! …"

Let us do this now…for our mothers…for our sisters and wives…let us kill, kill, kill—for the torsos of the women are tireless and the loins of the men are strong. [CHICAGO, *July* 29, 1919] (SS: 107)

The poem was created directly with the inspiration of a fact. It was on a Sunday of July 27, 1919. The black boy, seventeen-year-old Eugene Williams entered "white" water carelessly from "black" water on a beach in Chicago, and was believed by blacks to be brutally stoned to death by whites. But a coroner's jury concluded that he drowned "because fear of stone-throwing kept him from shore." Then this became the fuse of subsequent Chicago riots. Many were killed, and many injured. Sandburg was appalled at the savagery of events and he gave thoughtful coverage about the working class' cutting one another's throat. It is clear that the poem came from Sandburg's then irate mood for the blacks' and white's conflict. So he says in the poem "I am a hoodlum, you are a hoodlum, we and all of us are a world of hoodlums". And he borrows a person's instinctive and close relationship and emotion with family members to goad the people concerned to self–abuse and stop this kind of brutal action. So in the end he says, "Let us do this now··· for our mothers··· for our sisters and wives··· let us kill, kill, kill–for the torsoes of the women are tireless and the lions of the men are strong." It could be imagined that on the scene if each was given the poem to read, or Sandburg could have made such a speech using the poem, maybe the subsequent riots would have stopped. Hearing this, who wanted to be a "hoodlum"? For mothers and sisters, who wanted to be killed and kill women?

This event has its historical reason and background. In Chicago, after World War I, returning white veterans found many of their jobs filled by southern blacks coming to the city during their absence. Apparently the whites feared the blacks' growing strength and this fear came to change into a kind of hate. As mentioned, Williams Incident was only a fuse of subsequent riots.

After this, Sandburg finished writing *Chicago Race Riots: July*, 1919. It is his first book published by Harcourt's new firm, as well as his first commercial book of prose based on 1919 Chicago race riots. Meanwhile the poem "Crimson Changes People" (The poem has been partly analyzed, see Section III, Chapter Three, taken as an example here again.) is another one dropping a hint of the background and the trauma of the series of race riots:

···

Did I see the moths in your eyes, lost moths,

with a flutter of wings that meant:

we can never come again.

Did I see No Man's Land in your eyes

And men with lost faces, lost loves,

And you among the stubs crying?

Did I see you in the red death jazz of war

losing moths among lost faces,

speaking to the stubs who asked you

to speak of songs and God and dancing,

of bananas, northern lights or Jesus,

any hummingbird of thought whatever

flying away from the red death jazz of war?

Did I see your hand make a useless gesture

trying to say with a code of five fingers

something the tongue only stutters?

did I see a dusk Golgotha? (SS: 42)

The "moth" is the image and symbol of American blacks. A moth comes from night and darkness. It yearns towards light and often dies in fire. It gets light by mortgaging and pledging its life. When it goes near light from night, it goes near suffering and death. It's just like the situation of American blacks then. Many of them, whether they were whites or blacks, "never come again" in the conflicts. And in the conflicts, the working class themselves "lost faces" and "lost loves". Originally they should have this kind of friendship and love. And certainly "I" "stutters" to be able to say nothing in the imagination of "Golgotha". Though the title contains "crimson", in the whole poem, it cannot be found again. "Crimson" implies blood, the holy blood from "Golgotha" of Jesus Christ. And Jesus Christ's blood is for the ordinary people on the earth. So the blood is at the same time the common people's blood. "Crimson changes people", and "crimson" taught the people a lesson: Brotherhood is valuable. Cherish it! Don't cut one another's throat again! And this is what Sandburg hints.

Sharing the same emotion and impulsion from Sandburg with "Crimson Changes People", his "Man, the Man Hunter," is a description about a lynching, the stark metaphor for the race riots:

I saw Man, the man–hunter,

Hunting with a torch in one hand

And a kerosene can in the other,

Hunting with guns, ropes, shackles.

I listened

And the high cry rang,

The high cry of Man, the man–hunter:

We'll get you yet, you sbxyzch!

I listened later.

The high cry rang:

Kill him! Kill him! the sbxyzch!

In the morning the sun saw

Two butts of something, a smoking rump,

And a warning in charred wood:

Well, we got him,

The sbxyzch. (SS: 48)

Among the lines, the echo of race riots is echoing. Maybe the whites were killing the blacks, and maybe the blacks were killing the whites. "Guns, ropes and shackles" were their tools to kill each other. The "sbxyzch" stands for their "game". When the sun rose in the morning, what are the "two butts of something, a smoking rump"? They were probably parts of human body. Here human being seems to become brutal animals like tigers and wolves, or at least like wild beings. What does the "Man" hunt? Since he is a "man–hunter", he hunts man, his own kind.

Sandburg was so deeply worried about the lingering impact of the race riots. And at this time, his articles on the racial problems are generally considered to be his best reporting. It is the result and success of his going deep into the people and the society.

He went into the masses, learned from the people, and experienced the society. And even in his last years he did not forget to contribute his saving to society. When he was 81 years old, in 1959, Sandburg dedicated $ 2,000,000 to Carl Sandburg High School in Mundelein, Illinois, just a little north of Chicago. (LCS: 522) And about Carl Sandburg School, there are many schools named after Carl Sandburg. On December 3,2004, by searching "Sandburg School" in the searching engine "Google", the website (http: //www. google. com), 95300 results of all kinds of related information are given (Dct. 2004), from which the following different schools can be seen: Sandburg Middle School, Carl

Sandburg Elementary, Sandburg Elementary School, Carl Sandburg High School, Carl Sandburg Junior High School, and so on, with some of them having the same name. Meanwhile in Galesburg, Sandburg's birthplace in Illinois, the Carl Sandburg College was established by authority of the Illinois Community College Act of 1965 and was approved by voters in a September 1966 referendum. So many schools were built to commemorate the poet. This phenomenon shows Sandburg's popularity among the people and his affinity with the people. This is the payback to Sandburg from the people.

Sandburg, coming from and going into the people, rhyming for the people, was and is paid back by the people. What he did formed the basis of his poetics. What he did becomes part of his poetics: to play a role in society, and to function well for the people. His poetics is simple and difficult, because it involves simple, great, deep and profound people, and not every poet could and can step so deep into the people. He went deep into the people, while the people went deep into him and his poetry.

As an Extropoet

In terms of themes of poetry, poets can be roughly divided into two groups: intropoets and extropoets (with some being both). To compare with some other poets who tend to indulge in themselves and are called "intropoets" here, we can see Sandburg's impersonal themes are artery in his poetry. There are few people discussing the real himself. Even speaking in the voice of "I", it's the poetic "I" as Walt Whitman did in his *Leaves of Grass*, reinforcing readers' sense of self-exploring, not referring to a complete oneself at all. In this group of poems, "I" becomes the person involved in the poem, yet still remaining "Carl Sandburg." The kind of poets such as Sandburg can be classified into what I call "extropoet". An extropoet cares about the other people, (for Sandburg, the people). And he draws nutrition-poetic source from the others, for Sandburg, the people. That is to say: The kind of poets step into the people. By their going into and describing the demos, they find themselves and their own values. It's like the fact that a singer on the stage, sings the audience, and the audience acclaims the singer and becomes idolaters. It is easy for them to get resonance. This is also the case for a poet and his readers, and also for Sandburg: he rhymes the people, and the people acclaim him.

But for what is called "intropoet", it's the other way round. For an intropoet, he invites the people to step into him (sometimes he does not do it at all and only appreciates his poetry by himself), but it often leads to a failure of popularity among the common folk. An intropoet can seldom draw many people's attention into his poetry and his world. Intropoets often rhyme lyric poetry belonging to the Spring Snow[①], though they can have resonance with some of the people, they are not like extropoets'. In the meantime, poetry of intropoets may leave more poetic arts or poetics for the coming world, while extropoets can be socially and historically meaningful and can direct more contemporary people in practice and offer more historical lessons. Though the author here does not lean to express what kind of poet is better, but if to produce a people's poet like Sandburg, extropoets are more likely than intropoets to become the people's poets, because they tend to eye on the other people and impersonal topics, while intropoets like to limit their topics and world to the scope involving their own personal emotion. So we come to the definitions of "extropoet" and "intropoet". An extropoet is a poet whose poetic topics are often impersonal ones, and themes are of social and historical significance. An intropoet is a poet whose poetic topics are often personal ones and poetics may be of artistic value, often lacking social and historical significance. Now to put the two kinds together to have a clear comparison, Sandburg's "Blue Maroons" and William Shakespeare's Sonnet 111 are chosen here:

BLUE MAROONS
"You slut," he flung at her
It was more than a hundred times
He had thrown it into her face

---

① a melody of the elite in the state of Chu in the Warring States Period (403 BC — 221 BC) of ancient China, later, coming to refer to highbrow art and literature.

And by this time it meant nothing to her.

She said to herself upstairs sweeping,

"Clocks are to tell time with, pitchers

Hold milk, spoons dip out gravy, and a

Coffee pot keeps the respect of those

Who drink coffee—I am a woman whose

Husband gives her a kiss once for ten

Times he throws it in my face, 'You slut.'

If I go to a small town and him along

Or if I go to a big city and him along,

What of it? Am I better off?" She swept

The upstairs and came downstairs to fix

Dinner for the family. (SS: 46)

The poem directly shows us a wife's miserable situation in the family. Only by several words like "slut", "a kiss once for ten times", "fling", and "throw" the woman's place is awesomely shown on the paper. Sandburg purposely treats the title "Blue Maroons". Both words can mean color, but neither means color. "Blue" here means "gloomy, depressed, dismal, or dreary". "Maroon" means originally "a person who is banished or exiled, as on an deserted island". So we can also understand in this way: someone is blue and lost in the wilds. " The poem typically discusses a social problem—women's position in society, and it is significant to some extent in the society then, and in present society. Surely, we can consider it as the meaningful expression of an extropoet, and it is the embodiment of poet's function in the society of Sandburg. In Shakespeare's Sonnet 111, however, the poet focuses on the lament about his own misfortunes:

111

O, for my sake do you with Fortune chide,

The guilty goddess of my harmful deeds,

That did not better for my life provide

Than public means which public manners breeds.

Thence comes it that my name receives a brand;

And almost thence my nature is subdued

To what it works in, like the dyer's hand:

Pity me, then, and wish I were renew'd;

Whilst, like a willing patient, I will drink

Potions of eisel 'gainst my strong infection;

No bitterness that I will bitter think,

Nor double penance, to correct correction.

Pity me, then, dear friend, and assure ye

Even that your pity is enough to cure me. ①

Shakespeare resents that circumstances have forced him to behave as he did because fortune provided so meanly for his birth and " did not better for my life provide / Than public means which public manners breeds. " Here other than an allusion to work, his statement is generally vague and does not explicitly identify his profession. The phrase "public means," therefore, maybe mean he must try to find a patronage by "public manner" as others did then—for example, the pursuit of favor through flattering verse (in fact, he did some, Sonnet 18 is an example). "You" in the poem must be someone for whom he feels sorry. The remark "Thence comes it that my name receives a brand" expresses the poet's determination to make amends for the insincerity of his flattering eulogies and for his betrayal to "you". He apologizes for his materialist motives and asks the young man to "Pity me" for two times.

Since it is a sonnet, it carries the poetic characters and rules. The rhyme scheme is ababcdcdefefgg. The meter is iambic pentameter. The last two lines are a couplet. According to the definitions of extropoet and intropoet, the poem originates from an intropoet; or, when the poet rhymed the poem, he showed the nature of intropoet with personal topic, emphasizing the poetics he followed.

But honestly, it is very difficult to tell whether a poet is a complete extropo-

---

① Liang, Zongdai. *Selected Lyrical Poems of Shakespeare.* Changsha: Hunan Literature Press, 1996: 222.

et or a full intropoet. In any case, both are, from a certain angle, of great significance and importance. The author here would only like to prove what kind of poet is likely to become the people's poet. Most of Sandburg's poems are of an extropoet. Though an extropoet does not necessarily equal to the people's poet, the people's poet should, at least, tend to be an extropoet. Sandburg is such a kind.

Ⅲ. The Realistic Poet and His Circular Development

Sandburg once said: "Here is the difference between Dante, Milton and me. They wrote about hell and never saw the place. I wrote about Chicago after looking the town over for years and years. " ① Sandburg's words show not only the difference between Dante and Milton and him, but also tell realistic poets and writers from the others. It can be taken as Sandburg's manifesto of his being a realistic poet. In spite of this, he underwent a circular development from realism, idealism, to historical mode, and then went back to realism again. But generally, I would like to define Sandburg the poet as a realist.

As a Realistic Poet

According to *Oxford Concise Dictionary of Literary Terms*②, Realism is a mode of writing that gives the impression of recording or "reflecting" faithfully actual way of life. And most of Sandburg's poetry just meets the definition. He writes realistically about the people, general and specific. And because the common people's pursuit is actuality in concrete life day after day, Sandburg realistic aspects should be discussed here.

His realism comes from his basic attitude towards the function of a poet. He

---

① Sandburg, Carl. *Carl Sandburg: His Life and Works.* University Park and London: The Pennsylvania State University Press, 1987: 81.

② Oxford Concise Dictionary of Literary Terms. Shanghai: Shanghai Foreign Language Education Press, 2000.

believed throughout his career that a poet has an obligation to address the issues of his time, to articulate the problems in his world. (See CSB: 278) Sandburg did so all his life. Mark Van Doren[1] offers us testimony in his introduction to Sandburg's Harvest Poems: "The ideal poet, as Schiller had said, yearns only up and off. But the real poet studies the world as it is: lovely, terrible, sensible, grotesque; and would ask for no other one in its place. In this sense, Sandburg is a real poet, so that it is no wonder people trust him and adore him." (HP: 10) In many poems of Sandburg, "White Hands" is one that is real description about real society:

> For the second time in a year this lady with the white hands is brought to the west room second floor of a famous sanatorium.
> Her husband is a cornice manufacturer in an Iowa town and the lady has often read papers on Victorian poets before the local literary club.
> Yesterday she washed her hands forty–seven times during her waking hours and in her sleep moaned restlessly attempting to clean imaginary soiled spots off her hands.
> Now the head physician touches her chin with a crooked forefinger. (SS: 211)

Though it cannot be said to be of great importance and significance, it is the real description and reflection of the daily social life. Really we can from time to time meet this kind of ladies who have over–cleanliness, and actually it is a psychological illness. The ladies of this group often come from a high–fed class. The poem alludes that the illness is the result of idleness sometimes.

The world is this way, and that is the way it is. Sandburg's realistic poetic style liberates him so that he may manage all of this freely; it gives him entry in a large scale into the world, the society, and the daily life of common folks. In "The Harbor", Sandburg gives us the comparison of real society and ideal world:

---

① 1894–1973, American poet and critic.

Passing through huddled and ugly walls
By doorways where women
Looked from their hunger-deep eyes,
Haunted with shadows of hunger-hands,
Out from the huddled and ugly walls,
I came sudden, at the city's edge,
On a blue burst of lake,
Long lake waves breaking under the sun
On a spray-flung curve of shore;
And a fluttering storm of gulls,
Masses of great gray wings
And flying white bellies
Veering and wheeling free in the open. (CP: 3)

"The harbor" is a stop or a turning point. On the one side there are "huddled and ugly walls", the miserable urban world, which you have to "pass through" it with difficulty; on the other side, there is "a blue lake" with gulls flying freely in the open air. The lake mirrors the contrast between realism and idealism. Under this difference, hardship of earthly life looks prominent: "women looked from their hunger-deep eyes" "out of the huddled and ugly walls". This is the vivid portraiture of real life.

We cannot say Sandburg loved Chicago very much. At least, as we know, after many toilful years, he chose to flee from it-the metropolis. At times he surely detested what he saw:

They Will Say
Of my city the worst that men will ever say is this:
You took little children away from the sun and the dew,
And the glimmers that played in the grass under the great sky,
And the reckless rain; you put them between walls
To work, broken and smothered, for bread and wages,
To eat dust in their throats and die empty-hearted
For a little handful of pay on a few Saturday nights. (CP: 3)

On the way of the advancement of capitalism, the flesh and blood of children were once stuck to the rolling wheel of the development of the society. As seen, they were cruel enough and "took little children away from the sun and the dew". · They were "broken and smothered, for bread and wages" with "dust in their throats" and died "empty-hearted". But it was only "for a little handful of pay on a few Saturday nights". (Incidentally, some developing countries are facing the same severe social problems.) Sandburg, using his realistic writing, tells us development is brutal and ruthless. But if it is based on children's flesh and blood, it will be more inhumane. Then and there in America of the first half of the last century, American economy developed fast, and the phenomenon in the poem was very prevalent, which Sandburg witnessed and stung him greatly.

As a matter of fact, Sandburg found bitter with sweet. Almost regularly, it appears he swung on the pendulum from tears to laughter and he never found no happiness existing in Chicago:

HAPPINESS

I ASKED the professors who teach the meaning of life to tell me what is happiness.

And I went to famous executives who boss the work of thousands of men.

They all shook their heads and gave me a smile as though I was trying to fool with
　　them.

And then one Sunday afternoon I wandered out along the Desplaines river

And I saw a crowd of Hungarians under the trees with their women and children
　　and a keg of beer and an accordion. (CP: 9)

Sandburg finds commonness is happiness that lies everywhere and every minute. It does not necessarily lie in greatness. It depends upon a person's psychology and attitude towards life, and understanding about life. What he saw on a Sunday afternoon is just happiness— "a crowd of Hungarians under the trees with their women and children and a keg of beer and an accordion".

As a realistic poet, war theme is one of his main topics. Behind and in the front of the war, the people are the real victims. Sandburg treats most poems about war with low-key. And the most frequently appearing phenomenon before his eyes is dead bodies of the soldiers. Compared with other poets, Sandburg, in a unique way, treats war poems more graphically in imagery and more impressionistically. Among the poets of his time, he kept a singular focus on individual tragedies composing the terrible mosaic of the war. The poem "Murmurings in a Field Hospital" is such a one:

[They picked him up in the grass where he
had lain two days in the rain with a piece of
shrapnel in his lungs]

Come to me only with playthings now…
A picture of a singing woman with blue eyes
Standing at a fence of hollyhocks, poppies and sunflowers…
Or an old man I remember sitting with children telling stories
Of days that never happened anywhere in the world…

The explication under the title says the young soldier was picked up "in the grass where he had lain two days in the rain with a piece of shrapnel in his lungs." Only this is enough to pitch the whole poem and prove the cruelty of the war. The soldier may be young enough, inviting other people to "come to me with playthings now". Or playthings are more important than all the other things for him, which is a setoff of war's meaninglessness in his eyes. And the soldier's wish is simple:

No more iron cold and real to handle,
Shaped for a drive straight ahead.
Bring me only beautiful useless things.
Only old home things touched at sunset in the quiet…
And at the window one day in summer

Yellow of the new crock of butter

Stood against the red of new climbing roses⋯

And the world was all playthings. (CP: 39)

The action in the line "Bring me only beautiful useless things" seems what a child does. But it indicates the soldier's deep hatred for the war. To survive, to live on happily was enough and an extravagance for him. In the last line he thought that "the world was all playthings" including war. He regarded war as a game, and soldiers as playthings of warriors. So his "Among the Red Guns" tells us how people and soldiers dream and wish for peace and the end of war:

Among the red guns,

In the hearts of soldiers

Running free blood

In the long, long campaign:

Dreams go on.

Among the leather saddles,

In the heads of soldiers

Heavy in the wracks and kills

Of all straight fighting:

Dreams go on.

Among the hot muzzles,

In the hands of soldiers

Brought from flesh–folds of women–

Soft amid the blood and crying–

In all your hearts and heads

Among the guns and saddles and muzzles:

Dreams,

Dreams go on,

Out of the dead on their backs,

Broken and no use any more:

Dreams of the way and the end go on. (CP: 38)

"Dreams go on" is repeated four times in the short poem. Though the poet does not tell us clearly what the dreams are, we can strongly sense that they are the dream of ending the war. The red color is dominant, hinting blood of soldiers and passion of revolution; and in addition, it also implies his "red" background—a socialist.

Practically, during the period from 1914 to 1915, Sandburg paid more attention to the war in poetry than in his journalism. Mostly, his war poems were structurally lean and tight free-verse stanzas, carefully controlled with somber rhythms and the repetition or key phrases "Among the Red Guns" with the repetition of "dreams go on", is a case in point again. As Harriet Monroe said: "his rhythms pound like guns booming. " And in this period more and more often Sandburg's war poems appeared in journals, including Poetry and the International Socialist Review. In *Chicago Poems* Sandburg gathered them into one cluster entitled "War Poems (1914–1915)" including some in the above paragraphs. He revealed the carnage of the war, and the exploitation of many young men in battles started by war hawks. He found no one except the soldier's relatives would feel more sorrowful for the loss of sons, brothers and husbands. Sandburg's "Ashes and Dreams", published in the International Socialist Review in May 1915, is an ode to the mothers of the world whose sons and dreams were lost on the battlefields: Silence, /Dry sobs of darkness/In the houses and fields, /O mothers of the world, /Watching. (CSB: 259) The "silence" is dead silence. The "sobs" are dry sobs. They want to cry but have no tears. Mothers are "in the houses"; while sons are on the battlefield. The "mothers of the world" are "watching" with expectation and dreams to end the war, but Hour on hour /The trenches call /And the ditches want /And the shovels wait. (Ibid.) The four-line stanza discusses the busy phenomenon on the battlefield. But maybe they know or do not know they are busy going to die. The trenches and ditches, which can be used to burry themselves too, may be their end or result. He continues: White faces up, /Eyes wide and blind, /Legs stiffs and arms limp, /Pass them along /And pile them in /And tumble them over, /Ashes and dreams together. (Ibid.) Now, as a result, they die with "white faces up, eyes wide and blind" and "legs stiffs and arms limp" . Then they were passed along, piled up and tumbled over, gone with "ashes and dreams together". And: (Mothers of the world, /Your waste of work) (Ibid.) In the bracket, the only eight words seem to count for little, but they hold the balance for the whole poem. The death of the sons have become the mothers' waste work–their expectation, their dreams, their waiting, their dry sobs and their nursing.

No wonder Penelope Niven said: "The distant, growing war galvanized Sandburg's poetry. The form was sparse and rugged, the images violent and often repelling, the voice apolitical in its fervent attack on war in the abstract and its vivid depiction of the minute, realistic particulars–bloody injuries, individual agony, loss, death. " (CSB: 260) Very naturally and emotionally, the realistic poet's "realistic particulars" remind us of the cruelty of the war. For Sandburg, everything of the war will be forgotten and covered by grass:

Grass

Pile the bodies high at Austerlitz and Waterloo.

Shovel them under and let me work—

I am the grass; I cover all.

And pile them high at Gettysburg

And pile them high at Ypres and Verdun.

Shovel them under and let me work

Two years, ten years, and passengers ask the conductor:

What place is this?

Where are we now?

I am the grass

Let me work: (C: 60)

What the "Grass" says is the meaninglessness of war! "Grass" will "cover all". And all will be covered by grass. The bodies of soldiers will be nothing and not neither greater nor taller than grass. For three times "Let me work" is repeated, telling us war is to kill each other only. We are often asked to remember history, just because we are forgetting; in fact, we cannot remember history at times. War is mostly of temporary significance. Sandburg warns us that cruelty of war is a fact and peace is expected all the time. In the poem, it lacks the sturdiness of war, the greatness of heroes, courage of fighters, and martialism of warriors, but a grave mood hangs over and throughout the whole poem. We only feel all will be covered by silent grass.

Actually, during and after World War I, Sandburg repeatedly revealed his horror of war and its consequences in his writings. Although not a pacifist in his maturing years, he exposed the carnage of martial conflict in many of his poems with graphic language. He carried this realistic attitude into nearly all of his poetry. But in "The Four Brothers" (partly discussed in Section III, Chapter Three), which was first published in Poetry covering five pages in 1917, Sandburg changes his attitude towards war into a radical one. The following lines are to demonstrate this:

> The Four Brothers
> Notes for War Songs (November, 1917)
> Make war songs out of these;
> Make chants that repeat and weave.
> Make rhythms up to the ragtime chatter of the machine guns;
> Make slow-booming psalms up to the boom of the big guns;
> Make a marching song of swinging arms and seinging legs,
> Going along,
> Going along… (C: 67)

Starkly, Sandburg is singing for WWI. It seems a "marching song" acclaiming the war. It appears he is singing behind the four brothers—France, Russia, Britain, and America while they are fighting, drinking and cheering for the war. At this time he looks as if he had forgot the cruelty of war, any war:

> They are hunting death,
> Death for the one-armed mastoid kaiser.
> They are after a Hohenzollern head:

There is no man-hunt of men remembered like this.

The four big brothers are out to kill.

France, Russia, Britain, American—

The four republics are sworn brothers to kill the kaiser. (Ibid.)

The usage of " are hunting", " are after", " big brothers", " to kill" and " are sworn to kill" implies the inevitable victory and vigor of the war. But the use of " big" in " big brothers" shows somewhat Sandburg's arrogance for America and the other three. Though Kaisers in Europe should be killed, the people under them are harmless and the fighters are only victims of Kaisers. For Sandburg, the four brothers are killing in the right and with good reasons:

Yes, this is the great man-hunt;

And the sun has never seen till now

Such a line of toothed and tusked man-killers,

In the blue of the upper sky,

In the green of the undersea,

In the red of winter dawns.

Eating to kill,

Sleeping to kill,

Asked by their mothers to kill,

Wished by four-fifths of the world to kill—

To cut the kaiser's throat,

To hack the kaiser's head,

To hang the kaiser on a high-horizon gibbet… (Ibid.)

Sandburg regards the war as " the great man-hunt" . Soldiers have become killing-machine, " eating to kill, sleeping to kill" . Though when people kill Kaisers there must be victims of ordinary innocent persons, why does not Sandburg kill the victims with sympathy? Now Sandburg seems to become radical and Jacobinical. It is completely different from his previous attitude towards war. And by the subtitle, " Notes for War Songs" , even without reading the poem, we should have known it is song of war. He could not think of the cruel outcome of war this time.

The poem marks the turning point in Sandburg' attitude toward the war. Heretofore his war poetry attacked the brutality and hopeless tragedy of war. But to discuss it from the original angle, we can regard it as a realistic description about war. In Sandburg's eyes, the "Four Brothers" seem to be a statue of the four bound together, invincible, and all-conquering. He, the realistic poet, gives the confidence to defeat the enemy by his literary work.

Nevertheless, in "And So Today" of *Slabs of the Sunburnt West* Sandburg returns to his theme of lament for the war dead. Like the length of "The Four Brothers", it occupies 8 pages in the book. Since Sandburg had experienced war in the Spanish-American war in 1898, it is very easy to comprehend the depth of the poet's feelings about the horrors of war. Of course he had been exposed to the atmosphere of World War I, but not as a combat soldier. The description seems to show that Sandburg was on the scene and psychologically immersed himself in the locale. Vividly he expresses:

> And so today-they lay him away—
> The boy nobody knows the name of—
> the buck private-the unknown soldier—
> the doughboy who dug under the died
> when they told him to-that's him.
> Down Pennsylvania Avenue today the riders go,
> Men and boys riding horses, rose in their teeth,
> Stems of rose, leaf stalks, rose dark leaves—
> The line of the green ends in a red rose flash. (SSW: 20)

To "lay away" means to "bury". It appears on the first line of the long poem, giving prominence to the sad and severe mood dominating the whole text. The first two stanzas contain a sharp comparison between a war field and a peaceful world. One side is full of sorrow; the other side is filled with tender love. But in the final stanza, Sandburg mixes the two scenes into one, which still cloudy, though:

> And so today–they lay him away—
> the boy nobody knows the name of—
> they lay him away in granite and steel—
> with music and roses–under a flag—
> under a sky of promises. (SSW: 27)

The last stanza is almost the refrain of the first stanza, but "with music and roses–under a flag", and it is useless and meaningless now. The soldier has been dead and killed by war. He can hear nothing "under a sky of promises". Even "promises" have been nothing for him. Disappointment, pessimism and low–key, which congest the poem, are just the main characters of Realism.

About his realism, Harriet Monroe, after WWI broke out, argued in the September issue of Poetry that it was "immediately the poet's business" to join in the movement to "get rid of war." She predicted there would be a "new poetry of war," and offered as an example Sandburg's entry in a contest, "Ready to Kill" which she thought "significant in its huge contempt" (See CSB: 256):

> Ten minutes now I have been looking at this.
> I have gone by here before and wondered about it.
> This is a bronze memorial of a famous general
> Riding horseback with a flag and a sword and a revolver on him.
> I want to smash the whole thing into a pile of junk to be hauled away to the scrap yard.
> I put it straight to you,
> After the farmer, the miner, the shop man, the factory hand, the fireman and the teamster,
> Have all been remembered with bronze memorials,
> Shaping them on the job of getting all of us
> Something to eat and something to wear,
> When they stack a few silhouettes

Against the sky

Here in the park,

And show the real huskies that are doing the work of the world, and feeding people

instead of butchering them,

Then maybe I will stand here

And look easy at this general of the army holding a flag in the air,

And riding like hell on horseback

Ready to kill anybody that gets in his way,

Ready to run the red blood and slush the bowels of men all over the sweet new

grass of the prairie. (CP: 27)

What Sandburg contemns in the poem is the general, once in the past riding the whirlwind. It is the bronze hero in the park, with much admiration from many people. He even has the impulsion to "want to smash the whole thing into a pile of junk to be hauled away to the scrap yard". From Sandburg's view, the general is only a warrior "ready to kill anybody that gets in his way" and "ready to run the red blood and slush the bowels of men all over the sweet new grass of the prairie." Or the general can be considered an executioner. On the contrary, Sandburg defends the working people who are "the farmer, the miner, the shop man, the factory hand, the fireman and the teamster", and they should be idolized and remembered "with bronze memorials", for they could "get all of us something to eat and something to wear." The point is what just Harriet Monroe agrees with and favors. And what the general does in the poem is not what the realistic people care about. The poem is really "significant in its huge contempt" to the "significant" hero and general. It is thought-provoking. And Monroe's key comments fall into the point exactly.

Sandburg as a realistic poet, unlike some romantic poets paying less attention to their families in literary history (British poet Percy Bysshe Shelley and Chinese poet Li Po are examples.), thought a lot of and valued domesticity. Since his first daughter Margaret's birth in hospital had been easy, his wife Paula thought that a home delivery would be safe for the second birth. She engaged a homeopathic physician with good reputation. Unfortunately, when Paula

went into labor, the baby did not survive the birth because of the doctor's care-
lessness. He was deeply haunted by their loss, and expressed it in some poems.
"I am singing to you / Soft as a man with a dead child speaks" he wrote in the
later poem "Killers. " In the elegy "Never Born" for their aborted baby, he
shows more of his realism with pessimism:

> The time has gone by.
> The child is dead.
> The child was never even born.
> Why go on? Why so much as begin?
> How can we turn the clock back now
> And not laugh at each other
> As ashes laugh at ashes? (CP: 37)

After that, his world seemed to collapse. Though the "time has gone by",
his child has still been dead. Sandburg could not erase the shadow of the child's
death. In it, he feels life is of insignificance. So he says: "Why go on?" He e-
ven wants to "turn the clock back" to regain his baby. He uses his realistic vision to find living bodies as "ashes", for any body will become ash after death.
He sees through earthy human life. He ignores men's laughing at each other as
"ashes laugh at ashes". These are typical and classical words from a realist!

Reading the poem, who will not share the sorrow? Who will not have the
resonance? And the fascination of realistic poems lies right here. They can easily
draw the people's attention, and it is the very charm of extropoet. He writes a-
bout the deepest feeling of the commonest people. The communication between
the people and the poet occurs by this kind of realistic poems. And this is just
Sandburg, the people's poet and the realistic poet.

The Poet's Circular Development

From an overall view, Sandburg experienced four phases of development:
from realism to idealism, then from idealism to a historical mode, and at last

from historical mode back to realism again. But the four periods are not isolated. The division is only done to make it easy to study. Virtually it is a circular and compound developing process. Since this part relates not so much to the thesis, only a rough process and outline of his changes is to be given here.

First, he transferred from Realism to Idealism. After *Smoke and Steel*, Sandburg embarked on a deliberate excursion into the realm of fancy and myth, seeking a kind of consolation. He wanted to escape realism and retreat to the gentler world of his imagination. But Sandburg's progression from realism toward idealism coincided with a jolting family tragedy. Margaret, his daughter, was often sick in those days and was found to suffer epilepsy, and there was no effective treatment then. The adversity tortured his family and him very much. And this can be one of the reasons leading him into idealism to seek psychic consolation, while in fact, his poetry of this period also carries the color of realism as discussed in the above text.

In 1920 he and Paula voted for Eugene Victor Debs[①] for President was a gesture of his support of idealism, because Debs was a socialist leader and I believe that socialism, as well as communism of that time, contains component of idealism to a great extent. In spite of his many early socialistic activities, we cannot say he was an idealist then, the reason lying in the fact that at that time he only attended some socialistic activities, without going further to generalize them into socialism theory structure that contains some of idealistic goals.

And in journalism he also made a radical change: He relinquished his position as realistic labor reporter and editorial writer to turn to writing film criticism at the Chicago Daily News. Very soon, Sandburg had become the "cinema expert, the critic of the silent celluloid for the Daily News". (See CSB: 365) And during the next few years Sandburg reviewed an average of six films weekly and changed from interviewing labor leaders, criminals, or inhabitants of the Black Belt, to talking to movie star cowboys and ingénues. As journalist and poet,

---

① 1855–1926, American labor organizer and socialist leader who ran unsuccessfully for President five times between 1900 and 1920.

Sandburg had painted his times realistically as he saw them, for better or worse. Now he chose to move from truth to imagination, from the wrenching reality of "Liars" and "Hoodlums" to the fictional truth of fairy tales and motion pictures. It was a sweeping and pivotal change for him. And the change produced his first book for children—*Rootabaga Stories* published in 1922, Rootabaga Pigeons, the second book for children, published in 1923, and *Rootabaga Country* in 1929, these were all written for his children, and can be taken as his romantic literary creations.

To be exact, the then Sandburg roamed two primary landscapes: the realism of modern times, exemplified by "The Windy City" as the first poem published in *Slabs of Sunburnt West* in 1922, the same year with *Rootabaga Stories*, and the timeless fantasy of Rootabaga country. There are sharp contrasts in the images from the two worlds: In the Windy City—Chicago, "the monotonous houses go mile on mile / Along monotonous streets out to the prairies." (SSW: 8) While in the *Rootabaga Stories*, the character Gimme the Ax and his family break away from a house "where everything is the same as it always was." The enchanting White Horse Girl and the Blue Wind Boy meet and run away together in search of "where the white horses come from and where the blue wind begins," and find the place. "It belongs to us; this is what we started for," they say. Whereas a harsh fate confronts the boy and the girl in "The Windy City":

And if the geraniums
In the tin cans of the window sills
Ask questions not worth answering—
And if a boy and a girl hunt the sun
With a sieve for sifting smoke—
Let it pass—let the answer be—
"Dust and a bitter wind shall come." (SSW: 9)

Obviously, the Windy City is a rigorous, dull and unattractive society. The freedom and joyful civility of Rootabaga cities pose an ironic counterpoint to the disenchantment and resignation of life in the Windy City where "it is easy to die alive-to register a living thumbprint and be dead from the neck up. " (SSW: 5), implying the human beings' spiritual death in mind. This can be taken as another reason leading him into idealism—another timeless surreal fantasy of Rootabaga country to seek psychic console.

To prove Sandburg's moving into idealism, there are many points to support: he was a minstrel, a reciter of his own poems, a folk singer, and a guitar player. All this can more or less illuminate his tendency toward idealism. But this change is not absolute, as I mentioned above, sometimes he roamed two primary realms at the same time: the realistic world and idealistic world. However this did not alter his quality and nature of realistic poet. Idealism only functions as a balance and reconciliation for his realism.

From Idealism to Historical Mode

Introduction of the thesis herein tells us Sandburg's fame as a historian began from his writing and the publication of biography on Abraham Lincoln. And from then on he once more moved from children's Rootabaga country—idealistic and imaginative world to a historical mode.

Actually, the biography he created deviates from the traditional writing method of biography. Some critics condemned and looked down upon his biography, which is even without notes. There were no footnotes or endnotes. Some even thought Sandburg had written the biography as if it were a novel or a poem. The time for biographical writing extended from 1926 in which two-volume *Abraham Lincoln: The Prairie Years* was published on Lincoln's birthday to 1954 when *Abraham Lincoln: The Prairie Years and The War Years*, a condensation of the six volumes in one, was published. His Lincoln biography was epic in scale. Regardless of some critics said, publicly and widely, Sandburg was and is accepted as both a historian and a poet. And his Lincoln biography was once of great popularity. As for his biographic style, his realistic poetry writing must have influenced it. And history, from which biography cannot be separated, has to take reality as its basis.

During the same period, his autobiography *Always the Young Stranger*, the novel *Remembrance Rock* and other books including poems were published. This mixture, like the previous periods, shows Sandburg's several developing phases are not isolated. They are mixed, overlapped, simultaneous and relevant. To study each phase separately is difficult and impossible. After this time, we find the great book *The People, Yes* is a regress to realism again.

Back to Realism

The publication of *The People, Yes* was mixed with Sandburg's historical years. It was published in 1936. So as mentioned above, his developing phases were overlapped.

Most of its poems, as discussed in Section III, Chapter Four, give us a realistic description. The Depression of the 1930s made him see the people's sufferings. For example, more than fifteen million Americans were out of work in 1933, the year when Hitler became Chancellor of Germany and Roosevelt set to wage war against the economic emergency which crippled his country. Under this severe situation, he did not forget responsibilty of a people's poet and his poetic principle of the function of a poet in the society. He could not keep silent during the American ordeal of the 1930s. Naturally and fluently he produced *The People, Yes*, the realistic epic for the people, encouraging them to tide over and live through the Great Depression, pulling him into the real society again from previous idealistic, and historical mode step by step.

Briefly, Sandburg's development is from realism to idealism, then from idealism to a historical mode, and at last back to realism again. Each mode carries the characteristics of other kind of tendency. But realism is a keynote in his poetry. From another point of view, in this compound way the people's poet is more valuable, covering more topics, treating more people including children, popularizing Abraham Lincoln who had liberated the black people of America, and functioning his role of the people's poet in the society.

Ⅳ. "Sense of Nativeness" in Grain

Professor Ou Hong[①] discussed Sense of Nativeness as follows, "The core of Sense of Nativeness is the sense of a nation or a culture, that varies according to the change of time and people, including an individual's sense of belonging to a certain class. When people are studying, translating, teaching or learning from a certain foreign literature, they often, consciously or subconsciously, take their own culture as a reference, a medium or a selector."[②] As for the present author, it is natural for the study to carry more or less, consisously or unconsciously, a Chinese "Sense of Nativeness". However, that is an angle of view from me, a foreigner to Sandburg and Americans. And this viewpoint may not be easy to be found among Americans. And maybe a not-so-proper Chinese saying can be used to explain this: "The spectators see the chess game better than the players". So if a clearer and truer analysis about Sandburg's "Sense of Nativeness" could be given here, that would be the best wish.

Sandburg cannot be said to be the first-rate poet in the world. But in any case, he is a great American or Americanized poet. Among many reasons, his "Sense of Nativeness" played a great role in his popularity and greatness. Here in what is to be proved in the present dissertation—Sandburg as the people's poet, "the people" in fact mostly refer to Americans—the native Americans. This implies at some point Sandburg is a native poet with American "Sense of Nativeness" in grain. And there is enough evidence for this.

When he was young in primary school, in order to be Americanized and establish his identity as an American, at the age of eight he changed his surname spelling of Swedish "Carl" to the more American "Charles", and changed his surname spelling from Swedish "Sandberg" to American "Sandburg". (See

---

① Ou Hong (区铁), 1946-, a professor in Sun Yat-sen University, China. He firstly put forward in China the visual angle of "Sense of Nativeness" in foreign literature study.

② Ou, Hong. Sense of Nativeness: Trans-cultural Studies on Literature (unpublished), Preface, p. 1.

CSB: xvii) This can be regarded as the strongest desire to be Americanized and nativized in his childhood. This typically meets the famous Chinese saying, "While in another place, follow the place's custom", which is similar to English idiom "Do in Rome as the Romans do". And the saying can be thought of as the representation of "Sense of Nativeness". Sandburg tried and did.

In his poetry, the important thing to be noticed about the poet is his loyalty to American scene, American people, and American spirit expressed in his work. Irwin Shaw[1] once wrote about Sandburg: " I have never written any author to tell him that I liked his book, but I have just finished *The People, Yes* and I am moved to tell you that it is a kind of dictionary of the American Spirit, in which a writing man may look and find the exact word for an attitude, a shape, a longing, native to America, mixed with the soil of its farms and the dust of its cities. " (CSLW: 96) This talks about Sandburg's native sense. The piece excerpted from *The People, Yes* can be an example to prove it (See the quoted text in Section VII, Chapter Three). Under the Great Depression of the 1930s, many people were unemployed. They needed courage to recover American economy. Sandburg's punctual *The People, Yes* played a part in encouraging American people to weather through the crisis. From the poem, with this kind of American spirit, though they have nothing, not even " a stake in the country", they are marching everywhere with "dust", with "wind" "toward Omaha toward Tulsa". This is just what Irwin Shaw referred to as " the American Spirit" in Sandburg's poetry, and the following lines are a good example:

"What was good for our fathers is good enough
for us—let us hold to the past and keep it
all and change it as little as we have to. "
Since when has this been a counsel and light
of pioneers? of discoverers? of inventors?
of builders? of makers?

---

[1] 1913–1984. Prolific American playwright, screenwriter, and author of international bestsellers, of which the best-known is THE YOUNG LIONS (1948), one of the most famous novels about World War II.

Who should be saying,

"We can buy anything, we always have,

we can fix anything, we always have,

we're not in the habit of losing,

on the main points we have our way,

we always have"?

who should be saying that and why? (PY: 270)

In the past, "our fathers" struggled hard, and now "let us hold to the past and keep it all", keep the spirit and brave the difficulties and change the world better "as little as we have to" like our "pioneers", "discoverers", "inventors", "builders" and "makers". And it is "an attitude, a shape, a longing, native to America, mixed with the soil of its farms and the dust of its cities." With this of America, "we" can "buy anything", "fix anything", and "we" are not the habitual losers. "Who should be saying that and why?" The American people should. And "Why?" Because "we" are Americans who are brave, marching onward. It is a strong and complete "Sense of Nativeness"! Native to America, and sense of America in grain.

Unlike many of his contemporaries, Sandburg never went abroad for a literary pursuit. His native identity enabled him be able to help the American people discover their native sense and their national identity through poems, songs and his biography on Abraham Lincoln. William Allen White[①] told Sandburg that "you have put more of America in your verses than any modern poet." (CSLW: 85) While Sandburg himself in a letter to Alfred Harcourt on January 24, 1933 thinks: "too much of my language is a departure form the educated Englishman's speech, is too Americanese, and might seem almost nationalistic in its flaunting of the North American airs and syllables". (LCS: 286). He knew how to do and what he was doing.

And by investigating the frequency of some important names of places in

---

① 1868–1944, American newspaper editor and writer noted for his politically influential editorials and his autobiography (1946) .

The Complete Poems of Carl Sandburg can his sense of naitiveness be seen to some extent too:

Table 5   Frequency of Native Names of Place in CPCS

Of Places	America(n)	Illinois	Chicago	New York
Frequency (occurring times)	90	27	67	20

With the several key place names (or place correlative) as exemplification, only these 4 native words appear up to 204 times. On some level, it is enough to prove something about Sandburg's nativeness.

While in his children's book The Rootabaga Stories, Sandburg dedicated the book to Margaret and Janet, using their nicknames " Spink " and " Skabootch. " "I wanted something more in the American lingo," Sandburg said about his stories. "I was tired of princes and princesses and I sought the American equivalent of elves and gnomes. I knew that American children would respond, so I wrote some nonsense tales with American fooling in them. " In American native history, as we know, there is no "princes" and "princesses". (CSB: 389) Sandburg shapes the stories into American style without the traditional heroes in European children's stories to nativize it in America. In the book the rutabaga is a large yellow Swedish turnip; its name is derived from words meaning "a baggy or misshapen root. " Sandburg changed the spelling to "rootabaga" to Americanize it, or to emphasize its basic meaning by replacing "ru-" with "root-", implying he will root in America. About the stories, his wife Paula said: "Carl thought that American children should have something different, more suited to their ideals and surroundings. So his stories did not concern knights on white chargers, but simple people, such as the Potato Face Blind Man who played the accordion, the White Horse Girl and the Blue Wind Boy, or commonplace objects, a rag doll and a broom handle, a knife and fork" (CSB: 389-90) which belong to native Americans. The book *Rootabaga Pi* geons appeared in 1923, roughly similar to *The Rootabaga Stories* in style and contents.

But unlike many authors of children's stories, Sandburg did very little moralizing in his stories for children which can be considered as one of the traits of this style of literature, and meantime it can be taken as Sandburg's point of view, attitude and pursuit in literature of this kind: It is unnecessary to mix instruction with pleasure.

However, at times, Sandburg's Sense of Nativeness is parochial. Amy Lowell is an attestor. She once wrote a positive review in *The New York Times* on Sandburg's Smoke and Steel, and she told a friend in private that Sandburg sometimes overdid his Americanisms. (See CSB: 361)

About Nobel Prize, Harcourt and Sandburg talked privately about whether Sandburg could follow Harcourt's former star author Sinclair Lewis who received Nobel Prize for literature in 1930. Sandburg himself thought that he would never be considered because he was seldom heard of in Europe and his language was "too Americanese," and in "both the poetry and the Rootabaga stories there is a batty and queer, if not crazy approach. " In fact he never received the honor. (See CSB: 489). This unfortunate outcome is an inevitable regret, for his Sense of Nativeness was too much rooted in America in grain, instead of in a worldwide scale.

Again, the poem "The Four Brother" is not a bad example to investigate Sandburg's narrow Sense of Nativeness. (About the text of the poem and more discussions, see Section III, Chapter Three and Section II, Chapter Four.) Richard Crowder, biographer of Carl Sandburg[1], takes a dim view about the eloquent poem:

The limitations of Sandburg's vision are evident in this poem, and echoes of his early interest in Populism reverberate. The poem had the narrow view of a professional patriot in wartime. The armies of the allies represent the "People. " No notion is present that God might also be the God of the German people. The

---

[1] Crowder, Richard. Carl Sandburg. New York: Twayne Publishers, 1964.

idea that the true enemy is Kaiser Wilhelm may be sound enough, but the un-considered concept is that the Allied armies are fighting the common people of the other side, who also swear Gott mit uns. [1]

Certainly and naturally, native sense and global sense form a discordant contradiction. For either of them, we cannot say this one is right, and that one is wrong. Sense of Nativeness comes artlessly from Sandburg's native origin and birth, and from his loyalty to America and its people. Though he could not win Nobel Prize for his somewhat narrow Sense of Nativeness, his value is much higher than that. And Nobel Prize is not all to prove a writer's or a poet's value. Sense of Nativeness is like a vertical line, expressing the depth of sense; while global sense is like a horizontal line, expressing the extent of sense. They cross at "sense".

To sum up, Sandburg is American, his poetry is American, and his sense is native–American in grain, too. Anyway, Americanly or globally, both Sandburg and his poetry are of the people.

V. Common Subjects with Great Passion

In the last three sections of the chapter, the content treated can be roughly taken as the basis of Sandburg's poetics. Hereinafter till the end of the chapter, his poetics helping him become the people's poet with the guidance of function of poet in society is to be discussed.

In his poetry, most of the subjects are common. This attributes to his common origin and his love for the people, which produce his great and inextinguish-able passion for the people. And this makes his poetry readable for the ordinary persons, laying the foundation on his way to becoming a poet of the common persons.

Sandburg's non–sublime subjects acted much in popularizing his poetry.

---

[1]   Crowder, Richard. *Carl Sandburg*. New York: Twayne Publishers, 1964, 68.

He wrote about day–to–day subjects that the real attention was and still is paid to by the common people living day after day. And common subjects are the most sublime subjects because this kind of poetry has its great social value for its influence on the ordinary people.

After a survey of *The Complete Poems of Carl Sandburg*, many titles of his poems are found to contain such words as "people", "man", "woman", "baby", "me", "father", "flagman", "friend" …which point to the people directly; and many titles imply common people's daily life and events, even chores, such as "Shirt", "Brass Keys", "A Coin" and the other direct titles, indirectly treating people. These are all the common ones. About this, a study of titles in *The Complete Poems of Carl Sandburg* (CPCS) is necessary, and the study mainly includes *Chicago Poems*, *Smoke and Steel*, *Good Morning America*, *and others*. (*The People*, *Yes* is a single and long poem without subtitles in it, and the only theme is about the people, so it is not taken into consideration for the investigation). The investigation starts from Page 5, the pages followed is the multiple of 50, and the themes can be grouped into "things", general "life", "places" and "feeling":

Table 6　The Incomplete Investigation of Common Subjects in CPCS

Page	Title	Thing	Life	Place	Feeling
5	The Harbor			√	√
50	Joy		√		√
100	Wilderness		√		√
151①	Smoke and Steel	√	√		
200	Jug	√			
250	Baby Vamps		√		
300	Harsk, Harsk		√	√	

---

① On page 150, there is no poem, so the next page 151· is chosen.

Continued

Page	Title	Thing	Life	Place	Feeling
350	Crabapples	√			
400	Seven Eleven		√		
650	The Hammer	√			√
700	Fourth of July Night	√		√	
750	First Sonata for Karlen Paula		√		

It is an incomplete investigation, but it is optional enough, and the optional result can prove Sandburg's poetry is of common subjects in a way. As grouped, the chosen poems can be classified into four kinds. They are all common from ordinary people's eyes and they are sometimes earthy enough, such as "Crabapples" and "Jug", compared with Robert Frost's① "Stopping by Woods on a Snowy Evening". In The Complete Poems of Carl Sandburg, most of his poems are so common that the people like to read, because the subjects are not so far away from the ordinary people's day-to-day life and come from his deep understanding about and experiences from the lower class.

The poem "Hats" from *Smoke and Steel* is such a common thing, but under it Sandburg finds and thinks of more:

Hats, where do you belong?
what is under you?
On the rim of a skyscraper's forehead
I looked down and saw: hats: fifty thousand hats:
Swarming with a noise of bees and sheep, cattle and waterfalls
Stopping with a silence of sea grass, a silence of prairie corn.
Hats: tell me your high hopes. (CPCS: 160)

---

① Robert Lee Frost, 1874–1963, American poet whose deceptively simple works, often set in rural New England, explore the relationships between individuals and between people and nature. His collections include *A Boy's Will* (1913) and *In the Clearing* (1962).

"What is under you" —hat? The "skyscraper" can be both a real building and a person's mind. A mind is just like a skyscraper, and as high as skyscraper. "Hat" can see everything: "a noise of bees and sheep, cattle and waterfalls" and "a silence of sea grass, a silence of prairie corn". And hats, implying heads under hats, have "high hopes". What a common topic! But Sandburg finds what we can't find. We will be surprised to discover the real thing, the great thing—mind under the commonest thing—hats.

As is expressed in what I discuss about poetry translation in the article of "On the Principle of Poetry Translation and Orientation of Translation Style"[①], a translator should adopt a prospective way taking readers into consideration. And Sandburg, in poetry creation, unlike some other poets, does not indulge in self–admiration. He takes target readers—the common people into his poems. He knows what accompany them and what are near them. His themes are about the people; meanwhile he chooses the people as his target readers. He finds the people, and the people find themselves in his common subjects of poetry. Considering the need of common readers, Sandburg makes his poetry somewhat readerized in most of his poems.

Surely, if without passion and deep concern for the masses, nobody could have this kind of persistence to rhyme the people, the common persons! And this great passion comes from his origin of working class, and with it he tends to approach the masses. This is the very reason for his admiring Jack London's[②] open demonstration of alliance with the working class: he dressed as a worker in London slums, looked for a job among the jobless, applied for relief to support his survival, and slept where he could lie down to feel the lower situation. "If he were not a Common Man," Sandburg concluded, "I would call him a Great Man." So Sandburg once wrote an article to probe Jack London's personality, life and career, and traced the similar evolution of his socialism and analyzed so-

---

① Zhang, Guangkui. On the Principle of Poetry Translation and Orientation of Translation Style. *Journal of China University of Mining and Technology*, Vol. 5. No. 4. 2003: 156–160.

② Jack London is the pen name of John Griffith London. 1876–1916. American writer of rugged adventure novels, including *The Call of the Wild* (1903) and *The Sea Wolf* (1904) .

cialist color in his fiction such as *The Sea-Wolf*. (See CSB: 106)

In practice, like Jack London, Sandburg was always the friend of the down-trodden, and he had great passion to care about the poor and lowly people inclu-ding the blacks. In one of his letters to Professor Philip Green Wright in 1903, Sandburg mentioned a black slum: "Dover is about of [sic] the South type of city, and gives opportunity for study of the race question on the ground where the race question arises. I have trimmed myself on several points where I thot [sic] I was cocksure. The black slum that is fastened like a cancer on almost every southern town radiates its sensuality and shiftlessness, and the degree of this ra-diation is what is serious, what impresses the newcomer. " (LCS: 17) His ca-ring about blacks produces some of the poems of this topic. "Nigger" is both a song and a lament for blacks vended to America from Africa:

I AM the nigger.
Singer of songs,
Dancer···
Softer than fluff of cotton···
Harder than dark earth
Roads beaten in the sun
By the bare feet of slaves···
Foam of teeth··· breaking crash of laughter···
Red love of the blood of woman,
White love of the tumbling pickaninnies···
Lazy love of the banjo thrum···
Sweated and driven for the harvest—wage,
Loud laugher with hands like hams,
Fists toughened on the handles,
Smiling the slumber dreams of old jungles,
Crazy as the sun and dew and dripping, heaving life of the jungle,
Brooding and muttering with memories of shackles:
    I am the nigger.
    Look at me.

I am the nigger. (CPCS: 23–24)

Sandburg becomes the poetic "I" again, singing about the greatness of blacks, who are singers of songs, softer than fluff of cotton, and who are lamenting their sadness, brooding and murmuring with memories of shackles. They need the freedom as free as that in the "old jungles" in Africa. The last three lines are wail, wailing to draw attention. The last three lines are catchwords, catching other people's eyes to notice their greatness. And the last three lines, within which two lines are repeated, are courage, encouraging themselves to fight for freedom.

Besides poems, Sandburg wrote astute editorials on the role of the blacks in race riots. In this way he always showed a warm and sympathetic understanding of the condition of the colored people, showing his devoted spirit for his career and acutance as a newsman. No wonder Harry Hansen, an associate of the newspaper for which Sandburg worked, remembered that the newcomer had the same unruly shock of hair over his forehead and he wrote:

> The warmth that Carl had for people was something that you never forgot. He was from the beginning a newspaperman and he had the qualities of a newspaperman. He had awareness. A newspaperman somehow knows what is going on around him. He doesn't live in isolation. Carl had a keen sense of justice and it runs all through his career, runs in his poems. (CSLW: 61)

With the devotion to his career and his love for the people, and with his mean parentage from the working class, Sandburg holds great passion to work for the people, to create poems eulogizing the people, not from time to time, but all the time. The passion for the people is like burning fire undiminished in his heart and life. We often regard Walt Whitman as the first people's poet, and his exclusive poetry book *Leaves of Grass*① covers 501 pages; but for Sandburg, peo-

---

① Whitman, Walt. *Leaves of Grass* (1924, the inclusive edition) . Hai'nan Publishing House. Haikou: 2001.

ple's poet second only to Whitman, his complete poetry book *The Complete Po-ems of Carl Sandburg* covers 797 pages. Certainly, by this comparison we cannot say and judge which one was more passionate for the people. But here it can be seen Sandburg's passion for the people is just like, or as high as Whitman's passion for the common people. For Sandburg, if there would be no passion, there would be no writing; and if there were no passion for the people, there would be no Sandburg's poems.

Sandburg's theme and content about the people, which can be thought of as the "flesh" of his poetics, are decisive in building the poet; but the form, rhetoric and sound of poetics also play a key role making his poetry accepted widely. More will be revealed in the following: his heritage from Whitman, his unique poetic style, and musicality in his poetry.

VI. Heritage from Walt Whitman

Walt Whitman, to whom Sandburg is supposed to owe
an almost unpayable debt!

—Mark van Doren

In his preface to a Modern Library edition of the work of Walt Whitman, Sandburg wrote that Whitman was "the only established epic poet of America," and called *Leaves of Grass* a "massive masterpiece." (See CSB: xix) In fact, not only did he judge Whitman so but he also inherited much from Whitman's poetry. During his retreat from working in fire station in his hometown and his subsequent departure to Chicago, Sandburg had begun to write some poetry influenced by Whitman. It is just this sort of follow and heritage that makes Sandburg inherit Whitman's affinity with the commons and leads him into the people's poet after Walt Whitman.

Imitation of Theme and Contents

Since Sandburg would become the Poet of the People Whitman had hoped to be, indeed he encountered Whitman's poetry at a crucial time in his own journey toward creative writing. Whitman gave him a model for social idealism, poetry and the life of the soul. For example, "Fragments", Sandburg's unpublished poem that can be dated back to about 1906, appears to be an almost antiphonal response to Whitman's rousing challenge in "Passage to India." Whitman writes in the poem's finale:

O my brave soul!
O farther, farther sail!
O daring joy, but safe! Are they not all the seas of God?
O farther, farther, farther sail![1]

Whitman's heroic struggle here urges his audience to do joyous and fearless exploration "on trackless seas" marking the triumphant voyage of his soul. Meanwhile Sandburg profoundly struggled for self and work, he embraced Whitman's challenge. Sandburg writes in "Fragments":

I am Columbus
And out over seas uncharted,
I sail my fragile and battered craft;
I may wear chains and languish,
I may fall sick, to brood and curse,
But though I reach no palm-fringed, coral shore,
I will have sailed!
I will have sped o'er the trackless blue,
I will have known the love of the sky,
Rouse of the sea and talk of the stars—

---

① Whitman, Walt. *Leaves of Grass*. Hai'nan Publishing House. Haikou: 2001: 381.

I will have sailed!

I have comrades, out on the seas,

Brothers valiant, dexterous, true;

Their crafts are moving over the tides—

What of the Indies we shall find? (CSB: 103)

In the poem, we find in Whitman Sandburg discovers an extraordinary alliance of spirit, and validation of his own stubborn courage and unorthodox experiments in poetry. He finds his own soul's journey, but it is not terminal and the outcome, and he would sail the uncharted seas. "O my brave soul!" Whitman sang, "O farther, farther sail!" "I will have sailed!" Sandburg answered. "I will have sailed···What of the Indies we shall find?"

On the other hand, his poetry's being declined can also be used as a proof of Whitman's influence on Sandburg's poetry. In 1906, eagerly wanting to know whether he could be a poet, Sandburg sent some of his poems to the editor of Mirror—William Marion Reedy. He received a long letter with sympathetic but straightforward criticism; Reedy declined his poems for his over-resemblance to Whitman. "I know that you say that you are modeled more upon Henley[1] than Whitman," Reedy wrote, "And yes, to be quite frank with you, I do not think that you conform to Henley's idea of rhythm···. In your verse the Whitman idea seems to be dominant and, as I say, in the last batch of poems which you sent me there is but one thing which seems to me to be anything like poetry as I conceive it. " (CSB: 114) Boldly, we can guess that Sandburg must have over-imitated Walt Whitman then.

In fact, in later years Sandburg destroyed or withheld most drafts of his early work, but he published some of them in *Chicago Poems* in 1916. The poem "The Road and the End," (first entitled "Lands and Souls") was published in a magazine called The Fra in August 1908, conveying the information of Sand-

---

[1] Henley, William Ernest, 1849–1903, British writer and editor of the National Observer (1889–1903), in which he published the early works of George Bernard Shaw, Thomas Hardy, Rudyard Kipling, and other aspiring writers.

burg's early life while echoing Whitman's image of the traveled road:

> I SHALL foot it
> Down the roadway in the dusk,
> Where shapes of hunger wander
> And the fugitives of pain go by.
> I shall foot it
> In the silence of the morning,
> See the night slur into dawn,
> Hear the slow great winds arise
> Where tall trees flank the way
> And shoulder toward the sky.
>
> The broken boulders by the road
> Shall not commemorate my ruin.
> Regret shall be the gravel under foot.
> I shall watch for
> Slim birds swift of wing
> That go where wind and ranks of thunder
> Drive the wild processionals of rain.
>
> The dust of the traveled road
> Shall touch my hands and face. (CPCS: 42–43)

The first two stanzas are extracted from Whitman's "Song of the Open Road" totaling 250 lines:

> Afoot and light-hearted I take to the open road,
> Healthy, free, the world before me,
> The long brown path before me leading wherever I choose.
> Henceforth I ask not good-fortune, I myself am good-fortune,
> Henceforth I whimper no more, postpone no more, need nothing,
> Done with indoor complaints, libraries, querulous criticisms,

Strong and content I travel the open road···①

The initial word of the initial stanza is "afoot", while in Sandburg's "The Road and the End", the first line of it contains " "foot" . It is very difficult to call it coincident. Very likely, Sandburg read the poem before his "The Road and then End", since, at the same time, the two convey similar meaning: both express their courage to explore the unknown world. The big difference lies in that Sandburg's with only 19 lines is shorter than Whitman's with totally 250 lines. It is kind of imitation in theme and content.

Still like Whitman, Sandburg began to recall past journeys on "the traveled road," getting back and identifying his own soul, with his own past as subject for poetry. "Broadway" explores backward his 1902 sojourn in New York:

I shall never forget you, Broadway
Your golden and calling lights.
I'll remember your long,
Tall-walled river of rush and play.
Hearts that know you hate you
And lips that have given you laughter
Have gone to their ashes of life and its roses,
Cursing the dreams that were lost
In the dust of your harsh and trampled stones. (CPCS: 69)

But with the same title, Whitman has "Broadway" in his *Leaves of Grass*:

What hurrying human tides, or day or night!
What passions, winnings, losses, ardors, swim thy waters!
What whirls of evil, bliss and sorrow, stem thee!
What curious questioning glances—glints of love!
Leer, envy, scorn, contempt, hope, aspiration!

---

① Whitman, Walt. Leaves of Grass. Hai'nan Publishing House. Haikou: 2001: 136–46.

Thou portal—thou arena—thou of the myriad long-drawn lines and groups!

(Could but thy flagstones, curbs, facades, tell their inimitable tales;

Thy windows rich, and huge hotels—thy side-walks wide;)

Thou of the endless sliding, mincing, shuffling feet!

Thou, like the parti-colored world itself—like infinite, teeming, mocking life!

Thou visor'd, vast, unspeakable show and lesson![1]

Is this still coincidence? It is impossible at all. The same subject, the same place, and the similar contents and tone! More examples can be found to prove Sandburg's heritage, or imitation of Whitman, but it is meaningless and unnecessary to instance further, since some of the poems are really imitation in theme and contents. To continue with the topic, the following points will deal with Sandburg's heritage from Whitman in structure, rhetoric and skills in poetry, which become accepted by the common people.

Inheriting of Free Verse and Long Sentence

Sandburg's free style and usage of long sentence like Whitman's in his poetry are prominent. To be more exact, here are listed two typical poems about this, one is "To a Common Prostitute" of Whitman, and the other is "The Soiled Dove". The first one is:

Be composed–be at ease with me–I am Walt Whitman, liberal and lusty as Nature,

Not till the sun excludes you do I exclude you,

Not till the waters refuse to glisten for you and the leaves to rustle for you, do my words refuse to glisten and rustle for you.

My girl I appoint with you an appointment, and I charge you that you make preparation to be worthy to meet me,

And I charge you that you be patient and perfect till I come.

Till then I salute you with a significant look that you do not forget me. [2]

---

① Whitman, Walt. Leaves of Grass. Hai'nan Publishing House. Haikou: 2001: 465–466.

② Ibid. , 2001: 353.

At the same time, Sandburg's "Soiled Dove" is full of long sentences with free style, talking also about a "harlot" –prostitute:

Let us be honest; the lady was not a harlot until she married a corporation lawyer
　　who picked her from a Ziefeld chorus.
Before then she never took anybody's money and paid for her silk stockings out of
　　what she earned singing and dancing.
She loved one man and he loved six women and the game was changing her looks,
　　calling for more and more massage money and high coin for the beauty doctors.
Now she drives a long, underslung motor car all by herself, reads in the day's pa-
　　pers what her husband is doing to the inter–state commerce commission, re-
　　quires a larger corsage from year to year, and wonders sometimes how one
　　man is coming along with six women. (CPCS: 63)

Except the obvious free style of the two poems, apparently, Sandburg's sentences are even longer than Whitman's. And long sentences give Sandburg more chances and freedom to express his ideas. This can be treated as an advantage compared with rhymed verse. Of course, this kind of long sentence appears nearly everywhere in Sandburg's poetry and it is unnecessary for us to illustrate more.

Cataloguing Things

Amy Lowell once remarked: " No one hearing him can fail to see that Sandburg is one of the most important poets in American today. Something of the Whitman who loved to catalogue people and places···" (CSLW: 83) By cataloguing, the poet can produce many concrete images to support and emphasize the common or conjunct images. The extracted poems form only a small part of "Chicago" by Sandburg and the poem " I Hear America Singing" by Whitman (the underlined and bold words are marked by the author here to draw readers' attention to the usage of catalogue) . The latter one is as follows:

I hear America singing, the varied carols I hear,

Those of mechanics, each one singing his as it should be blithe and strong,

The carpenter singing his as he measures his plank or beam,

The mason singing his as he makes ready for work, or leaves off work,

The boatman singing what belongs to him in his boat, the deck–hand singing on the steamboat deck,

The shoemaker singing as he sits on his bench, the hatter singing as he stands,

The wood–cutter's song, the ploughboy's on his way in the morning, or at noon intermission or at sundown,

The delicious singing of the mother, or of the young wife at work, or of the girl sewing or washing,

Each singing what belongs to the day—at night the party of young fellows, robust, friendly,

Singing with open mouths their strong melodious song. ①

Sandburg grasps the function of catalogue in poetry started by Walt Whitman. His "Chicago" is a good example of using catalogue:

Hog Butcher for the World,

Tool Maker, Stacker of Wheat,

Player with Railroads and the Nation's Freight Handler;

Stormy, husky, brawling,

City of the Big Shoulders:

… (CPCS: 3)

The underlined and bold words show us the obvious usage of catalogue in Sandburg's "Chicago" and heritage from Whitman. More examples are relatively at random given from in CPCS: "Theme in Yellow" on Page 56, "Places" on Page 190, Section 24 of PY (*The People, Yes*) on Page 465, Section 100 of PY on Page 600 and "Timesweep" on Page 771 (last page of the text in the book), all bearing the rich usage of cataloguing.

Sandburg catalogues the common things or persons that the people are very

---

① Whitman, Walt. *Leaves of Grass*. Hai'nan Publishing House. Haikou: 2001: 12.

familiar with. And this corresponds to Sandburg's common subjects, showing Sandburg's subjects come from common materials with the purpose for the common people.

Parallelism and Reiteration

Sandburg scoops some nutrition in rhetoric from Whitman too. Parallelism and reiteration are two ways frequently used in Whitman's poetry (In the total 10500 lines of *Leaves of Grass*, the lines with the reiteration of initial words cover 41% , and meanwhile parallelism is everywhere) , and Sandburg borrows this into his poetry. The following table is an illustrative, not inclusive investigation about the usage of parallelism and reiteration in Sandburg's CPCS compared with those in Leaves of Grass. ①

Table 7   **Usage of Parallelism and Reiteration**

Page	Anthology	Parallelism and Reiteration of Initial Words
42	LG	"A", 4 times in 4 lines. "Comrade of "'s reiteration and parallelism, 4 times in 2 lines.
	CPCS	"In the + n. "'s reiteration and parallelism, 9 times in 9 lines.
100	LG	"The", 8 times in 8 lines. "O", 11 times in 7 lines.
	CPCS	"And ", 5 times in 3 lines.
179	LG	"Dwellers", 3 times in 3 lines. "Shapes of…"'s reiteration and parallelism, 4 times in 4 lines.
	CPCS	"There's + n. "'s reiteration and parallelism, 3 times in 3 lines. "There + n. "'s reiteration and parallelism, 3 times in 3 lines.
286	LG	"Give me…"'s reiteration and parallelism, 8 times in 8 lines.
	CPCS	"or", 8 times in 8 lines. "Said" & "When", separately, two times in 2 lines.

① Whitman, Walt. *Leaves of Grass.* Hai'nan Publishing House. Haikou: 2001: 381.

Continued

Page	Anthology	Parallelism and Reiteration of Initial Words
317	LG	"In" & "For", separately two times in 2 lines "He", 2 times in 2 lines. "Songs of…" 's reiteration and parallelism, 2 times in 2 lines.
	CPCS	"Poetry" as the initial word in each line. And first half of each line is parallelism.
499	LG (501 pages)	"I am…" 's reiteration and parallelism, 2 times in 2 lines. "They + V…. " 's reiteration and parallelism, 3 times in 3 lines.
	CPCS (771 pages)	"In + n. + they + v. " 's reiteration and parallelism, 3 times in 3 lines.

Note: CPCS stands for the edition mentioned above of The *Complete Poems of Carl Sandburg*; LG stands for the edition mentioned above of *Leaves of Grass*.

The comparison in the table explains Sandburg's heritage of reiteration and parallelism in his poetry from Whitman. The pages taken here are meant to cover the whole books nearly. And as we have seen, reiteration and parallelism can be found in many, or almost all pages of Sandburg's poetry. On this level, Sandburg chose a way trodden by Whitman who was considered the first people's poet of America. At least, the path trodden by Whitman had once been a successful one. This popularized Sandburg's poetry very much.

VII. Unique Poetic Style

Sandburg came to grow toward poetry as unorthodox and independent as his politics. He learned from his study of Whitman that "first-class" poems should "grow of circumstances and are evolutionary. " He drew subject matter and vision from "these incalculable, modern, American, seething multitudes around us, of which we are inseparable parts!" (See CSB: 225) From this kind of soil and in this way, Sandburg developed his own poetic style, and from those circumstances his poems were evolving. Though he inherited much from Whitman, he was becoming a truly original poet, a pioneer using his realism and free verse to explore America, Americans and their dreams in his own manner, and this is just what his teacher Philip Green Wright encouraged him in early years. He urged Sandburg to walk on his own way to find his own unique voice. Sandburg mentioned Wright's influence in his life in *Ever the Winds of Chance* (discussed in Chapter Two), as well as in an unpublished poem "To a Poet". In it, Sandburg writes:

> I would find my way.
> But you were the strongest person I had known.
> You were the morning wind, and you were stone.
> You said: I know that you will go your way.
> Whatever horse you want to ride is yours,
> And night is yours, and the evening gleams, and day.
> I can tell you nothing you have not known.
> I said, I go with you; I am your own.
> But I went alone. (CSB: 111)

Following his teacher's direction, Sandburg "went alone" into his unique style, bearing his own marks, becoming more and more mature in language, materials, rhetoric and narrative methods.

Conventional Early Style

Before his coming to Chicago, Sandburg wrote poetry deeply influenced by the traditional romantic and classic poetry he read, as well as poems by his teacher Professor Wright, and the free ones by Whitman and Henley. After arriving in Chicago, maybe because of geographical and intellectual liberation from his hometown Galesburg, he began to transform his poetry. Most of the surviving poems during this period concern Chicago with a freer and more economical form. The images are often simple and clear. "Docks" is a typical one of this kind from Chicago Poems. In rhythmical free verse, Sandburg portrayed the silently departing ships with the sustained simile of the "mastodon":

> Strolling along
> By the teeming docks,
> I watch the ships put out.
> Black ships that heave and lunge
> And move like mastodons
>
> Arising from lethargic sleep.
> The fathomed harbor
> Calls them not nor dares
> Them to a strain of action,
> But outward, on and outward,
> Sounding low—reverberating calls,
> Shaggy in the half—lit distance,
> They pass the pointed headland,
> View the wide, far—lifting wilderness
> And leap with cumulative speed
> To test the challenge of the sea.
>
> Plunging,
> Doggedly onward plunging,
> Into salt and mist and foam and sun. (CPCS: 65)

   This one is very different from his later poems. Sentences are short. Image is simple and clear. And it contains end rhymes and internal rhymes. We can broadly call it traditional verse. But before the publication of Chicago Poems, Sandburg had begun to release his own fluid free—verse style from the conventional verse forms. And meanwhile he could convey images simply and change them easily and quickly, without the crutch of effusive description:

The Red Son
I LOVE your faces I saw the many years

I drank your milk and filled my mouth

With your home talk, slept in your house

And was one of you.

            But a fire burns in my heart.

Under the ribs where pulses thud

And flitting between bones of skull

Is the push, the endless mysterious command,

            Saying:

I leave you behind—

You for the little hills and the years all alike,

You with your patient cows and old houses

Protected from the rain,

I am going away and I never come back to you;

Crags and high rough places call me,

Great places of death

Where men go empty handed

And pass over smiling

To the star—drift on the horizon rim.

My last whisper shall be alone, unknown;

I shall go the city and fight against it,

And make it give me passwords

Of luck and love, women worth dying for,

And money. ⋯ (CPCS: 74)

    The poem was to cherish his memory of his departure from Galesburg in 1906. Who is the red son in the poem? Sandburg is. Images change very quickly from Galesburg to Chicago, from "little hills" to "crags and rough places"; from old "faces" and "house" to "luck and love, women worth dying for". Now in the poem Sandburg is very good at dealing with the changing images and he does it so smoothly with no overfull and excessive emotional description.

    His early style, generally, is simple and clear in image, economical in structure and tends to be more conventional in rhyme. This has some relationship with his simple origin in Galesburg and his early reading about the conventional poems. But we can regard it as the source, or start of his mature poetics later.

Transitory Nature of His Language

Sandburg was fascinated very much with the transitory nature of language. In his eyes, language is transitory and dynamic. In the poem "Languages", he discusses the nature and quality of it:

> There are no handles upon a language
> Whereby men take hold of it
> And mark it with signs for its remembrance.
> It is a river, this language,
> Once in a thousand years
> Breaking a new course
> Changing its way to the ocean.
> It is mountain effluvia
> Moving to valleys
> And form nation to nation
> Crossing borders and mixing.
> Languages die like rivers.
> Words wrapped round your tongue today
> And broken to shape of thought
> Between your teeth and lips speaking
> Now and today
> Shall be faded hieroglyphics
> Ten thousand years from now. (CPCS: 72–73)

He considers language as a "river" flowing forward, maybe with a history of "a thousand of years", but always trying to break "a new course". What you see about river is present, not past, nor tomorrow. And this is the nature of language. In it, Sandburg is found not to care about the future very much. So his poems are often about situations here and now, and he often chose to sing about today, and he continues:

Sing—and singing—remember
Your song dies and changes
And is not here tomorrow
Any more than the wind
Blowing ten thousand years ago. (Ibid.)

But this is only his discussion about language. The concrete poems about people and things containing the transitory nature of language are everywhere in CPCS. "Half Way" is about a little horse, in which Sandburg does not open his imagination about its past or its surrounding:

At the half-way house the pony died.
The road stretched ahead, the sunny hills,
people in the fields, running waters;
towns with new names, windmills pointing
circles in the air at holy crossroads.
It was here we stopped at the half-way house,
here where the pony died.
Here the keeper of the house said, "It is strange
how many ponies die here. " (CPCS: 388)

In it, Sandburg only emphasizes that after the pony's death, all things still go on: people are still working in the fields, waters are still running⋯. The four "here" s are used, showing his poetry's pointing to "here" and "then" . Other examples are "Branches" on Page 257, written about "the dancing girls"; "Couples" on Page 297, about men and women's cheating each other without any imagination forward or backward; "Swell People" on P669, about people's quality, and so on.

This kind of tendency, basically, comes from Sandburg's deep understanding about the people, because the people living day after day are concerned about only today, here and now relatively. They are unlikely at all times to think of all the time the history and tomorrow. And Sandburg, as the people's poet, also comes from the masses, the commons. Naturally and certainly, this situation makes Sandburg and his poetry more popular with time spirit in his own time and marked with the brand of his time. (This also expresses the weakness and shortcoming of transitory nature of his language, so since his death and his time, he has been less noticed than some other great poets and writers.)

Raw Material, but Refined Poems

Daniel Hoffman[①], once Consultant in Poetry at the Library of Congress, remarked about *The People, Yes*: "Nobody in America could have written those lines but Sandburg. They have the thumbprint of his personality, his ear for a good yarn, his sense of the revealing detail, his empathy with the folk wisdom, his unique ability to transform the raw materials of common speech into a lyricism with a swing and rhythm recognizably his own. " (CSLW: 96) Hoffman stresses here Sandburg's unique ability to make raw materials drawn from the common people's life into refined product—his poetry. In fact, the representative poem should be still *Chicago* (about the text, see the quoted part in Section II, Chapter Three).

Most of the materials of the poem "Chicago" are raw, and very raw materials such as "hog butcher", "tool maker", "stacker of Wheat", "Nation's Freight Handler", and some rough words like "stormy, husky, brawling", "wicked", "brutal", "crooked", "kill", "sneer", "curse", "lure" and so on are found. It is just these "raw materials" that Sandburg uses to make "refined" product—poems.

Raw materials unnecessarily refer to rough words, things or people. They can at the same time mean raw or common theme like that of "Sweeping Wendy: Study in Fugue" listed below:

Wendy put her black eyes on me

---

① Daniel Hoffman, 1923—, served as Consultant in Poetry to the Library of Congress from 1973 to 1974 (the appointment now called the Poet Laureate).

and swept me with her black eyes—
sweep on sweep she swept me.
Have you ever seen Wendy?
Have you ever seen her sweep
Keeping her black eyes on you
keeping you eyeswept? (CPCS: 653)

It is a very common theme, only a simple, rough, and raw expression in Wendy's eyes. But Sandburg grasps it and hammers it into a poem, a refined poem. When a gentleman reads, likely he will be moved and willing to meet a lady like Wendy in the poem. This is where the fascination or enchantment lies. So do you regard it raw or refined?

And raw can mean vernacular he uses in his poetry. During the decade in his twenties, Sandburg was once a soldier, a college student, an itinerant salesman, an aspiring orator and poet, recording American vernacular permeating his poetry later. This point needs no further proof at all, for when you open his poetry, it is not easy to find vernacular language. However, his vernacular comes from his hobo life giving him much time to approach and go into many hobos and the common people and getting and enriching his original language, which proves to be of great use in his poetry. And Sandburg afterward just wove the vernacular he collected into his poetry and prose. No his hobo life, perhaps, no his poetic style.

Recurring Symbols

Another one that shows the uniqueness of his writing lies in his use of recurring symbols. One symbol that can be easily noticed in his poems is a red bandana. In "Muckers", the red bandana is used as a method of wiping the sweat off the muckers' heads:

Twenty men stand watching the muckers.
Stabbing the sides of the ditch
Where clay gleams yellow,

Driving the blades of their shovels
Deeper and deeper for the new gas mains
Wiping sweat off their faces
With red bandanas⋯ (CPCS: 10)

Sandburg writes about these muckers to show how tenacious people are. They work very hard just to make a few dollars to support their families. The symbol recurs in order to give prominence to this group of common people, showing the position of these people in Sandburg's mind. So "bandana" appears again (at least 8 times in CPCS) in "The Right to Grief":

Take your fill of intimate remorse, perfumed sorrow,
Over the dead child of a millionaire,
And the pity of Death refusing any check on the bank
Which the millionaire might order his secretary to scratch off
And get cashed⋯.
Yet before the majesty of Death they cry around the coffin
And wipe their eyes with red bandanas and sob when the priest says, "God have mercy on us all. " ⋯ (CPCS: 12)

It deals with a man who has just lost his three–year old daughter. In the poem, Sandburgshows how compassionate he really is. But this time they used the red bandanas to wipe their tears instead of "sweat" in "Muckers": "Yet before the majesty of death they cry around the coffin and wipe their eyes with red bandanas". The bandana also symbolizes a sense of balance in spirit and relief of pains for the family members as they experience the worst feelings in the world.

Another recurring symbol, for example, is "poppy". In CPCS, on Page 60 is the poem "Poppies", on Page 365 is "Crossing Ohio When Poppies Bloom in Ashtabula", on Page 683 is "Psalm of the Bloodbank" containing "poppy" ⋯ The symbol "poppy" appears 18 times.

The recurring symbols chosen here happen to be with red color in the poems. It seems we can try to conclude that Sandburg likes the color— "blood red" as he describes in "Poppies" on page 60 in CPCS. And what does "red" stand for? It can stand for "passion", "revolution" of his socialism, and can be nothing, only the color and things he likes. But it is one of Sandburg's unique characters in his poetry. At least the recurring symbols emphasize some images.

Free and Narrative Style

Sandburg's free style has been mentioned many times in the thesis here. It is unnecessary to discuss more about the obvious style playing a role in his poetry's popularity. But one thing, that is, William Butler Yeats' coming to America and his encouragement should be mentioned.

In 1914, the great Irish poet and playwright Yeats came to Chicago. Sandburg and his wife were invited to attend the banquet. Yeats challenged his select audience that night to "encourage American poets to strive to become very simple, very humble. You poet must put the fervor of his life into his work, giving you his emotions before the world, the evil with the good…. Poetry that is naturally simple, that might exist as the simplest prose, should have instantaneousness of effect, provided it finds the right audience. " Furthermore, Yeats said, "A great many poets use vers libre because they think it is easier to write than rhymed verse, but it is much more difficult. " (CSLW: 87) Sandburg listened and got enthralled, then he stood up to read his new poem. And then he confirmed his style, and in high spirits he began to write more and more poetry with new vigor that spring.

About his narrative style, since his college days he had begun to show his narrative characteristics in his poetry creation. In the spring of 1901 in Lombard College, Sandburg was elected the editor of *The Lombard Review*, then he began to rhyme: "Under the headings of 'Roundabout' or 'At the Sign of the Brass Facet' I threw in a variety of scribblings, even rhymed verse. " (EWC: 111) The following pieces are to exhibit his narrative style:

PUMP POPPYCOCK

"Have a drink?"

"You drink. "

"No, you go on. "

"O, pshaw now, I pumped this; drink. "

"No, you go ahead. "

" Well, if you insist, then, but—" (EWC: 111)

It is short, but narrative enough. To open CPCS, narrative poems are not difficult to find, and the most striking one is the long single narrative poem *The People, Yes* (from Page 439 to 617). But for convenience, I would like to choose a short one to study:

AMBASSADORS OF GRIEF

There was a little fliv of a woman loved one man and lost out. And she took up with another and it was a blank again. And she cried to God the whole layout was a fake and a frame–up. And when she took up with Number Three she found the fires burnt out, the love power, gone. And she wrote a letter to God and dropped it in a mail–box. The letter said:

O God, ain't here some way you can fix it so the little flivs of women, ready to throw themselves in front of railroad train for men they love cab have a chance I guessed the wrong keys, I battered on the wrong panel, I picked the wrong road.

O God, ain't there no way to guess again and start all over back where I had the keys in my hands, back where the road all came together and I had pick?

Washington, D. C. , dumped into a dump where to God—and no house number.

The way used in the poem is just the way of writing a short story about a lady's unfortunate fate. Fully it expresses Sandburg's narrative style. Also this style draws the common readers to read his poetry. It can also explain among the common people why short stories and novels are more popular than poems. The ordinary people tend to read more narrative things. So, narration in his poems should be another reason to make Sandburg's poetry accepted widely by the people, leading him to the people's poet a step forward again.

His Emphasis on Style

"Each authentic poet makes a style of his own. Sometimes this style is so clearly the poet's own that when he is imitated it is known who is imitated. Shakespeare, Villon, Li Po, Whitman—each sent forth his language and impress of thought and feeling from a different style of gargoyle spout. " [①] They are Sandburg's words about style from "Notes for Preface" of The Complete Poems of Carl Sandburg. Sandburg, after many experiments in poetry, decided to go his own way in style. He attached the importance to his own style all the time. For this purpose, he wrote "Style" to discuss it specially:

Style–go ahead talking about style.
You can tell where a man gets his style just
        as you can tell where Pavlowa got her legs
        or Ty Cobb his batting eye.
        Go on talking.

Only don't take my style away.
        It's my face.
        Maybe no good
                But anyway, my face.
I talk with it, I sing with it, I see, taste and feel with it, I know why I want to
keep it.

Kill my style
        and you break Pavlowa's legs,
        and you blind Ty Cobb's batting eye. (CPCS: 24)

---

① See "Notes for Preface" of The Complete Poems of Carl Sandburg, p xxx.

He thinks that asking where to get style is to ask "where Pavlowa got her legs". Style is important to him, so he begs: "Don't take my style away. /It's my face / Maybe not good / But anyway my face." Sandburg wrote so, and he did so. On his own way, he went on and on with his poetry. Style is his life of poetry. Without his own style, he has no popularity in his poetry.

Except the above, another feature of his poetry is, more often than not, his unity of poems was generally achieved not in the line itself (for he often divided clauses in the middle or even into thirds and fourths, for example in "Style" above), but through frequent rhetorical repetitions, and through modestly climactic conclusions.

Maybe the uniqueness of Sandburg's poetry is not so prominent, but it is this kind of uniqueness that makes it possible to distinguish his poetry from the others'. And it is this kind of unique feature that creates a unique Sandburg into the people's poet.

Ⅷ. Musicality in Sandburg's Poetry

Musicality concerns aesthetics, and poetics relates with aesthetics. And therefore musicality is chosen for discussion. But because of the ignorance in music of the author here, it is impossible to study Sandburg's poetry in terms of music. So, only through some superficial aspects will the musicality of his poetry be discussed, including how his poems were adapted into opera and music, how even his letter writing is poeticized, and how some of the elements contributing to his poetry's musicality work.

Adapted into Opera and Music

We know that opera and music are complexly beautiful. If works can be adapted into the two, most original works must be musical enough. We cannot say all of Sandburg's poems are musical, but some of them are really musical enough. But some of the poems in *Wind Song*, in which most are short ones, can be set into music, while some of the other longer ones can be adapted into opera.

The People, Yes is a long poem. American Playwright Norman Corwin and composer Earl Robinson created a one–act opera basing upon it and it was broadcast over the CBS (Columbia Broadcasting System) radio network on May 18, 1941. (LCS: 395)

About adaptation for music, at the Library of Congress, Archibald MacLeish, and Marian Lorraine, together with Sandburg himself, for a program given, set "Mr. Lincoln and His Gloves" and "Mr. Longfellow and His Boy" to music. (See LCS: 405) Take the latter poem as an example:

Mr. Longfellow and His Boy
(An old–fashioned recitation to be read aloud)

MR. LONGFELLOW, Henry Wadsworth Longfellow,
　　the Harvard Professor,
　　the poet whose pieces you see in all the schoolbooks,
"Tell me not in mournful numbers life is but an empty dream ···"
Mr. Longfellow sits in his Boston library writing,
Mr. Longfellow looks across the room
　　and sees his nineteen–year–old boy
propped up in a chair at a window,
home from the war,
a rifle ball through right and left shoulders···. (CPCS: 632–3)

Though the adapted music cannot be found, the original poem is like a nostalgic song. And by the line "Tell me not in mournful numbers", immediately we can think of Henry Wadsworth Longfellow's[1] beautiful poem "Psalm of Life". Really some of his poems had been set to music. Another instance is that in a letter to Harry Golden in 1961, Sandburg writes: "A phone call came today

---

　　[1]　Henry Wordsworth Longfellow, 1807–1882, the best–known 19th–century poet in the United States, he wrote *The Song of Hiawatha* (1855) and a translation (1865–1867) of *Dante's Divine Comedy*S.

form Gwynn Steinbeck saying she has done music to eight poems of mine and that music people who have heard the discs say they are great. She is bringing the discs out here next week and I will hear them and we will discuss them. " (LCS: 538)

And even in the year of 2002, Sandburg's poems were used to set to jazz music as "The Carl Sandburg Project" in his hometown Galesburg, Illinois. Here is the key part about this from an article with the title of "Jazz Concert to Feature Works Based on Sandburg Poems" (attention to the underlined part by the author herein.):

> The Matt Wilson Quartet with guest vocalist Dawn Thomson will perform selections from Wilson's jazz composition "The Carl Sandburg Project" at 8 p. m. , Friday, April 19, in Jay Hall (rescheduled from Kresge), Ford Center for the Fine Arts, at Knox College, Galesburg, Illinois. The free, public concert is presented as part of the Sandburg Days Festival.
>
> "Sandburg's poetry has an honest and free-flowing style," said Wilson, a native of Knoxville and an award-winning jazz percussionist and composer. "The Carl Sandburg Project explores a broad range of improvised styles, including use of an electronic sampler as a part of the sonic palette. "
>
> "Sandburg was 'the people's poet' and a musician," Wilson said. "In one of his poems Sandburg wrote, ' Music is when your ears like what they hear'. "①

But because of shortage in this material, the author here feels sorry not to give more proofs to study this point further. Maybe that has been enough to say Sandburg's poetry is musical since our contemporary musician still tries to connect Sandburg's poetry with music.

Poeticized Letter Writing

The musicality not only lies in his poetry but also in his letter writing. A-

---

① See http: //deptorg. knox. edu/newsarchive/news_ events/2002/matt_ wilson_ sandburg. html. 18 May 2004.

mong many of his letters to many of his friends and other correspondents, some letters are actually poems; that is to say, he tried to make his letters musical by poeticizing his letters. Alfred Harcourt later recalled: "···and what correspondence! Every letter he wrote, even of humdrum details, seemed to sing. Everything Carl writes is music and full of wisdom." (CSLW: 72)

In July 1917, Sandburg wrote to Mrs. William Vaughn Moody:

Dear Harriet Moody,

  From strong hills about Omaha

  and singing bushes of prairie roses

  I send you a Sunday afternoon greeting.

  Luck and health to you.

       Carl Sandburg (LCS: 120)

In about March 1918, Sandburg wrote to Henry Justin Smith in the same way:

Dear Henry:

  I find the scenery

  along the Northwestern Railroad

  in the Minnesota river bottoms

  up to specifications.

  Keep the hills

      as they are.

  And let the birches be.

  These are my recommendations.

  Do as you like about them.

  Only remembering I send

      a special prayer

      for the birches.

  I pray for all standing white memorials

  of people I care for.

     C. S. (LCS: 127)

The two letters extracted from The Letters of Carl Sandburg can be regarded as pure poems except with the letter format. Actually in the book LCS (The Letters of Carl Sandburg) there are many similar poeticized letters. It contains at least about 16 letters that can be absolutely considered to be poems, and some others are more or less, or half like poems. To make it clear, the following table concerns the letters that can be seen as real poems according to their letter bodies:

Table 8　　　　　**Poeticized Letter Writing in LCS**

Date	Addressee	Page
May 1, 1898	The Sandburg family	3
June 4, 1907	Reuben W. Borough	47
May 9, 1908	Lillian Paula Steichen	70–72
May 13, 1908	Lillian Paula Steichen	72
Nov. 21, 1908	Paula Sandburg	80
July, 1917	Mrs. William Vaughn Moody	120
Circa March, 1918	Henry Justin Smith	127
Sept. 27, 1918	Alice Corbin Henderson	141
Oct. 10, 1918	Amy Lowell	142
Circa September, 1919	Edward Steichen	167
Dec. 27, 1920	Alfred Stieglitz	195
September, 1922	Paula Sandburg	217
Nov. 19, 1922	Eugene V. Debs	219
March 3, 1928	H. L. Mencken	257
Fall, 1939	Helga Sandburg	376
Circa 1951	Don Shoemaker	474
Circa July 1, 1957	William G. Stratton	514

Note: The book contains 551 pages. And the letters spans 65 years from 1898 to 1963.

For comparison, now a short one of the sixteen letters is taken as an illustration from Page 219 to 220 of the book, and a poem with similar length is extracted from CPCS, to give further explanation:

1

There was a tree of stars sprang up on a vertical panel of the south.

And a monkey of stars climbed up and down in this tree of stars.

And a monkey picked stars and put them in his mouth, tall up in a tree of stars shining in a south sky panel.

I saw this and I saw what it meant and what it means was five, six, seven, that's all, five, six, seven.

Oh hoh, yah hay, loo loo, the meaning was five, six, seven, five, six, seven.

Panels of changing stars, sashes of vapor, silver tails of meteor streams, washes and rockets of fire—

It was only a dream, oh hoh, yah, yah, loo loo, only a dream, five, six, seven, five, six, seven. (CPCS: 401–2)

2

You will always be close to us. The only way we can decently remember you and what you left with us here will be a certain way of living it, may dying it.

And some day I hope to get the strong truth about those hands of yours into a poem. It's only a hope but I'll try for it and learn something.

My signature goes for the whole bunch under our roof. As you went away out the front door one of them said, "He's a big rough flower."

With you it isn't really a good—by because you are still here. (LCS: 219–20)

Without the immediate notes, most people would feel it difficult to judge which one is the original poem and which one is the letter at the first glance. To study in detail from the appearance, the only difference lies in the fact that the first one is with the first line indented and the second one is with hanging indent. In fact the first one is a poem with a title of "Monkey of Stars" from CPCS, and the second one is from LCS.

Additionally, some of his letters are very poetic, though they don't bear the arrangement of poetic lines. Here is a letter from Sandburg to Paula:

It's been mystically wonderful lately, that backyard, with a half moon through the poplars to the south in a haze, and rustlings⋯on the ground and in the trees, a sort of grand "Hush–hush, child. " And as the moon slanted in last night and the incessant rustlings went on softly, I thought that if we are restless and fail to love life big enough, it's because we have been away too much form the moon and the elemental rustlings. (CSB: 230)

And we can try to change it into a poem of free verse:

It's been mystically wonderful lately, that backyard,
With a half moon through the poplars to the south in a haze, and rustlings⋯
On the ground and in the trees, a sort of grand "Hush–hush, child. "
And as the moon slanted in last night and the incessant rustlings went on softly,
I thought that if we are restless and fail to love life big enough,
It's because we have been away too much form the moon and the elemental rustlings.

Clearly, Sandburg inserts his poetry writing into letter writing and he emotionally melts musicality into his letter writing too! About this, he says: "Writing letters too is writing" (CSLW: 94) .

To go back to the table hereinbefore, because the book is edited chronologically, according to the study of the dates herein discussed, the table shows that before Sandburg was fifty years old he was energetic and his letter writing of this time is more poeticized, and more musical. After about his fifty, most of his letters are of only one long paragraph. And before this, especially when he was young, a letter was usually paragraphed into several paragraphs; it's like or completely free verse!

To be brief, Sandburg's letter writing is poeticized, and some are even real poems, showing a tendency of musicality of his letter writing. And so his letter writing is mentioned and analyzed.

Key Elements of Musicality in His Poetry

The musicality of Sandburg's poetry contains several basic and necessary elements. Generally, three points can cover them nearly: the rhythm and rhyme in his poetry, lyric—like structure and theme of lyric.

First, the rhythm and rhyme in his poetry is analyzed. In spite of free verse, Sandburg's poetry bears much rhythm and rhymes. For example, in rhyme, sometimes end rhymes, sometimes internal rhymes, and sometimes slant rhymes are used within his poetic lines. Rhythm is one musical element in music too. The study of the poem "The Windy City" (used once more as an instance) can lead us to share the musical rhythm and rhyme (the numbers on the right stand for the line of the quoted part.):

The lean hands of wagon men	1
put out pointing fingers here,	2
picked this crossway, put it on a map,	3
set up their sawbucks, fixed their shotguns,	4
found a hitching place for the pony express,	5
made a hitching place for the iron horse,	6
the one—eyed horse with the fire—spit head,	7
found a homelike spot and said, "Make a home",	8
saw this corner with a mesh of rails, shuttling	9
people, shunting cars, shaping the junk of	10
the earth to a new city···. (CPCS: 271)	11

This is the first stanza of the poem. Taking it as lyric to analyze, we can group the rhymes into three, the first one broadly includes the italicized bold sounds as alliterative [s] and [s]; the second group is broadly the bold alliterative rhyme [p]; the third group includes the underlined slant rhymes as [s], [z] and [θ]; and the last rhyme is dynamic bold and shadowed sound of "ing" –[iŋ] . Meanwhile some slippery and smooth vowels make the lines sound more musical: [ʌ], 6 times; [ɔ] and [ɔː], 10 times; [au], 3 times; and [aiə], 4 times. These are all the key sounds to make a poem, or even an article and speech. Meanwhile in rhythm, for instance, some lines contain symmetrical and paralleled structure as in Line 3, Line 4 and Line 10. And since they are paralleled and symmetrical, the rhythm is finger-popping with a strong sound followed by one or two weak sound (s) like that in Line 2 ("∨" for strong, "—" for weak): ∨ — ∨ — ∨ —; in Line 4: ∨ — ∨ — ∨ — ∨ —; and in Line 10: ∨ — ∨ — ∨ — ∨ —. Generally and roughly, they show a kind of rule and rhythm.

The second element is his lyric—like structure. We take the same stanza to prove. We know that in a song, refrain is necessary. Though in it there is not complete refrain, for a poem, if we compare "a hitching place for the pony express" with the immediately following line "a hitching place for the iron horse" and "the one-eyed horse", we can in fact call them refrains of "a hitching place" and "horse". Simultaneously, in the last second line, "shunting cars" and "shaping the junk" can also be considered partial refrains, which are often necessary in a song. As sentences, they are short, simple and easy to understand, just meet the need of lyric.

Usually, lyric needs clear, profound and chantable theme with real emotion and popular language. [①] For Sandburg's poetry, mostly it bears such traits. So chantable theme is the third element of the musicality in his poetry. Because many of his poems are narrative, themes are very clear and profound. Like "The Windy City", it centers upon Chicago and Chicagoans as its theme; because of its rhythm, the lines are chantable. And of course Sandburg's emotion for Chicago was real and unusual since he lived there for so many years and was deeply attached to it, and meanwhile it was the place that he rose from and where he became a success.

As for language, it has been discussed in several places in the thesis: his language is common and vernacular, and can be an additional element of the musicality in his poetry. Therefore, most of his poetry must be, and in fact is, very popular among the people, like how pop songs work among the people, because most people are common ones, most of whom have no background of higher education, and colloquialism is what they love to speak and hear.

---

① See http: //www. music1234567. com/bbs/showthread. php? t = 1188. 31 May 2005.

Except "The Windy City", poems from CPCS like "Early Moon" on P86, "Laughing Corn" on P87, "Village in Late Summer" on P88, "Sand Scriplings" on P214, "Spring Grass" on P337, "People of the Eaves" on P418 and so on, are all of great musicality. But it does not mean these poems can be used as lyric directly without any adaptation. And of course it does not mean all Sandburg's poems bear these traits.

To have a retrospect of Chapter Four, it treats Sandburg's poetics on the basis of the commons, which turns into a mature people's poet. Throughout his practice and poetry, he insisted on his basic principle as a poet: A poet should function in the society. He did what he persisted. But what creates the people's poet on earth? Now it is clear that his poetic basis coming from and going into the people supports his poetics, and then his poetics creates his poetry of and for the people, and then his poetry creates the great people's poet. Concretely, his going into the people plays a basic role; his realistic principles direct him to write many realistic poems for the realistic people; his "sense of nativeness" makes him natively popular among the people; his common subjects and language draw the ordinary people's attention to read his poems; his heritage from Walt Whitman leads him on a trodden successful way to the second (to Whitman) people's poet's success; but finally, it's his unique poetic style and quality in his poetry that creates the people's poet to a greater degree.

In a word, Sandburg, the people's poet, creates his popular poetics fitting for the common people, and in return, his popular poetics plays a great role hammering him into the people's poet. They interbuild, intercreate and interact.

Chapter Five
The Sandburg Range and His Influence

Sandburg's range covers widely: From poetry to history, novel to prose, tales to music; from children to adults, whites to blacks, individuals to nation, and Americans to foreigners, etc.. As an extended part of the poet, his role of minstrel and musician, from which some elements of popular poetics can be abstracted, are within his range. He knows poetry can be both for reading and for reading aloud, and reading aloud and singing can be more touching than silent reading, and he brings poetic function and effect into the most degree. For being a minstrel, Sandburg popularized his poems and popularized poetry reading among the people; as a collector of *The American Songbag* and the people's poet, he studied music and ballads collected from the people and elementarily contributing to the formation of his popular poetics.

I. The Minstrel

The New Princeton Encyclopedia of Poetry and Poetics[1] defines a minstrel as "a general term for a professional performer of medieval lyric or narrative poetry." So, according to this definition, Sandburg was an approximate (not a strict) minstrel, because he really traveled around much and sang folk songs and his own poems which are narrative enough.

Sandburg as a minstrel can be traced back to 1920. When he gave a lecture

---

① Preminger, A. & T. V. F. Brogan, etc.. *The New Princeton Encyclopedia of Poetry* and Poetics. Princeton, New Jersey: Princeton University Press, 1993.

at Connell College, Iowa, he found a guitar behind the lectern and started to sing songs and his own poems. From then on, on more or less important occasions, he often traveled and tried to find chances to sing folk songs, ballads, and his own poems. And some of his poems were composed to music for his performance and other purposes as mentioned in Chapter Four. Another story and example occurred in 1925 for a dinner for Sinclair Lewis[1] who had just returned from England; Sandburg was invited to be present and asked to sing. And he sang with a borrowed guitar "The Buffalo Skinners" which is about starvation, blood, fleas, hides, entrails, thirst, and bad Indians. When Sandburg had finished, Sinclair Lewis cried, with tears streaming down his face and saying: "That's the America I came home to. That's it." (See CSLW: 118) How deeply Lewis was moved! And how soulfully Sandburg performed.

Not only songs did he sing, but he also read his own poems. On December 21, 1919, Sandburg gave a joint lecture–recital with another one, during which Sandburg read his poems (and, to his own guitar accompaniment, sang folk songs he had collected in his travels). He crooned his songs to an enthralled audience and discovered a new way to express himself and earn money at the same time. Later Emanuel Carnevali, associate editor of Poetry at that time, reviewed the show in February 1920. (CSB: 347) Starting from 1920 Sandburg spent many days each year giving lecture–recitals of poetry and folk songs, thriving on the travel and the stimulation of a live audience, and gathering an ever–growing repertoire of folk music and folklore.

As time went on, Sandburg was becoming a literary celebrity. His lectures broadened his audience and readers of his poetry. Every lecture–recital he gave brought new songs and variations of old songs for his ever–growing bag of music for playing and singing. Wherever he went he would discover more songs. And this kind of traveling brought his *The American Songbag* into birth.

In 1921, Sandburg had the second westward trip: minstrelsy. It was an ex-

---

① Lewis, (Harry) Sinclair, 1885–1951, American novelist who satirized middle–class America in his 22 works, including Babbitt (1922) and Elmer Gantry (1927). He was the first American to receive (1930) a Nobel Prize for literature.

tensive and successful trip west. He traveled and worked in California, Utah, Arizona, New Mexico, Texas, Arkansas and Tennessee. His lecture-recitals brought him the excitement and adulation of a live audience, which in turn boosted the sales of his books and enlarged greatly the number of his readers for his poetry. During the travel, he entertained various hosts, sometimes on borrowed guitars, trying out new songs he picked up from many places he visited.

The five-week six-thousand-mile journey offered him vivid colors and sparse, rugged western landscapes and he began to displace the city and the prairie as the terrain for his poetry. By "Prairie Woodland" we sense the heritage of his western journey of this time:

> Yellow leaves speak early November's heart on the river.
> Winding in prairie woodland the curves of the water course are a young woman's
>   breasts.
> Flutter and flutter go the spear shapes—it is a rust and a saffron always dropping
>   hour on hour.
> Sunny and windy the filtering shine of air passes the drivers, cornhuskers, farm-
>   ers, children in the fields.
> Red jags of sumach and slashes of shag-bark hickory are a crimson and gray cram-
>   ming pictures on the river glass···. (CPCS: 746)

This time Sandburg toured the country, and baptized his soul again as one of the commons. During the process, he kept in deep touch with the ordinary persons, dug out their happiness and pains, powerfulness and weakness. He not just read his poems, but also played the guitar and sang folk songs. He collected some songs, ballads and ditties into his The American Songbag (New York: Harcourt, Brace & Company, 1927). Meanwhile, his tour of reading, singing and playing, on the other hand, popularized his poetry among the common people. And the journey drew him again near the ordinary people. Compared with his first western hobo journey, this one was successful. After the journey, Sandburg told Louis Untermeyer that there was vitality in contemporary American literature which was "entirely lost on distant, dozing New York editors and columnists. " (CSB: 376–77) Maybe because of this kind of deep sentiment, for the rest of his life, he contributed more poetry and songs directly to the people. And the people not only became his subjects, but also his audience and his readers.

The following event can be regarded as the climax of Sandburg's being a minstrel. At the end of 1933 when he was 55 years old, Sandburg received a letter on White House stationery from Eleanor Roosevelt, who was American diplomat, writer, and First Lady of the United States (1933–1945) as the wife of President Franklin D. Roosevelt. It says: "Miss Frances Perkins [Roosevelt's Secretary of Labor and the first female Cabinet member] tells me that you will be good enough to come sometime for the night to play for my husband. I think a Sunday night in January will be perfect, if you and Mrs. Sandburg can come, and practically any night that you find convenient will do. " He did not expect Paula to travel with him, and he responded with pleasure to Eleanor Roosevelt's invitation. (See CSB: 495) He offered his service with pleasure and pride, and this was the highest recognition for his role as a minstrel.

Being partly a minstrel, Sandburg collected many folk songs and ballads and popularized his own poems and poetry reading by reading them aloud and singing. And it drew his poetry closer to the common people, and it further improved his poetry's nature of affinity with the people.

II. "Mr. Song–Bug's Sand–bang" [①]:
The American Songbag

On the way of Sandburg's development into the people's poet, growing into a minstrel is the secondary line for the poet's maturity to some degree. It was just this secondary line that produced finally *The American Songbag*. And his second western journey as analyzed above especially contributes to the publication of his *The American Songbag* in 1927.

[①] See *Letters of Carl Sandburg*, p. 70.

The American Songbag is a collection of 280 songs, ballads, ditties, coming from voices of common men and women, who, "speak, murmur, cry, yell, laugh, pray"[1] . Herein, originally the songs and ditties are not the thesis's purpose, and not the emphasis of the study. But ballad, again according to *The New Princeton Encyclopedia of Poetry and Poetics*[2] , is "one of the if not the most important forms of folk poetry", and often "short and narrative". As defined here, it concerns, or, is, poem, so several ballads are selected to show in terms of theme and contents how Sandburg, both as a minstrel and a people's poet, approaches and expresses the things about masses.

From his second western journey, we see how he approached the people and collected folks and ballads. He collected songs even since his hobo days, filling his pocket notebooks with lyrics and using his own simple notation system to jot down melodies he heard and collected. And audience and readers were willing to offer him more songs and ballad; these people, most of who were anonymous, included IWW leaders and labor organizers feeding him prison and jail songs and labor anthems.

And at the Eclectic Club at Wesleyan University in Connecticut, he first heard "Foggy, Foggy Dew," which became one of his favorite ballads and songs, and which he collected into his *The American Songbag*:

When I was a bach'lor, I lived by myself,
I worked at the weaver's trade;
The only, only thing I did that was wrong
Was to woo a fair young maid.
I wooed her in the winter-time
And in the summer, too;
And the only, only thing I did that was wrong,
Was to keep her from the foggy, foggy dew.

---

① Sandburg, Carl. *The American Songbag*. New York: Harcourt, Brace and Company, 1927: viii.

② Preminger, A. & T. V. F. Brogan, etc.. *The New Princeton Encyclopedia of Poetry* and Poetics. Princeton, New Jersey: Princeton University Press, 1993.

Oh, I am a bach'lor, I live with my son;

We work at the weaver's trade;

And ev'ry single time I look into his eyes

He reminds me of the fair young maid.

He reminds me of the winter–time

And of the summer too;

And the many many times that I held her in my arms,

Just to keep her from the foggy, foggy dew. (AS: 15)

And the explanatory words of the melody goes like this in the book: "After hearing it sung with a guitar at Schlogl's one evening in Chicago, D. W. Griffith telegraphed two days later from New York to Lloyd Lewis in Chicago, 'send verses Foggy Dew stop tune haunts me but am not sure of the words stop please do this as I am haunted by the song.'" [sic] (AS: 14) Obviously, it was a love story of an ordinary person, and the song was moving. No wonder Sandburg takes it as "a great condensed novel of real life."

Robert Frost gave Sandburg the tune and verses of "Whisky Johnny" (See AS: 403) and "Blow the Man Down," (See AS: 404) which he had learned when he was a boy in San Francisco. (See CSB: 443) And "Hallelujah, I'm a Bum," is a ballad he learned "from harvest hands who worked in the wheat fields of Pawnee County" in Kansas during his 1897 hobo journey west. During the height of the IWW movement, it was adopted as Wobbly theme song. The original verse reads as follows:

1. Oh, why don't you work

           Like other men do?

           How the hell can I workP

When there's no work to do?

           Hallelujah, I'm a bum,

           Hallelujah, bum again,

           Hallelujah, give us a handout,

           To revive us again.

2. Oh, I love my boss

And my boss loves me,

And that is the reason

I'm so hungry,

    Hallelujah, etc..

3. Oh, the springtime has came

And I'm just out of jail,

Without any money,

Without any bail.

    Hallelujah, etc..

4. I went to a house,

And I knocked on the door;

A lady came out, says,

"You been here before. "

    Hallelujah, etc..

5. I went to a house

And I asked for a piece of bread;

A lady came out, says,

"The baker is dead. "

    Hallelujah, etc..

6. When springtime does come,

O won't we have fun,

We'll throw up our jobs

And we 'll go on the bum.

    Hallelujah, etc..

    (AS: 184)

    Typically it is a ballad containing 5 stanzas with recurrent refrains as "Hallelujah, etc" appearing in each stanza, and "I went to a house" two times in Stanza 4 and 5. Though it is a ballad from the commons, it seems a description of Sandburg himself. For example, "I am bum", and Sandburg was once a bum; "I knocked on the floor; / a lady came out, says, / 'You've been here before. '", here it seems to be about the experience that after his first time hobo journey west he came back into his own home—the only door without knocking. In fact, from the ballad, we see through a bum, or an ordinary person's hard and tough life. But they still wish spring come to "go on the bum". Sandburg was so curious about the vagrant past of songs in which he could recall and share sense of hobo life he once experienced and the feeling vagrants had on their way from overseas to the American highlands, prairies and frontier. And the study of musical migration could often mirror the nation's history.

After he came back from his second westward journey of minstrelsy, his A-merican "songbag" had been filled with country songs, prairie songs, war songs, jail songs, songs of love and cities and death, and all other kinds belonging to the people. Sandburg was such a minstrel and poet who hunted for the songs people made up, and then sang them.

The American Songbag was published in 1927 by Broadcast Music Inc.. And Sandburg was regarded as the father of the current interest in American Folk music. Finally, Sandburg's own words are used to end the topic of discussion:

> The book begins with a series of Drama and Portraits rich with the human diversity of the United States. There are Love Tales Told in Song, or Colonial Revolutionary Antique, some of them have the feel of the black walnut, of knickerbockers, silver shoebuckles, and the earliest colonial civilization. Out of the selection of Pioneer Memories, one may sing with the human waves that swept across the Alleghenies and settled the Middle West, later taking the Great Plains, the Rocky Mountains, the West Coast. The notable distinctive American institution, the black-faced minstrel, stands forth in a separate section. Mexican border songs give the breath of the people above and below the Rio Grande. One section contains ballads chiefly from the southern mountain. (CSLW: 119)

Sandburg, both the minstrel and musician, extracting nutrition from the common people, and again feeding back the people, is such a great poet of the people.

III. Obliging the Young

Sandburg never forgot to foster young poets and educate the people. He often encouraged children to write poetry to become poets. To arouse children, in the preface of his *Early Moon*[①], Sandburg writes: "Should children write poetry? Yes, whenever they feel like it. If nothing else happens they will find it a graining for writing and speaking in other fields of human work and play. No novelist has been a worse writer for having practiced poetry. Many a playwright, historian, essayist, editorial writer, could have improved his form by experimenting with poetry." (SR: 113) Sandburg takes writing poetry as a basic education for children and even writers. He is right. (Many nations take poetry into consideration in basic language education, among which China has been doing so.) And he stressed the importance of poetry writing in other styles of writing such as those of playwright, historian, essayist, etc. Really many famous novelists wrote poetry before novel writing, and many wrote poetry while they did other style of writing. Sandburg himself is a good example. He produced much poetry, while he was writing biography on Lincoln. And to judge him fairly, sometimes his Lincoln biography is more popular than his poetry in the United States.

To foster more young poets, Sandburg always could give helpful advice to those who aspired to become poets. He was all the time to pull no punches to the young promising ones as shown in a letter he wrote to a Mrs. Cox: "The only procedure by which you can find out whether you have salable poetry is to type it neatly and send it to all editors of periodicals and publishers of books whom you think might possibly be interested. This is the only practical suggestion I can make as to the very practical problem you present. Considering the time I have given to the writing of verse I have received in payment of a wage per hour considerably less than a CWA worker and therefore do not qualify as an advisor from

---

① Sandburg, Carl. *Early Moon*. New York: Harcourt, Brace and Company, 1930.

the practical viewpoint. " (CSLW: 101) It is both a kind suggestion from Sandburg and his attitude towards poetry. He thinks by writing poetry as an art seldom can a poet make a living. If one wants to earn a living by poetry, maybe and mostly he will be a failure. To write poetry, one must like it instead of making money by it. As he says his earning in poetry per hour should be "considerably less than a CWA (Civil Works Administration) worker". For Mrs. Cox, practically he suggests she send her "salable poetry" to "editors of periodicals and publishers of books". That is to say, the poems should and have to be accepted by the market, means that poems should be judged by the people; or as an extropoet (see Section I, Chapter Four) does, a poet should not indulge in himself so much, and he should choose his subjects more impersonal subjects to make him and his poetry more popular.

Ⅳ. His Influence on Modern Poetry

As the people's poet, Sandburg's influence on modern poetry is powerful, and some of his poems have been analyzed as a necessity in Chapter Three and Chapter Four. For example, his succession to Whitman–style free verse is a continuous influence. He carries this style forward and melts it into today's free verse and fills something new into poetry as Mark Van Doren, in his introduction to Sandburg's Harvest Poems, stated: "Carl Sandburg, like all of the other American poets who came into prominence with him, brought something back to poetry that had been sadly missing in the early years of this century. It was humor, the indispensable ingredient of art as it is of life···a proof that reality is held in honor and in love. " (HP: 9) Also he was one of the representatives of Chicago Renaissance① and one of the pioneers of Beat Generation. Here in the

---

① The Chicago Renaissance, providing one example of a literature growing self–consciously out of its region, may be narrowly defined as covering the period from 1900–1920, when its most characteristic productions appeared; but, broadly conceived, it embraces the years 1890–1925, including earlier writers and journalists such as Eugene Field, George Ade, Henry Blake Fuller, Hamlin Garland, Robert Herrick, and William Vaughn Moody.

following is a concise summary.

Firstly, during the period of Chicago Renaissance, Sandburg was one of the three voices most typically associated with Chicago's literary heyday, with the other two being Vachel Lindsay and Edgar Lee Masters. They are undisputedly considered to be the main poets of the Chicago Renaissance, and for a time they were very highly regarded and widely read. Also Sandburg was involved into one of the several crucial focal events: the creation of Poetry: A Magazine of Verse (1912), the publication of Edgar Lee Masters' Spoon River Anthology (1915) and Sandburg's Chicago Poems (1916), and the two texts are credited with inventing "modern" poetry in the United States. Sandburg, like other early practitioners, discovered the city of Chicago and the common people and common things as a possible literary subject; and he was, still like his other companioss, the first to document Chicago's unique scenery, the people's speech rhythms, ethnic dialects, and their diverse occupations.

Secondly, he liberated poetry from genteel tradition. Before Sandburg, roughly speaking, Whitman was alone. One of Sandburg's great contributions to modern poetry should be his succession to Whitman's free verse. He carried it much forward. Readers can find Sandburg's views are that of the Populist—the idea that the people should be central and focus. And his use of the idiom of the streets—words and phrases uttered by what he called "the mob" is everywhere in his poetry. In his poetry, Sandburg never feels unabashed to express anger, pride in strength and tender compassion, but he never tries to show sharp ironies or the bookishness in his poems. Actually his mood is partly of American bard, but completely breaking away from the genteel tradition.

And Sandburg did his best to loosen poem's structure and make it more flexible. He liberated poetic line endings from the restriction of rhyme, broadened poetic language by using words and rhythms of the streets and workers. Poetry, under his pen, is much freer than ever before; and poetry, under his pen, can express more than past; and poetry, under his pen, voices more for more people than foretime.

Thirdly, Sandburg insisted on being unaligned, and so he kept poetry varied in form. Ever since Sandburg's first poems were published in Poetry, Ezra Pound and Sandburg had begun to exchange poems and compliments. But later, when Pound tried to advise him to join the new movement of Imagism, Sandburg expressed that he preferred to prefer his own unaligned way to continue to narrate and rhyme the common people as the center of his interest.

After World WarI, some of American writers left America for Europe, as Eliot and Pound had done earlier. But Sandburg stayed on with some others such as Frost staying in New England, William Carlos Williams in Rutherford, Wallace Stevens in Hartford, and Marianne Moore in Brooklyn and so on. But the poets in America seldom visited Pound and Eliot and they did not appear to follow them. In his poems, Sandburg attacks injustice and hypocrisy with anger and in compassion for the ordinary and the underprivileged people and expresses constantly his love for family, friends, and humanity—especially the masses. In such a way, Sandburg stayed firmly rooted in the States, going on his own unaligned way, writing about American native subjects, and keeping modern poetry varied.

Fourthly, Sandburg has been regarded as one of the pioneers of Beat Generation. Though Eliot, Pound, and the New Critics' powerful influences lasted to the end of World War II, their influence was somewhat only modish to be corralled into European culture. At this time near Sandburg's last years, Beat Generation rose in another direction. Allen Ginsberg (1926–1997) as its representative was among the foremost spokesmen for a new freedom, taking Emerson, Whitman, and Sandburg as their pioneers in structure and language.

For the Beat Generation, they felt that Sandburg–like liberation from poetic genteel tradition was perhaps much closer to the American temperament of that time than Eliot and Pound and other poets' poetry. The first three lines of Ginsberg's "Howl" may remind us of the difference and similarity between the two:

I saw the best minds of my generation destroyed by madness, starving hysterical naked,

drag ging themselves through the negro streets at dawn looking for an angry fix,

ange lheaded hipsters burning for the ancient heavenly connection to the starry dynamo in the machinery of night, ...①

Generally, the lines are a little longer than Sandburg's, but we see more similarity: freedom of diction and that from linear restriction, native subject matter from the streets, the real (like Sandburg) American temperament. Good or bad, they are American.

Finally, as to the comparison between Sandburg and T. S. Eliot, in Section III, Chapter Three, there is a discussion about Sandburg's *Four Preludes* and Eliot's *The Waste Land*, and more details can be seen in the section. But without specific data, it is difficult to tell whether Sandburg had an influence on Eliot. Yet, one thing can be sure that Sandburg's *Four Preludes* was written before Eliot's *The Waste Land*, and even without the objective reasons analyzed in Section III, Chapter Three, at least it is likely for the two to be equally influential in modern poetry.

Sandburg's influence on modern poetry is not limited to America. We will have more discussion in the immediate Section V. But here we quote a professor's statement to give us a glance into it. Professor Royal Snow, from Queens University in Kingston, Ontario, Canada gave such comments on Sandburg: "Your reading here has done a world of good. It represented the first invasion of modern poetry into Canadian universities; somewhat earthquake – like in its effects, but a lot of crystallized opinion had been cracked. " (CSLW: 100)

V. Among the People

Among the people, Sandburg's influence is undoubtedly great. Two points can testify this. One is to see who read Sandburg; and the other is how the people admit him. But the two points can only be like the Chinese saying: A leaf before the eye shuts out Mount Tai. That is to say, the analysis here is impossi-

---

① See *The Norton Anthology of Modern Poetry.* New York: W. W. Norton and Company Inc. , 1973: 1121.

ble to involve all his influence among the people.

First of all, who Read Sandburg? The 40th President of the United States (1981–1989) Ronald Wilson Reagan (1911–2004) should have read Sandburg. The excerpt is a proof, which is from Reagan's speech about Nation's economic recovery: "···The poet Carl Sandburg wrote, 'The republic is a dream. Nothing happens unless first a dream. ' And that's what makes us, as Americans, different. We've always reached for a new spirit and aimed at a higher goal. ··· As Sandburg said, all we need to begin with is a dream that we can do better···All we need to have is faith, and that dream will come true. All we need to do is act, and the time for action is now. "①

Not only once did Reagan cite Sandburg's words and thoughts. On May 9, 1982 the famous Eureka Speech was given as Commencement Address on the Eureka College Campus on the fiftieth anniversary of his graduation. It was about major foreign policy challenging the Soviet Union to a new era of negotiations to reduce nuclear arms and this speech heralded the beginning of the end of the cold war:

The fourth point is arms reduction. I know that this weighs heavily on many of your minds. In our 1931 Prism, we quoted Carl Sandburg, who in his own beautiful way quoted the Mother Prairie, saying, "Have you seen a red sunset drip over one of my cornfields, the shore of night stars, the wave lines dawn upon a wheat valley?" What an idyllic scene that paints in our minds—and what a nightmarish prospect that a huge mushroom cloud might someday destroy such beauty··· ②

The citation by Reagan can be found on P80 of CPCS, in "Prairie" of Cornhusker. Even if at this time Sandburg had not been so famous, after President Reagan's citation and advertisement, Sandburg would have become famous. In fact, it was because of his great influence that his words were quoted. And his position as the people's poet in the common people's heart, even in a president's heart, was obviously high enough.

---

① See: http://www. reaganlegacy. org/speeches/reagan. economic. recovery. htm. 8 March 2004.
② See: http://reagan. eureka. edu/beyond/speech_ text. html. 26 March 2005.

Another president—the 35th President of the United States (1961–1963) is J. F. Kennedy (1917–1963) who was likely to read Sandburg. Because in a letter to Harry Golden in 1961 Sandburg writes: "Do I recall your saying that J. F. Kennedy recited 'Cool Tombs' or did he merely mention that he was familiar with it?" (LCS: 539) However, further argumentation cannot be given for lack of data. But we can guess it was probably a fact.

And netizens have become his readers. On the front page of the special website of Sandburg-http: //www. carl–sandburg. com, the following words are shown: "This website is dedicated to Sandburg–Chicago Poems. On the bottom of front page is the statistics of visitors of the website since Sept. 1998, the displayed number is 350369 at 5: 06: 31 PM, Sunday, January 9, 2005 while I am reading the website. This is another evidence of his great number of readers in the past and at present.

Next, let's get to know a reader from natural science—Frank Lloyd Wright (1869–1959), a famous American architect writing a letter of praise for Sandburg's Rootabaga Stories: "I read your fairy tales nearly every night before I go to bed. They fill a long felt want–poetry ···. O man! the beauty of the White Horse Girl and the Blue Wind Boy. And the fairies dancing on the wind–swept corn. All the children that will be born in the Middle West during the next hundred years are peeping at you now, Carl—between little pink fingers—smiling, knowing that in this Beauty they have found a friend. " (SR: 91) We can imagine the excitement of Frank Wright when he was reading Sandburg. And we can imagine his readers involve many from different careers.

But the most elaborate and professional investigation about who read Sandburg was done by Charles H. Compton of the St. Louis Public Library. The results show his readers can be grouped into various categories of people:

> To the stenographer: "By day the skyscraper looms in the sun and has a soul···It is the men and women, boys and girls, so poured in and out all day, that give the building a soul of dreams and thoughts and memories. "
>
> To the typist: "Smiles and tears of each office girl go into the soul of the

building, just the same as the master–men who rule the building. "

To the Negro reader: "I am the nigger. Singer of songs, Dancer····. Softer than fluff of cotton····. Harder than dark earth Roads beaten in the sun by the bare feet of slaves. "

To the minister: "Lay me on the anvil, O God. Beat me and hammer me into a crowbar. Let me pry loose old walls. Let me lift and loosen old foundations. "

To the newspaper reporter: "Speak softly–the sacred cows may hear. Speak easy–the sacred cows must be fed. "

To the police clerk: "Out of the whirling womb of time come millions of men and their feet crowd the earth and they cut one another's throats for room to stand and among them all are two thumbs alike. "

To the musician: "A man saw the whole world as a grinning skull and cross bones····. Then he went to a Mischa Elman concert····. Music washed something or other inside him. Music broke down and rebuilt something or other in his head and heart····. He was the same man in the world as before. Only there was a singing fire and a climb of roses everlastingly over the world he looked on. "

To the waitress: " Shake back your hair, O red–headed girl. Let go your laughter and keep your two proud freckles on your chin. "

To the manager of a beauty parlor: "The woman named Tomorrow sits with a hairpin in her teeth and takes her time and does her hair in the way she wants it and fastens at last the last braid and coil and put the hairpin where it belongs and turns and drawls: Well, what of it? My grandmother, Yesterday, is gone. What of it? Let the dead be dead. "

To the book agent: "This is a good book? Yes? Throw it at the moon–Let her go–Spang–This book for the moon····. Yes? And then–other books, good books, e-ven the best books–shoot ' em with a long twist at the moon–Yes?"

To the man who puts himself down a laborer: "Men who sunk the pilings and mixed the mortar are laid in graves where the wind whistles a wild song without words. " (CSLW: 102)

As shown above, people from nearly every walk of life express what they feel after reading Sandburg's poetry. The concrete people can all be found and located in CPCS. Stenographer in "Skyscraper"; typist in Section 89 of PY;

Negro in "Psalm of the Bloodbank"; minister in "Mag"; reporter in "Fellow Citizens"; police in "Fame If Not Fortune"; musician in "Prairie Waters by Nights"; waitress in Section 44 of PY; a parlor worker in Section 47 of PY; an agent in "Onion Days"; and a laborer everywhere in CPCS. From what they say we sense the value of Sandburg's poetry in the common people's minds. And the common persons are able to find their prototype and their own value in his poems. A lieutenant uses his words to explain the reasons in his letter crossing from Tokyo to Seattle with four other Navy men in October 1945: "I had brought with me a copy of *The People, Yes*. We read the book and it was a great source of reassurance. We were able to feel a sense of inclusion, of participation in a heritage which we had come close to forgetting while we were supposed to be fighting for it. " (CSLW: 99)

Clearly, Sandburg's readers involve many. It is the most powerful evidence of his poetry's powerful influence on modern poetry and among the people. As a representative of blacks, Langston Hughes (1902–1967), a well-known black poet, said "For Carl Sandburg–the American poet whom I most admire. " (CSLW: 100) . Hughes, also claimed Sandburg as one of his primary influences, and in his eyes, Sandburg did "an insightful, colorful portrayals of black life in America from the twenties through the sixties. "[1] Really Sandburg did much work for American blacks as discussed in Chapter Two.

How is his influence abroad? In March, 1920, the conservative French journal Mercure de France printed a twenty–six–page article by Jean Catel praising the poetry of Sandburg and Frost. He admired Sandburg's "broad vision, profound human sympathies," his forceful personality and his original poetic forms. (CSB: 350-1) And he once went to visit Sweden and was welcomed warmly, and his poems were once exhibited in former Soviet Union. And surely, many scholars all over the world are studying him, and many students from many countries are reading him from literary books. (For instance, many Chinese College students know his famous "Fog" .)

---

[1] http: //www. poets. org/poets/poets. cfm? prmID = 84. 6 March 2004.

After his death, nearly six thousand people gathered at the Lincoln Memorial in Washington in September 1967 for a national Sandburg tribute sponsored by Chief Justice Earl Warren; United Nations ambassador Arthur Goldberg; and, personages from Sandburg's home state of Illinois, including Governor Otto Kerner, Senators Everett Dirksen and Charles Percy, and former senator Paul Douglas. With Margaret, Helga and Barney, Paula Sandburg was there to hear poets Mark Van Doren and Archibald MacLeish giving eulogies. President Lyndon Johnson arrived unannounced to praise "this vital, exuberant, wise and gentle man. " (CSB: 703–4)

Among the people, this is Sandburg, the people's poet, and his sweeping influence via popular poetics! He "not only sings the people but is sung by them. "

Conclusion

I. "Tradition Is a Bottomless Hole!"

For Sandburg, it is important for a popular poet to break through the restrictions of traditional poetry. The free style permits him to express the voices of the people unrestrictedly, giving him wider scope of common expressions to speak out what metrical verse cannot do. The breakthrough in tradition is a footstone of his popular poetics, and it is crucial for later development of modern poetry.

Talking of art tradition, a Chinese artist Zhan Wang[①] once said: "Tradition is a bottomless hole!" He meant if you want to have a development in modern art, you have to try to deviate from tradition. A piece of traditional work is like a drop of water in the sea. Even if you put a drop of holy water in it, you cannot find it at all in the boundless sea. And Sandburg should understand this point. So he liberated himself and poetic lines from tradition to some degree and freed modern poetry in some aspects.

Since all civilization is the product of the corresponding historical society and culture, the tradition of metrical verse can be regarded historically as one of social products. As time goes, society develops forward, and the production of a society will be surely different. The form of metrical verse is unlikely to be unchanged. So for any kind of poets, intropoets or extropoets, it is better to change their poetry to adapt to his contemporary society and its culture. The society

---

① Zhan Wang (1962–): a conceptual artist, who teaches at the Central Institute of Fine Arts in Beijing, China.

changes, the persons are different, and then there should be the possibility of poetic change. On the other hand, tradition including poetry becomes and should become reminiscence if it is still beautiful and useful, and this kind of tradition cannot be thrown off completely, for it will die out gradually on the course of inheritance. Sandburg's free verse is a timely change and product of traditional poetry. He might have realized if he had gone on along the poetic tradition, his poetry would have been "a drop of water in the sea." Though we cannot deny he could have been a successful traditional poet, it was not a must. However, his non–traditional free verse proved his success and drew much attention from many people. But how do we judge a successful traditional poet? We still take Robert Frost as an example. Though he was a poet of traditional verse forms and metrics and remained steadfastly aloof from the poetic movements and fashions of his time, and he is anything but a merely regional or minor poet, his achievements lie in his artistic conception and meaning on deeper layer. And his poems cannot be said to function more and have had more readers than Sandburg's in the then society.

For contemporary poetry, where will it go? It is in the hands of contemporary poets. Under the influence of pioneers like Whitman and Sandburg, free verse has its full development, and it will still roll forward from this tradition to another one. More extropoets like Sandburg are expected to experiment with poetry; while more intropoets are expected to care about society and the people's life instead of their own inner world. Though people need both, they need more extropoets like Sandburg. By making the intropoets themselves melt into a society and the people, their bosom will be open enough and then it can be much easier for them to break through the bottomless tradition to develop modern poetry into a more timely style. Tradition exists necessarily, but most of it exits bottomlessly, and poetry will burgeon forward endlessly too. And there may be another Carl Sandburg or more in China or other places; at least this is the strongest wish from the author herein.

II. Yes! The People's Poet, and Popular Poetics

> What even the future will say about him, he will be
> there; like Whitman, he is one of our literary land-
> marks. (LCS: 512)
>
> —Norman Rosten[①]

To sum up Sandburg, his friends should have more rights to voice. Ben Hecht, one of his best friends from the *Chicago Daily News* for which Sandburg once worked for a long time, gave him a rousing review in slang to echo Sandburg's poetic slang: "…He's our Chicago bard, minstrel of our alleys, troubadour of the wheat patches outside our town. Homer of our sunsets and our stockyards…. There's more smoke to his song and kick to his heartbeat than Whitman ever coaxed out of his mellow, windbaggy soul…A man in love with life is Sandburg, looking at the world through his heart…The Peepul's [sic] Poet is Sandburg, poet for the great and egg-headed public who laugh at him, for the beetle browed wobblies who are sore at him because he won't throw bombs and be a regular red, for the cud-chewing pedants who perspire with rage at the right of vers libre [sic]. To all of them he makes love. He plays their dreams on a mouth organ. He tells them their secrets on a banjo. There's a snarl and a whine to him and he sometimes writes with his fists…. Out of the slang of his street, out of the brotherhood hokums and the turkey in the straw aesthetic of his day, Sandburg is making the new poetry. He doesn't belong to any of the art movements…. He's a movement all himself. He's the only genuine jazz motif in the letters of the day-a motif sonorous and quick, brazen and elusive. " (CSB: 335) Such a quotation may be long. But from this angle, Sandburg is uncovered nearly in all aspects: his hobo life, his activities in Chicago, his creative poetic

---

① American poet and playwright, 1914-1995.

style, his great passion for his fraternal people and so on.

And reviewed as a people's poet, Sandburg came from the Mid-west and the common folk. His origin and his hobo life in the west can be taken as his foundation of his poetry. Then to some degree, his socialistic political tendency can be his action principle to guide his poetry. Because of his identification with working people, Sandburg dedicated himself to the service for the people. And among his poetry, *Chicago Poems* and *The People, Yes* are the two important and representative books showing his deep affinity with the ordinary people.

As a people's poet, Sandburg had his own poetics, he insisted that a poet should play a role in the society, and he did so throughout his life and poetry. He based his poetry and poetics upon his mass groundwork, going into the people, discovering the people and rhyming the people. Coming from the realistic world, he chose common subjects to treat in his poetry. And except for his poetic heritage from Walt Whitman, Sandburg has his own unique poetics. His language is full of vernacular from ordinary persons. His style is free and narrative. His symbols are recurring. His materials are raw, but produce refined poetry. All this shows his admiring quality of one of the commons and a poet of the people.

Also, Sandburg is a popular lecturer and minstrel. He wrote and gave his famous lectures, singing his folk songs collected from the people, reading his own poems to the people, picking up the people into his poetry, and making the people realize themselves. And in return, the people read him, admire him and honor him.

In conclusion, Sandburg is a poet of the people to the highest degree, for his life and poetry were heavily influenced by his identification with the commons andbelief in the power of the people as his brothers. As a dedication to the people's beloved poet, some titles of his poems are selected from CPCS (with only four italicized words in brackets as exceptions) containing Sandburg's favorite word "people" to imitate a poem with his style, and it reads as follows:

I Am the People, the Mob

People Who Must①

For Crimson Changes People.

People with Proud Chins and People of the Eaves,

I Wish You Good Morning, Anywhere and Everywhere People.

White Elephants② Are Different to Different People:

My People—Swell People, Sandhill People, Field People, Moist Moon People,

　　And More Country People.

The People, Yes!!

Yes! Each pore of his is filled with people, just as his poetry is full of people too. But it is unnecessary for the people to compose epitaph to memorialize him, because in the following September after Sandburg's death on July 22, 1967, President Lyndon Johnson③ issued a statement as an eloquent reason at the Lincoln Memorial, which in part read, "Carl Sandburg needs no epitaph. It is written for all time in the fields, the cities, the face and heart of the land he loved and the people he celebrated and inspired."④

Sandburg, with his perseverance, sang fraternal songs all the way for his eternal commons—the ordinary people with his functional poetics—popular poetics. And his everlasting poetry will be monumental witness to tell his readers: Sandburg as the people's poet "will live on" among his poetic lines! His popular poetics, like and as popular culture, can work on, too, for its popularity, wide acceptance and demotic instruction.

---

① "Must" here means "go moldy".

② "White elephant" means here "heavy burden" of life.

③ Lyndon Johnson, 1908–1973, the 36th President of U. S. from 1963 to 1969.

④ Lee, Hopkins. *A Poetry of Workshop: In Print of Teaching Pre K-8*. Norwalk: Jan. 2005. Vol. 35, Iss. 4; p. 74.

Bibliography

Works by Carl Sandburg

Abe Lincoln Grows Up. San Diego, New York, London: Harcourt, Brace and Howe, 1954.

Always the Young Strangers. New York: Harcourt, Brace and Company, 1953.

Chicago Poems. New York: Dover Publications, Inc. , 1994.

Cornhuskers. Mineola, New York: Dover Publications, Inc. , 2000.

Early Moon. New York: Harcourt, Brace and Company, 1930.

Ever the Winds of Chance. Urbana and Chicago: University of Illinois Press, 1983.

Good Morning, America. New York: Harcourt, Brace and Company, 1928.

Harvest Poems 1910–1960. San Diego, New York and London: Harcourt Brace & Company, 1988.

Rootabaga Stories. Bedford, Massachusetts: Apple Wood Books, 1922.

Slabs of the Sunburnt West. New York: Harcourt, Brace and Company, 1922.

Smoke and Steel. New York: Harcourt, Brace and Company, 1920.

The American Songbag. New York: Harcourt, Brace & Company, 1927.

The Chicago Race Riots. New York: Harcourt, Brace and Howe, 1919.

The Complete Poems of Carl Sandburg. San Diego, New York and London: Harcourt Brace Jovanocich, Publishers, 1970.

The Letters of Carl Sandburg. New York: Harcourt, Brace & World, Inc. , 1968.

The People, Yes. San Diego, New York and London: Harcourt Brace & Company, 1964.

The Sandburg Range. New York: Harcourt, Brace and Company, 1957.

The Wedding Proceession of the Rag Doll and the Broom Handle and Who Was in It. San Diego, New York, London: Harcourt Brace & Company, 1950.

Wind Song. New York: Harcourt, Brace & World, Inc. , 1960.

Works on Carl Sandburg

Callahan, North. *Carl Sandburg: His Life and Works* University Park and London: The Pennsylvania State University Press, 1987.

Fetherl, Dale, ed. *Carl Sandburg at the Movies*, 1920–1927: A Poet in the Silent Era. Metuchen, N. J. : Scarecrow Press, 1985.

Golden, Harry. *Carl Sandburg* Cleveland and New York: The World Publishing Company, 1961.

Hallwas, John & Dennis Reader. *The Vision of This Land.* Macomb: Western Illinois University, 1976.

Niven, Penelope. *Carl Sandburg: A Biography.* New York: Charles Scribner's Sons, 1991.

Other References

Bell, Andrew. The Popular Poetics and Politics of the Aeneid. *Transactions of the American Philological Association.* Vol. 129. 1999.

Benjamin, P. A Poet of Common–Place. *Survey* 45, 1920.

Ferguson, M. , M. Salter & J. Stallworthy. *The Norton Anthology of Modern Poetry.* New York: W. W. Norton & Company, 1996: 971.

Ou, Hong. *Sense of Nativeness: Trans–cultural Studies on Literature* (unpublished) .

Oxford Concise Dictionary of Literary Terms. Shanghai: Shanghai Foreign Language Education Press, 2000.

Preminger, A. & T. V. F. Brogan, etc. . *The New Princeton Encyclopedia of Poetry and Poetics.* Princeton, New Jersey: Princeton University Press, 1993.

Shakespeare, William. *Slelected Lyrical Poems of Shakespeare.* (Liang,

Zongdai, Trans.) Changsha: Hunan Literature Press, 1996: 222.

Whitman, Walt. *Leaves of Grass.* New York: Caxton House, 1900.

Zhang, Guangkui. On the Principle of Poetry Translation and Orientation of Translation Style. *Journal of China University of Mining and Technology*, Vol. 5. No. 4. 2003.

Zhang, Guangkui. Carl Sandburg's Heritage in Poetry from Walt Whitman: Style, Language and Rhetoric. *Journal of Xuzhou Institute of Technology*, Issue. 2. 2005.

http: //infotrac. galegroup. com/menu (Gale–Literature Resource Center) .

http: //library. zsu. edu. cn/mdb/database/cnki. html (China Academic Journal Electronic Database) .

http: //millercenter. virginia. edu/scripps/diglibrary/prezspeeches/lincoln/al_ 1861_ 0704. html.

http: //reagan. eureka. edu/beyond/speech_ text. html.

http: //www. bartleby. com/65/so/socialis. html.

http: //www. music1234567. com/bbs/showthread. php? t = 1188.

http: //www. poets. org/poets/poets. cfm? prmID = 84.

http: //www. reaganlegacy. org/speeches/reagan. economic. recovery. htm.

http: //www. thezephyr. com/archives/universm. htm.

http: //www. uua. org/aboutuua/principles. html.

梁实秋编. 桑德堡. 台北: 名人出版社, 1980.

赵萝蕤译. 惠特曼诗选. 济南: 山东大学出版社, 1999.

赵毅衡译. 桑德堡诗选. 北京: 人民文学出版社, 1987.

后 记

　　本书的原中文主标题为《人民诗人卡尔·桑伯格》。虽然这个名称从一定程度上也说明了美国诗人桑伯格的诗学特征。但是，后来逐渐考虑到我国民众由于历史的原因对于"人民"的理解和西方人的理解会有一定的区别。再后来，在师从复旦大学陆扬教授做博士后研究期间，由于接触到了陆先生所研究的大众文化，也就突发奇想，桑伯格的人民诗学不正是大众诗学吗？于是，也就有了现在的中文主标题《大众诗学》。而原来的英文主标题 Fraternal Songs for Eternal Commons 也自然改成了 Popular Poetics，我自认为显得既简洁，又有力。更自然的是，"Popular Poetics"也似乎提炼、升华了"Fraternal Songs for Eternal Commons"的内涵；同时，"Fraternal Songs for Eternal Commons"在一定层面和程度上似乎应当是"Popular Poetics"的特性之一。在此，向陆扬教授表示我由衷的敬意。

　　虽然在本书的致谢里已经表达了对我的导师中山大学区鉷教授的诚挚感谢，但总觉得还是意犹未尽。因为他给我的影响是深远的、重大的、启蒙的。对于我本人来说，最让我感动的是区鉷教授的严谨。斗胆地说，如果近年来在陆扬老师的熏陶下算是有了不小的进步的话（请允许我稍微骄傲瞬间，以满足我实实在在的虚荣心），这个根基肯定是来自区鉷教授。我相信我自己会继续自勉下去，以诗歌研究为核心，去诠释诗歌，去研究诗学；去翻译诗歌，去研究诗歌翻译，去探讨诗歌翻译美学；去创作诗歌，并进一步把诗歌创作的直接经验应用到研究诗歌和研究诗歌翻译中去。

　　桑伯格创作的诗歌数量甚丰，但他的精品和经典似乎也可以说不多。不过，这并没有影响他成为人民诗人或大众诗人。从另一方面来讲，他之所以能成为人民诗人是和他的大众诗学密不可分的。他的诗歌是给大众欣赏的，所以他受到了大众的推崇与爱戴。和晦涩难懂的诗人相比，桑伯格更伟大。他的诗歌体现了，也实现了一个诗人的社会价值。但是，当今的国内外诗坛似乎搞晦涩创作的人越来越多，也不知是为了猎奇，还是为了炫耀。无论如何，我一直主张让别人看不懂的诗歌以自赏为好，最好不要发表，浪费资源！

　　《大众诗学》的出版，从一定程度上也表明了我的诗学观点和倾向，而且，我会继续努力。同时，我还相信，桑伯格式的大众诗学也同样可以成就经典，美国诗人罗伯特·弗罗斯特（Robert Frost，1874－1963）不也是一个很好的例证吗？

2008 年 5 月 18 日

于广州珠江花园鹏庵